# Readers love K.C. WELLS

## *Step by Step*

If you love a feel-good, super-sexy, relationship-centered story, go check this one out.

—Sinfully MM Book Reviews

Once I started reading I didn't want to stop for even a minute. It was the perfect book for me at the perfect time. Highly recommended.

—On Top Down Under

## *Bromantically Yours*

"This novella is a sweet friends-to-lovers tale with lots of romance along the way and a perfect little treat for Valentine's Day."

—Gay Book Reviews

"Anyone who is a fan of this author will recognise the unique voice that she expresses herself in and if you've never read her before, this would be a great place to get started."

—Love Bytes

## *Out of the Shadows*

"As always, this is beautifu[...] gaging story that will keep y[...] recommend this feel good r[...]

D1221674

By K.C. WELLS

Published by DREAMSPINNER PRESS
www.dreamspinnerpress.com

# TRUTH WILL OUT

# K.C. WELLS

Published by
DREAMSPINNER PRESS

5032 Capital Circle SW, Suite 2, PMB# 279,
Tallahassee, FL 32305-7886 USA
www.dreamspinnerpress.com

This is a work of fiction. Names, characters, places, and incidents either are the product of author imagination or are used fictitiously, and any resemblance to actual persons, living or dead, business establishments, events, or locales is entirely coincidental.

Truth Will Out
© 2018 K.C. Wells.

Cover Art
© 2018 Kanaxa.
Cover content is for illustrative purposes only and any person depicted on the cover is a model.

All rights reserved. This book is licensed to the original purchaser only. Duplication or distribution via any means is illegal and a violation of international copyright law, subject to criminal prosecution and upon conviction, fines, and/or imprisonment. Any eBook format cannot be legally loaned or given to others. No part of this book may be reproduced or transmitted in any form or by any means, electronic or mechanical, including photocopying, recording, or by any information storage and retrieval system, without the written permission of the Publisher, except where permitted by law. To request permission and all other inquiries, contact Dreamspinner Press, 5032 Capital Circle SW, Suite 2, PMB# 279, Tallahassee, FL 32305-7886, USA, or www. dreamspinnerpress.com.

Mass Market Paperback ISBN: 978-1-64108-067-5
Trade Paperback ISBN: 978-1-64080-630-6
Digital ISBN: 978-1-64080-629-0
Library of Congress Control Number: 2018930570
Mass Market Paperback published October 2018
v. 1.0

Printed in the United States of America
∞
This paper meets the requirements of
ANSI/NISO Z39.48-1992 (Permanence of Paper).

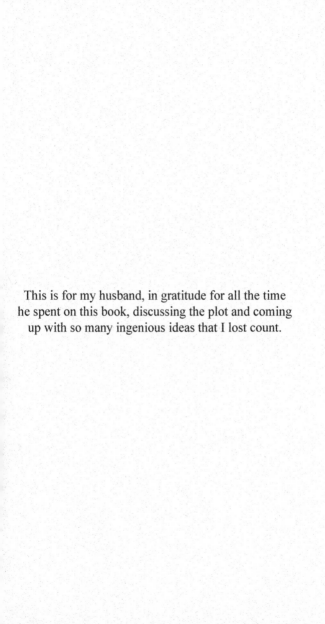

This is for my husband, in gratitude for all the time he spent on this book, discussing the plot and coming up with so many ingenious ideas that I lost count.

# Acknowledgments

Thanks to my wonderful team of betas—Jason, Helena, Daniel, Mardee, Sharon, and Will.

My especial thanks to Daniel, for a coffee session that was really a plotting session.

# CHAPTER ONE

JONATHON DE Mountford had forgotten how charming Merrychurch railway station was. From its quaint black-and-white mock wattle and daub exterior, to the colorful bunting decorating the arch above the door, to the troughs, pots, and hanging baskets filled with flowers everywhere he looked. The yellow-painted warning line toward the edge of the platform was bright, as if freshly done, and the station sign, with its white lettering on a dark blue background, was free from the graffiti Jonathon had seen in such plentiful supply only a short time ago in Winchester.

Only one thing was missing: there was no sign of his uncle, Dominic.

Jonathon checked the time on his phone. Ten minutes had elapsed since he'd gotten off the train, and the platform was deserted. The station guard had disappeared into his office, but Jonathon could hear him whistling cheerily. Then his mind snapped back to Dominic. Okay, it had been a very early train, but Dominic had assured Jonathon that he was still a habitual early riser and that collecting him from the station would be no trouble at all.

*Maybe he's waiting outside.*

Jonathon adjusted the strap of the backpack slung over his shoulder, grasped the pull-up handle of his suitcase, and trundled through the open doorway into the station, with its ticket counter and bright posters. The only incongruity was the self-service ticket machine, but he assumed even Merrychurch had had to succumb to some of the demands of the twenty-first century.

Passing through the wide wooden door onto the pavement beyond, Jonathon found himself standing alone, a car park to his left, surrounded by a picket fence. Nothing else to be seen but the lane, with tall trees on both sides. No traffic. No noise, except for the birds chirping away.

And still no sign of Dominic.

Jonathon checked his texts, but there was nothing. Sighing, he scrolled through to find Dominic's number. When all he got was his uncle's recorded message, the first tendrils of unease began to snake through his belly. This really wasn't like Dominic.

A glance up the empty country lane, a glance down, and he made his mind up. There seemed little point in waiting any longer. The best thing to do would be to make his own way into the village and then on to the manor house. He knew that Merrychurch was only a mile or so away, and, based on experience, it wasn't worth waiting for the local bus, which only ran once an hour. With the happy chirping of birds in the trees to accompany him, Jonathon headed toward the village, pulling his suitcase behind him.

It was a beautiful late-July day, just the right temperature that he didn't need a jacket. As he walked along, he recollected the recent emails and conversations he'd had with Dominic. There was nothing he could put his finger on, but Jonathon had gotten the definite impression that all was not well. The speed with which Dominic had agreed to Jonathon coming to stay had been enough of an indication.

*So why isn't he here to meet me like he said?*

Jonathon cast his mind back to their last conversation, a week ago. They'd spoken about the village fete, due to take place on the grounds of the house in early August. Dominic loved doing his Lord-of-the-Manor routine, and from what Jonathon could recall from past visits, it was usually a fun day. They'd also talked about Jonathon's latest book, a collection of photographs taken on a recent trip to India. More than once, Dominic had expressed his pride in Jonathon's work.

*Maybe we should have discussed what was bothering him.* Because it had been plain to Jonathon that something was definitely on Dominic's mind.

From behind came the sound of a vehicle, and Jonathon squeezed himself into the hedge, pulling in the case to stand it beside him. It surprised him when the car came to a stop in the road next to him.

"Do you need a lift?" The voice was male, deep, and cheerful.

Jonathon regarded the driver of the 4x4. He was in his late thirties, maybe early forties, with dark brown hair cut short and neat. Warm brown eyes peered at Jonathon from behind a pair of rimless glasses. "If you're going to Merrychurch, then yes."

The driver smiled. "I didn't think you'd be walking any farther. The next village after Merrychurch is Lower Pinton, and that's four miles from here." He nodded to the seat beside him. "Hop in. There's room in the back for your case."

"Thanks." Jonathon crossed to the passenger's side, stowed the case, then clambered into the front seat. "It was nice of you to stop." He clasped the backpack to him, his precious camera safely protected within it.

"I figured you'd missed the bus. Easily done, now they've reduced the timetable." He waited until Jonathon had fastened his seat belt before moving off. "Where are you staying in the village?"

"Excuse me?" Jonathon arched his eyebrows.

The driver laughed. "Okay, yeah, that was presumptuous of me, but the suitcase was a bit of a giveaway. And I'm only asking because if you don't have anywhere to stay, I own the local pub, and there are rooms if you need one."

"Ah." Jonathon kept his gaze focused on the passing landscape. "I'm staying with my uncle, but thanks all the same."

The lane leading to Merrychurch hadn't changed in all the years Jonathon had been visiting his uncle: trees met in a leafy arch over the road, the odd house here and there....

"Have you been to Merrychurch before?"

Jonathon smiled to himself. "A few times, yes."

"You probably know the place better than I do, then. I've only lived here for the past eleven months."

Just then a rabbit darted out from the hedgerow, and the driver swerved the car violently to avoid it. Jonathon found himself holding his breath, but fortunately the rabbit escaped injury and reached the other side of the road.

The driver expelled a low growl, then glanced across at Jonathon. "I hate it when the little buggers do that. One of these days, I'm not gonna be able to stop in time."

The fact that he'd swerved at all was a plus in Jonathon's book.

A minute later they were in the heart of the village. The driver stopped the car in front of the charming, picturesque pub, leaving the engine running. "So, can I drop you someplace? Where does your uncle live?"

Jonathon was overcome with an unexpected rush of nerves. He knew there were those in the village who resented his uncle—Dominic had intimated as much on several occasions—and he didn't want to say something, only to find his Good Samaritan harbored a grudge and turned out to be a psychopath. Then he pulled himself together. The stranger had already admitted he was a recent addition to the village population, so it was highly unlikely that he bore Dominic any ill will.

"My uncle had agreed to meet me," Jonathon explained, "but—"

"But he wasn't there when you arrived," the man concluded. When Jonathon lifted his eyebrows once more, he smiled. "That much was obvious, or you wouldn't have been walking into the village. Has he messaged you to say he was delayed?"

Jonathon shook his head. "Which is… weird."

The man gave an emphatic nod. "Right. In that case, I'll take you to him. That way, if he's not there, I'll bring you back here and you can wait in the pub until he surfaces. What do you think?"

Jonathon thought it was about time he knew the name of his Good Samaritan. "Sounds great to me." He extended a hand. "Jonathon de Mountford."

The man shook it. "Mike Tattersall. Pleased to meet you." His eyes widened. "Ah. I guess I don't have to ask who your uncle is, then."

Jonathon had suspected that might be the case. Even if Mike was a recent addition to Merrychurch, he would have known about de Mountford Hall, the imposing manor house on the outskirts of the village.

Mike's face clouded over, and he switched off the engine. "Your uncle is a sore point at the moment."

Jonathon stilled. "Why?"

"My sister, Sue, is his cleaner. She's worked up at the house for the past three years. Everything was fine, until last month."

Jonathon had the impression that Mike's sudden change of mood was more to do with his sister than Dominic. "What happened?"

Mike sighed. "Sue's a member of an animal rights activist group. I try not to get involved, partly because it gives me the willies to hear she's off on some protest. What I don't know can't keep me awake at night." When Jonathon frowned, he gave a shrug. "Comes with the territory. I'm an ex-copper. I've tried telling her to stay on the right side of the law, but it's not easy. She can be bloody stubborn when she wants to be. Anyway, last month she got wind of something and went charging off to the manor to see your uncle. Turns out he's given permission for the local hunt to go across his land, which also means they'll be close to the village."

"But… didn't they ban fox hunting? It's just hunting with dogs now, isn't it?"

Mike nodded. "Sue has got it into her head that the local hunt bigwigs will be ignoring that part. No idea where she's getting her information from. But yeah, things got a bit… ugly."

That fitted in with Jonathon's uneasy feelings. Something *had* been wrong after all. "I think I'd like to go to the manor, please."

Mike appeared to shrug off his mood. He straightened in the driver's seat and nodded briskly. "Sure thing. Let's get you up there." He switched on the engine and pulled away from the curb.

Jonathon gazed at his surroundings. The village seemed as it always had: a few shops huddled together, the pub, and the post office. Then there were the houses, many of them thatched. The church tower rose above the trees, square and solid. The river still wound its way through the village, dipping below the picturesque stone bridge with its graceful arch. Ducks squatted along its banks, heads tucked under their wings, while others swam in the slow-moving, clear water, bobbing their heads below the surface, their rear ends stuck up in the air, as comical as Jonathon remembered from his childhood.

"Merrychurch hasn't changed," he murmured as they sped through the narrow, leafy lanes.

Mike chuckled. "Oh, you think so? I've learned from experience that things are seldom as they appear.

You have no clue what's lurking below the seemingly tranquil surface." He snorted. "Yeah, there speaks an ex-policeman, always expecting the worst."

Jonathon studied him carefully. Mike was obviously too young to have retired. "How come you left the force? Where did you work?"

"London Met. And I was invalided out when I lost my foot in a raid."

Jonathon couldn't help the automatic glance toward Mike's feet.

Mike obviously caught the movement. "I have a prosthetic foot now. You'd never know it wasn't real if you saw it." Then he sighed. "At least that's what I tell myself every night when the shoes come off. Anyhow, as I was saying… when they gave me my compensation, I was at a loss. I'd been a copper since I was nineteen, and there I was, nearly forty, with no clue what I was going to do for the rest of my life."

"So you bought a village pub. Quite a change of pace from London, I imagine."

Mike laughed. "You have no idea. The pub was Sue's brainchild. She'd moved here with her husband, Dan, but things didn't work out for them. When he left, she stayed, although that meant finding work. The pub came up for sale, and she thought of me. I did suggest that she could work there if she wanted, but she soon scuppered that idea." He gave a wry chuckle. "She had a point. We'd have been at each other's throats within minutes. Chalk and cheese, us two." Mike nodded toward the windscreen. "There you are."

Jonathon followed his gaze. On either side of the lane stood the old stone gateposts that he recalled from his childhood, the ones that bore the family crest.

Except the crest had worn away during the two centuries or so that the family had owned the manor house, and the gateposts were beginning to crumble too. They marked the boundaries of the original estate. Subsequent members of the de Mountford family had sold off parts of it, and now all that remained were the one hundred or so acres that surrounded de Mountford Hall.

"And there it is," Jonathon said softly. The manor house was just visible above the tree line, perched on top of a gently sloping hill, its white facade standing out against the green, glowing in the early-morning sunshine. As Mike passed through the gateposts and followed the gravel-covered lane, Jonathon peered up at the hall. "I can't imagine what he finds to do all day in that place. He must really rattle around in there." Dominic was a confirmed bachelor and had lived alone since he'd inherited the house. Up until fifteen years ago, he'd worked in London, in the family law firm, but he had surprised everyone by announcing his retirement at the age of forty-five.

Mike took a left turn, and the gravel lane became a driveway that looped in front of the house, circling a grassy knoll where an ornate fountain stood, its wells dry. He pulled up in front of the wide arched entrance. "Delivered to the door. How's that for service?"

Jonathon smiled and held out his hand again. "Thanks, Mike." He glanced around. There were no cars in sight, but that might simply have meant they were in the garage.

"It's very quiet. Mind you, it *is* still early. Maybe he overslept."

Jonathon cocked his head and listened. Even the birds seemed to have ceased their happy song. That

only served to add to his returning unease. He put
down his backpack, got out of the car, and walked toward the heavy oak door, darkened by the shadow of
the stone arch above it. Jonathon pulled on the central
knob of the brass door bell, hearing the clang within
the house. He took a step back and waited, his gaze
fixed on the door.

After a minute of silence, he turned to Mike.
"Looks like he's gone out."

"He has servants, right? At least that's what Sue
says."

Jonathon tried to recall. "He used to, but that was
a few years ago. I haven't been here for two years, so I
don't know. He certainly didn't mention getting rid of
them." In which case it either appeared to be their day
off, or they hadn't arrived yet, which seemed unlikely.

"Try the door. Maybe he left it unlocked." When
Jonathon stared at him, Mike snickered. "Yeah, I know.
Since when does anyone go out and leave a place like
this unlocked these days? It was just a suggestion."

Nevertheless, Jonathon felt compelled to try. He
grasped the heavy doorknob and turned....

The door swung open with a creak.

"Uh-oh," he whispered.

Mike was out of the car and at his side in an instant.
"That's a bit odd. Want me to go in there with you?" he
asked in a low voice. "Just in case there are...."

"What? Just in case there are what?" Icy fingers
traced over Jonathon's skin.

"Burglars, maybe?" Mike peered at the door.
"Look, it could just be me with my overactive imagination. Or it could be something as simple as your
uncle forgot to lock the door when he went out."

Jonathon was praying for the latter. "Okay, you can come with me."

Mike puffed out his broad chest. "And stay behind me. If there's anyone in here, let me deal with them, okay?"

It took a moment or two to realize Mike was acting with such bravado to ease Jonathon's nerves. He gave a mock sigh of relief. "Absolutely." Not that he was afraid of taking on a few bad guys, but they'd have to be smaller than him, and since he was five feet six and as skinny as a rake, he thought that extremely unlikely.

Mike stepped into the cool interior, the white marble floor reflecting the sunlight that spilled in through the open door. He crept forward, his boots squeaking slightly against the tiles, his head to one side as he listened.

The house was as silent as the grave, and Jonathon ceased to see the funny side. "I don't think he's here."

Mike came to a stop and peered up the staircase. "Well, if there are burglars, they're quiet as bloody mice," he whispered. "I'm going to check upstairs, but I don't think there's anyone here."

Jonathon nodded. "I'll take a look around too." There was no way he was going to wait there, feeling as useful as an inflatable dartboard.

Mike narrowed his gaze. "Be careful."

It was rather sweet, Jonathon thought, considering Mike had known him for all of five minutes. Well, he could be sweet too. "I will if you will." Without waiting for Mike's reply, Jonathon crept over to the sitting room door. One glance around it convinced him that room was empty. He moved from room to room, the soles of his trainers making the same squeaky noises as Mike's boots.

No signs of disturbance. No signs of a break-in. Nothing.

When he reached the door of his uncle's study, he paused. As a child, this room had always been off-limits. Dominic's refuge for when visitors became too much, his sanctuary. Finding the door ajar only added to the panic fluttering in his belly.

"Dominic?" He pushed it cautiously, took two steps into the room—and froze.

"What's wrong?" Mike hissed from behind him.

Jonathon swallowed hard. "I think we need to call the police. And an ambulance." He tried to take another step, but his legs were like lead.

Mike pushed past him and came to a halt. "Oh, Christ."

Uncle Dominic lay in a heap on the floor by the fireplace, the harsh red of the blood pooled around his head stark against the white marble. Jonathon could only watch as Mike hurried over to the prone form and bent over to place two fingers against Dominic's neck. The silence stretched as Jonathon waited, unable to tear his gaze from the sight.

Finally Mike straightened and looked Jonathon in the eye. "I'm so sorry. He's dead."

His words didn't compute. Dominic couldn't be dead.

Mike walked over to him and grasped his upper arm. "Okay," he began, his voice calm and even. "I'm going to take you out to the car, and then I'll call the local police." When Jonathon gazed at him, blinking, Mike patted his arm. "You can't stay in here, Jonathon. This could be a crime scene."

That was when the shivers set in.

# CHAPTER TWO

JONATHON STARED through the windscreen at the house, his body and mind numb.

*I can't believe this is happening.*

Mike had gone inside when the local police had arrived, after giving Jonathon strict instructions to stay put. Jonathon had barely registered his words. He kept seeing Dominic lying there, his eyes open, and God, the blood....

It took a moment to realize Mike was back in the car. He studied Jonathon carefully before speaking. "Right. There's nothing you can do here, so I'm taking you back to the pub. Constable Billings will be over when they're done processing the scene. Doubtless he'll have a few questions."

Jonathon swallowed. "What did you mean, this could be a crime scene?" He opened his eyes wide. "What do you think happened?"

Mike's gaze flickered to the windscreen. "At first glance it looks like he fell and caught his head on the hearth. His feet were all tangled up in a rug, so maybe he tripped."

Jonathon frowned. "First glance?"

Mike shrugged. "Sorry. That's the copper in me talking. Never assume anything until the coroner has had a look."

*Coroner. Postmortem.* Jonathon shuddered. Then Mike's words sank in and he shook his head. "Tripped? No way."

"What makes you say that?"

Jonathon pointed toward the house. "That man climbed Everest! He was a sailor! Trip? He had the balance of a mountain goat."

Mike held up his hands defensively. "Hey, I'm telling you what I saw. And you don't know. Maybe he had a dizzy spell."

Jonathon stuck out his jaw. "And maybe he fell because someone pushed him."

There was a silence, broken only when Mike cleared his throat. "Okay, yeah, that's a possibility too, but unless there's evidence of a struggle…." He sighed. "You can't jump to conclusions. You have to look at the evidence." Mike glanced at Jonathon's face. "Come on, let's get out of here. SOCO and the—"

"SOCO?" Jonathon searched his befuddled brain for the term.

Mike gave him a gentle smile. "Scenes of Crime Officers. So yeah, SOCO and the coroner will be here soon, and I don't want *you* here when they carry out your uncle's body." Jonathon shivered, and Mike sighed. "That does it. I don't know about you, but I need a drink." He switched on the engine and drove around the knoll to head back along the driveway to the lane.

Jonathon leaned his head against the window, the passing scenery just a blur. He was grateful not to be on his own right then. Mike's solid, practical presence was the only thing holding him together. He closed his eyes, but Dominic was still there in his head. Still dead.

*Twenty-eight is way too young to have your first brush with death.*

When the car came to a stop, he opened his eyes. They were behind the pub in a car park that might have had room for maybe twenty cars.

Mike regarded him, his concern obvious. "Are you okay?"

"As well as can be expected, considering the circumstances." Jonathon picked up his backpack and opened the door.

"I'll get your case." Mike had already opened the rear door and was lifting it from the back seat. "Now, do you want me to show you to your room, or do you want a drink too?" When Jonathon gave another involuntary shiver, Mike nodded. "Drink first." He locked the car, then led the way to the solid back door. "I'll leave the case in the kitchen. It'll be safe there. Abi won't be here for an hour or two, and we're not open yet."

"Abi?"

"She makes the food." Mike closed the door behind them, and Jonathon followed him into the large kitchen, then through into the warm-looking bar, its chairs covered in a rich red that complemented the white-painted walls and black beams. The bar itself was a dark wood, varnished to a high gloss. The place had a cozy, old feel, nothing like the pubs Jonathon frequented.

"You said you own this?" Usually landlords were appointed by the brewery that owned the pub.

Mike nodded and patted the bar top. "I've worked hard to give the place an atmosphere. When I bought it, there was no food provided and little in the way of comfort. There was, however, a huge TV screen. Apparently the former owner was a big sports fan, and that was all you could watch here. I didn't feel a TV went with a pub this old, so I took it down. No one's complained so far." He went behind the bar, grabbed two glasses, and held them up to a bar optic. "Here." He placed the squat glasses on the black bar mat.

Jonathon eyed the amber liquid. "What's this?" He sat on one of the stools in front of the bar.

"Brandy. By the look of you, you need it."

Jonathon wasn't about to disagree. He lifted the glass and drained the contents in one long gulp before coughing violently when the fiery liquid hit his throat. He wiped his mouth and grimaced. "God, how can people like that?"

Mike chuckled. "Well, if you toss it back like it's water…." He took a sip and then regarded Jonathon's backpack, still over his shoulder, with interest. "You're very careful with that bag. What does it contain, your life savings?"

Jonathon placed the backpack on his knee and opened it. "My most precious possession." He took out the camera and held it up for Mike to see. "He goes everywhere I go."

"He?" Mike smirked.

"Definitely."

"And is this a hobby or something more than that?"

Jonathon placed the camera on the bar top and then reached into the bag. He handed Mike a large book with a glossy cover. "I was bringing this to give to Dominic. It's my latest book."

Mike stared at the cover, which was an image of a stunning waterfall, tumbling down a precipice. His eyes widened. "Oh my God. Of course. You're *the* Jonathon de Mountford. I thought it sounded familiar, and not just because of your uncle. I love your work."

"Really?" No matter how many times people professed to love his photographs, it still felt as new as the first time it had occurred. And Jonathon still couldn't get used to it.

Mike nodded, his eyes shining. "I have your book on Australia. Some of the images in there are simply stunning. You have a great eye for capturing the essence of a place." Then he laughed. "Get me. I'm *fangirling* Jonathon de Mountford."

Jonathon's cheeks felt like they were on fire.

Mike handed the book back to him. "I'm just sorry we had to meet under these circumstances."

And just like that, Jonathon was plunged into the present. For one brief moment, he'd forgotten the day's horrible event.

"Let me show you to your room."

It was like Mike could read his emotions, and Jonathon was grateful for the intervention. He nodded. "Thanks." He put the book and camera away and slid off the stool.

Mike led him toward the signs indicating the toilets, but then opened a door marked Private. Beyond was a wooden staircase, with a red carpet covering the center of each tread.

"The bed isn't made up, but I can soon sort that out," Mike said from in front of him. When they reached the landing, Jonathon saw five doors leading off it. Mike pointed to the farthest door. "That's where I live, so if you need anything and I'm not downstairs, feel free to knock on my door." Then he opened the nearest door. "This will be yours, for as long as you need it."

Jonathon stepped into a large room with a huge bay window at the far end, bracketed by deep blue curtains from floor to ceiling. There was a heavy stone fireplace, cleaned out but with a basket of logs beside it. The bed was wide, covered with a floral quilt, and had a small oak cabinet on either side. The varnished wooden floorboards were partially obscured by two or three matching rugs.

"There's only one bathroom up here, I'm afraid. It's two doors down. I haven't got around to fitting en suites yet."

Jonathon shook his head. "I wouldn't want one. It would spoil the room." The bedroom was full of olde world charm. He wandered over to the window and traced the leaded panes with his finger. *Real* leaded windows, not the modern attempt to copy them. "How old is this place?" His room overlooked the front of the pub, and he could see people below, going about their daily lives, with no clue as to the horrific tragedy that had taken place.

*How many of them will be sorry he's dead?* It didn't sound like Mike's sister would be among that number.

"I've seen documents that claim there was an inn first registered here back in 1458. There's a chair downstairs that your ancestor used to sit in, so they say."

Jonathon whirled around to stare at him. "John de Mountford, Earl of Hampshire? That was back in the late 1700s."

"Which is why no one is allowed to sit in it," Mike remarked dryly. He exited the room briefly, only to return with a pile of folded bed linens. "I'll just make up the bed. I only do it when I know I'm expecting guests."

"Can I help?" Anything to take his mind off the current situation.

"Sure." Between them, they pulled off the quilt and covered the bed with soft, fresh-smelling cotton sheets. "So, how long were you intending to stay with your uncle?"

Jonathon was busy stuffing a pillowcase that smelled of lavender. "A couple of weeks. He wanted me to accompany him to the village fete." His throat tightened, and across on the other side of the bed, Mike stilled.

"I shouldn't have reminded you."

Jonathon held his head high. "Yes, you should. I'm going to have to talk about it, deal with it, so there's no point avoiding the subject." Then it hit him, and he felt the realization like a body blow. "I have to phone my father. He has to be told, and I'd rather he heard it from me than from the police."

Mike nodded. "I'll leave you to it. Come down when you're done, and I'll make us some tea, coffee—whatever you want. Besides, Constable Billings should be here soon." He left the room.

Jonathon fished his phone out of his jeans pocket and then stared at it. "What the hell do I say to him?" he whispered to himself. Then he scrolled through, clicked Call, and wandered back to the window to gaze out at the village.

"I take it you're at Dominic's."

The sound of his father's voice, so cheerful and… normal, made Jonathon's stomach clench. "Not quite. You need to sit down, if you're not already doing so."

There was a moment's pause. "What's wrong?"

"There's no good way to say this, so I'm just going to come out with it. Dominic is dead."

The hitch in his father's breathing was audible. "Oh God. What happened?"

"The police are there now, but it looks like he fell and hit his head on the hearth."

More silence followed. Jonathon couldn't imagine how it would feel to lose a brother. His father had to be devastated.

"I see…. Wait a minute. Police? From where?"

"The local constable, I think." Jonathon didn't see why that should be of importance.

"Absolutely not. This needs to be handled by someone with authority, not some village PC Plod. I'll get on to Scotland Yard immediately." There was a crisp, authoritative edge to his father's voice that Jonathon recognized instantly. This was Thomas de Mountford, barrister, a man who didn't take no for an answer. A man who always got what he wanted. And apparently not a man to let grief stop him for more than a few minutes.

"I don't think that's necessary." Not to mention Jonathon couldn't see the local police taking kindly to being descended upon by detectives from London. Not for what had all the markings of an accident.

"Well, you should, given the situation we now find ourselves in."

Something in his father's voice made the hairs on the back of Jonathon's neck stand up. "What situation?" he asked guardedly.

A sigh from the other end. "I suppose I'd better tell you. It makes no difference now because you'd learn soon enough, when the will is read."

That uneasy feeling in the pit of Jonathon's stomach was spreading its tendrils again. "Okay, what's going on?"

"Because Dominic has no heir, the house passes to the next male in line."

"Which is you, as his younger brother."

His father coughed. "Actually, no. Your uncle and I agreed that you should inherit the hall."

"Me?" The word came out as a squeak, and he cleared his throat. "Why?"

There was a moment of silence before his father responded. "Put quite simply, I have no intention of giving up my career, not when there is the possibility of becoming a High Court judge."

Jonathon had long known of his father's judiciary ambitions. "You can't have both?"

He didn't miss the noise of irritation. "Jonathon, de Mountford Hall is a huge responsibility. Why do you think the family crest can be seen all over that village? Because as the owner of the hall, the incumbent has an obligation to take care of its inhabitants. Such a responsibility requires being physically present."

"We've talked about this. The title died out many years ago. There hasn't been an earl, or a lord, or a viscount in the family for how many generations?"

"The title may have disappeared, but the hall remains, and as long as the family line continues, there will be a de Mountford living there." A pause. "And as I am speaking to the last of the de Mountford family, there—"

"Don't." The demand came out harsher than Jonathon might have wanted. "We are *not* going to discuss this again." Only his father could take a tragic death and turn it into yet another opportunity to argue that Jonathon needed to be married and working on producing the next generation.

Jonathon had no problem with the idea of marriage in principle. Where he and his father differed was with the gender of his future spouse.

"I'm sorry," he whispered. "I know you two were close." It felt mean-spirited to deliberately bring the conversation back to its painful origins, but it was better than letting his father continue in his usual vein.

"God, the things we got up to when we were younger." There was a softness to his father's voice that Jonathon hadn't heard in a long time. Then he cleared his throat and it was obvious the moment had passed. "I want you to keep me informed on everything that happens there, do you understand?" That hard edge was back.

"Yes, sir." Jonathon knew from experience that was the only response his father expected.

"Are you staying at the hall?"

"Right now I have a room at the local pub. I'm waiting to hear from the police."

"I imagine they're going over the house with a fine-tooth comb. Well, they'd damn well better be. As soon as you're given permission to go to the hall, I want you staying there. I don't want it left empty."

Jonathon had a nasty feeling he knew where this was going. "But... I only intended spending two weeks here. Then I was going to Vietnam." He'd spent months putting the trip together.

"Your little... hobby can wait, surely? Until it's been established how Dominic died. And after that, well... you'll have new responsibilities."

Jonathon's heart sank. Sometimes he hated being right. "Can we talk about this another time?"

"Of course. You must be feeling pretty low right now. If you need me to come down there, call. I can take a brief leave of absence in the circumstances."

After Jonathon had sent his love to his mother, they said their goodbyes, and he ended the call. With a heavy heart, he left the room and went down the stairs and into the pub.

Mike was sitting at a table near the bar, talking earnestly with the police constable who'd been first on the scene. "Hey, come and sit down. You look haggard."

*Hardly surprising*, Jonathon thought. He joined the two men and stared questioningly at Constable Billings. "Well? Do you still think it was an accident?" He sat on the remaining empty chair.

Constable Billings frowned and looked at Mike, who gave him an apologetic smile.

"Jonathon voiced the opinion that given his uncle's remarkable good balance, someone might have pushed him, causing him to fall."

The constable's furrowed brow smoothed out. "Oh, I see." He gave his attention to Jonathon. "It still looks like an accident to me, sir. Of course, things might change once the coroner's report comes out. We'll have to wait and see." He got out his notebook. "I have a few questions for you, if that's all right. I know you've been through a lot this morning."

"Please, ask away."

"When did you last speak to your uncle?"

"Last week. He called me to check that I was still coming to stay with him. He was supposed to meet me at the station this morning."

Constable Billings nodded, making notes. "Who is the next of kin?"

"That would be my father." Jonathon rattled off details, impressed that the officer kept up.

"Just one more thing. Would you know where Bryan Mayhew is right now?"

Jonathon froze. "Who the hell is Bryan Mayhew?"

Constable Billings frowned. "I thought you'd know. He's the student who's staying up at the manor."

"Oh yeah, I know him. He's been a regular for the last couple of weeks. Didn't your uncle mention him?" Mike asked.

"No, he didn't." Which again was odd. Dominic had certainly been acting out of character lately. "Why do you want to find him?"

"I just find it strange that he's not there. He's been investigating the history of the hall and the de Mountford family for the past four weeks. I assumed your uncle would have spoken about him."

"There's no sign of him?"

"None. His bike isn't anywhere that I could see. He rides a motorbike," Constable Billings added. "He's always zipping along the lanes on that thing. Gave poor old Mrs. Dawkins a scare when he drove past her one day last week." He shrugged. "I wanted to ask him when he last saw your uncle alive."

"You... you don't think he had something to do with Dominic's death, do you?" It seemed awfully coincidental to Jonathon's mind. His uncle had died, and this student was nowhere to be found.

"And there you go again, jumping to conclusions." Mike patted Jonathon's arm. "What did I say about evidence?"

Jonathon addressed Constable Billings. "What happens to my uncle's... body?"

"He's been taken to the mortuary at the Fareham Community Hospital. Oh, and there'll be no need for you to identify the body, sir, seeing as you were the one who found him." The constable rose to his feet. "Will you be staying here, sir? If I need to ask more questions."

"Yes, I'll be here. When will you get the postmortem results? They *will* examine his body, right?"

"I did say there'd be a coroner's report, didn't I?"

"Yes, you did," Mike interjected. "You can't blame Jonathon for being a little... distracted right now, given the current state of affairs."

Jonathon arched his eyebrows at that but said nothing.

"Of course. Entirely understandable. I'll be in touch as soon as there's any news." Constable Billings spoke with a calm, soothing voice. "Don't you worry, sir. I'm sure it was just a tragic accident." He shook Mike's hand. "I'll talk to you later, Mike."

"Sure." Mike got up and walked him to the door.

Jonathon would have liked to believe that they were right, that it really was just an accident, but something in his gut was telling him that was merely wishful thinking. There was one thing he was certain of, however.

He needed to talk to this Bryan Mayhew.

# CHAPTER THREE

JONATHON REGARDED what was left of his ploughman's lunch with disinterest. It wasn't that the food had been poor—far from it. Abi had put together a huge plate heaped high with three different kinds of cheese, salad, freshly baked, crusty bread, butter, and pickles, not to mention a thick slice of a pork pie. It was just that his appetite appeared to have deserted him. Not surprising, given the circumstances. It seemed a shame. That pork pie deserved to be enjoyed with more gusto than Jonathon could muster right then.

He was sitting at a table in the huge bay window, looking out at the village beyond. The pub had begun to receive its first patrons not long after Mike had opened the doors at eleven thirty, and once Abi had arrived, Mike had given instructions that the first order of the day was to feed Jonathon. *He's only just met me and yet he's taking such good care of me.* Of course, that was probably due to the fact that Jonathon had just found his uncle dead, but deep down, he couldn't help wishing the root of Mike's attention was for an entirely different reason. Then he admonished himself. He couldn't go around fantasizing about every gorgeous guy who strayed across his path. And Mike *was* gorgeous, no two ways about it. It didn't help matters that he was built like a bear, all rugged, muscled, and with a sexy beard to boot. Add to that the fact that he was older than Jonathon and wore glasses, and Mike was pretty much Jonathon's ideal man.

*Except this is neither the time nor the place to be having such thoughts.*

"You're not enjoying that." Mike's quietly uttered question dropped Jonathon smack into the present.

He sighed. "Sorry. It's great, really. It's just that I seem to have lost my appetite."

"Yeah, I can understand that." Mike glanced around them, his attention directed toward the bar. "Look, it's not a particularly busy time—that comes later, when everyone finishes work for the weekend—so why don't you let me get you a coffee or something, and then we can chat when the lunchtime rush dies down." He chuckled and shook his head. "Rush. Listen to me. We're talking six or seven regulars who come in for a pint and a sandwich. Not exactly swamped, right?" He nodded toward Jonathon's lunch. "Let me cover that up and put it in the fridge. Then if you feel peckish later, just help yourself. And you can come and go around here, okay? You want anything, feel free to wander into the kitchen. That goes especially for when you can't sleep and you want to make cocoa or Horlicks or whatever else you feel like."

Jonathon stared at him. "Why are you being so nice to me? You don't even know me."

Mike tapped his temple. "Instincts. I've always relied on mine, and right now they're telling me I can trust you. Besides, it strikes me that you could use a friend."

That much was certainly true. What Jonathon really wanted was for someone to give him a good hug and tell him it would all work out in the end, even it that turned out to be a lie.

Mike disappeared but returned with a mug of coffee. "Here. I'll be over soon." He took away Jonathon's plate and headed for behind the bar.

Jonathon sat back in his chair, facing the pub's interior, and indulged in his favorite pastime, people-watching. Except this time, the objects of his attention were regarding him with equal interest. He pondered on this for a moment, until he reasoned that news generally spread throughout the village like wildfire, and doubtless word had already gotten around about Dominic's death. It was disconcerting to feel their gazes crawl over him, and he wondered what they were thinking. Had they liked Dominic? Despised him? Or had he been of little consequence to them? Did they know who Jonathon was?

Usually, people-watching kept his mind distracted and was a good way to pass the time, but not today. There were too many thoughts in his head, clamoring for attention.

An older man walked in, his bald head reflecting the pub's lights. He paused at the bar to speak to Mike, and Jonathon was seized by the resemblance to his uncle. A wave of sorrow washed over him and his throat tightened.

*He really is gone.*

Jonathon sat in the grip of a flood of memories. Watching his uncle at the helm of his boat, steering as it cut through the waves around the coastline, not far from the village. Sitting on his uncle's lap, leafing through photo albums, listening as Dominic told him stories about the family. Jonathon at age thirteen, playing croquet with Dominic on the lawn to the rear of the hall, laughing at his uncle's attempt to cheat. They hadn't spent all that much time together, he supposed, but the time they had shared had been rich and vibrant.

*Time we'll never get to share again. And all because of something as trivial as tripping on a rug.* It didn't seem fair. Jonathon hadn't even given a moment's thought to the fact that he was going to inherit the hall. That was something to be pushed aside, to be considered later, when the initial throes of sorrow had passed.

He couldn't sit still and allow those memories to get the better of him.

Jonathon got to his feet and went over to the bar. "I'm just going for a walk," he told Mike. "I… I need some air."

Mike nodded, his brown eyes kind and compassionate. "Take as long as you like." He reached under the bar, grabbed a notepad, and after hastily scribbling on it, tore off the top sheet and handed it to Jonathon. "That's my phone number if you need it." Then his attention was claimed by the older guy with the bald head, the one who'd set off Jonathon's bout of reminiscing.

Jonathon folded the paper and pocketed it. Then he left Mike to it and exited the pub. The sun was high in the sky, and in the distance, he caught the cries of seagulls. He turned right and strolled along the lane that passed in front of the church, to the old covered gate with its white-painted gable, where notices were pinned under its moss-covered tiled roof. He peered at them, barely taking in the announcement of a bring-and-buy sale in the church hall, a bright poster about the village fete, and the times of the services. Jonathon was no stranger to St. Mary's. As a child, visiting the hall with his parents, he'd attended the Sunday service with them, sitting in the front pew, which bore the de Mountford crest, a further reminder of the family's importance in the village.

On impulse he pushed open the gate and walked at a leisurely pace along the cobbled path that dissect-ed the lush green of the churchyard. Ancient, mossy gravestones, their engravings almost obliterated by the passage of time, marked the route to the main church door. Wildflowers, bright and colorful, sprang up between the stones, a sharp reminder of life among so much death. Now and again, he spied bunches of flowers arranged in urns or simply tied in a bunch and laid to rest against the stone, and the sight comforted him. Even in death, those who rested there were not entirely forgotten.

"Good afternoon."

The sweet, melodic voice stopped Jonathon in his tracks, and he lifted his chin to see who'd spo-ken. An elderly lady, her gray-blonde hair resting on her shoulder in a fat braid, a straw hat on her head, regarded him with clear blue eyes. Over her arm she carried a basket, and in one hand, she held a pair of pruning shears. Poking over the rim of the basket were the heads of some of the wildflowers.

"Good afternoon. I hope I'm not disturbing your gardening." He had a vague recollection that this was Melinda Talbot, the vicar's wife. He'd only seen her on a few occasions, but he remembered her being kind to him when he'd first attended the church.

She smiled. "You've grown a lot since I last saw you. It's Jonathon, isn't it? Dominic's nephew?"

Jonathon returned her smile, pleased to have been remembered. "Yes, Mrs. Talbot."

She laughed. "Go on, make me feel really old and tell me how old you are now. Because the last time I saw you, I think you were still in your teens. Or maybe you were at university. I forget."

"I think your memory is excellent," he complimented her. "And I'm twenty-eight."

She nodded eagerly, but then her smile faltered. "I would say I'm pleased to see you, but word gets around fast in this village." Melinda stepped forward, her hand extended. "My condolences. What a terrible thing to have happened."

Jonathon took her hand and she covered his with her other, both sheathed in deep green suede gardening gloves. She glanced down and shook her head. "Look at me. Silly old woman." She released his hand and removed the gloves. Her gaze met his. "Where are you staying? Not at the hall, surely."

"Mike, the pub landlord, gave me a room there. He's sort of taken me under his wing since I got here."

Melinda nodded, her expression pleased. "Mike's a good man." Her eyes widened. "Would you like to come to tea tomorrow afternoon? I'd love it if you could. I know my husband would like to talk to you."

"Tea?" For a moment the concept didn't compute.

She smiled. "Yes, I know it feels strange to be thinking about tea in such circumstances, but life goes on, my dear boy. Besides, when was the last time you had a proper English afternoon tea?" When he opened his mouth to reply, she shook her head. "I know all about you, young man. You're forever jet-setting off around the world, taking your marvelous photos." Jonathon blinked, and she gave him a sad smile. "Your uncle was always talking about you, where you were, showing us your photos in magazines and on his laptop. So I know what a wonderful life you lead. But I bet you can't remember the last time you sat down to tea, cake, and sandwiches." Her eyes twinkled.

Jonathon admitted defeat. "You know what? You're right. I can't remember. What time?"

"If we make it about four o'clock, then you can bring Mike along as well. The pub will be closed by then and it won't open again until six." She smiled mischievously. "Mike looks like he could use some tea too."

"I'll tell him." Jonathon held out his hand, and she clasped it briefly in her cool one. "Thank you. This is very kind of you."

"Nonsense," she said with a wave. "Haven't you heard? This is what vicars' wives do." Her eyes sparkled with good humor. Then she glanced over Jonathon's shoulder and smiled. "Good timing, Sebastian."

Jonathon turned around to see a tall, bearded man walking along the path, pulling a bike beside him. He gazed at Jonathon inquiringly before returning his attention to Melinda.

"Afternoon, Melinda. Who's this, then? Another waif and stray?" He smiled.

Melinda laughed. "Not quite." She glanced at Jonathon. "Allow me to introduce our curate, Sebastian Trevellan. Who thinks he's funny." She gave Sebastian a mock glare before continuing. "Just because I make a habit of bringing people home with me." She arched her thinning eyebrows. "I believe *you* were the last stray, if memory serves." She indicated Jonathon with a flick of her head. "This is Jonathon de Mountford. Dominic's nephew."

Sebastian's eyes widened. "Oh. Oh, I see. I'm sorry for your loss. Everyone is talking about it, of course. Such a tragic accident. Your uncle was well respected in the village."

Melinda huffed. "By most people, yes."

Jonathon longed to ask her what she meant by that, but Melinda gave him a smile.

"I'd better take my husband a cup of tea. Once he starts leafing through those hefty tomes in his study, he loses all track of time. And if he *is* writing Sunday's sermon, he'll need tea. It fuels the brain cells."

"The sermon is already written," Sebastian interjected. "I'm preaching this Sunday. That's what I was working on last night."

"Ahh. Is *that* why you were burning the midnight oil? I saw the lights from the house." Melinda turned to Jonathon. "Sebastian lives in the cottage at the end of the garden. We *have* told him there's plenty of room for him in the vicarage, but no, he prefers to stay there." She gave an elegant shrug. "I can't blame him,

I suppose. Who would want to live with a pair of old codgers like us?"

Sebastian gave her a fond glance. "As if either of you fits that description." He addressed Jonathon. "Glad to meet you. Sorry about the circumstances."

"You can talk to Jonathon tomorrow. I've invited him and Mike Tattersall to tea."

Sebastian blinked. "Oh. Oh, right. The more the merrier." He smiled. "I'll see you tomorrow, then." He continued along the path, his hands on the handlebars of the bike.

Melinda watched him. "He's a pleasant man. He came to us a year ago. This is his first parish. Not a talker, however. Very private, and likes to keep to himself. I keep telling him to go for a drink in the pub once in a while. It would do him no harm, and he might actually enjoy it." She faced Jonathon and grinned. "Maybe you could try inviting him when you see him tomorrow. He might listen when the suggestion comes from a younger man, rather than his mentor's elderly wife. And now I really must go. Until four o'clock tomorrow, Mr. de Mountford."

Jonathon nodded. "I look forward to it." He watched as she headed up the path toward the church, then followed another path around the old stone building, doubtless going to the vicarage. The conversation had done him a lot of good. He felt calmer, and the recent bout of melancholy had departed. He was left feeling tired, however.

Maybe a nap was a good idea.

THERE HAD to be between twenty to thirty people in the pub, hardly packing it to the rafters.

Jonathon liked the atmosphere. There was a mixture of chatter, laughter, passionate discussion, and whispered conversations. He sat at the bar, drinking it all in, watching as Mike interacted with his customers, exchanging banter and smiles.

"Anyone would think you've been doing this all your life," Jonathon commented when Mike took a moment to drink from a pint glass of water.

Mike's face lit up. "That's possibly the nicest thing you could have said. I love this. It's so different from my career, and the change of pace seems to suit me. That's not to say that sometimes I don't miss the old life."

"What was your rank when you left?"

"Detective Inspector. I had no aspirations to go any higher. A desk job was definitely not for me." He left to serve a couple of old men their pints but came back when the bar was free of customers. "Tell me about your uncle."

Jonathon arched his eyebrows. "Is this you being polite, or are you asking out of habit, Mr. Detective?" He grinned. "Was it difficult to give up the sleuthing?"

Mike laughed. "Okay, you got me. It's just that I've been thinking about him ever since this morning. Understandable, really. But I don't know that much about him." He glanced at Jonathon's empty beer glass. "Can I get you another?" He gave a wicked grin. "Alcohol gets the tongue working better."

Jonathon laughed and held out his glass. "Go on, then." He watched as Mike expertly pulled a pint, getting the head just right. "Dominic was a barrister in London, working for the family firm."

"The de Mountfords are barristers?"

Jonathon nodded. "My father is aiming to be a High Court judge one of these days. Law seems to run in the blood. Present company excluded."

"I won't ask how *that* went down in a family of lawyers." Mike flicked a glance in his direction, and Jonathon shook his head. "Thought as much. So, back to Dominic. When did he leave London to lord it over the inhabitants of Merrychurch?"

"About fifteen years ago, when my grandfather died and he inherited the hall. He gave up his career and moved here, a decision that apparently surprised a lot of people." Jonathon frowned. "Except my father. I was only thirteen at the time, but I seem to recall him accepting the situation with little or no fuss, which really isn't like him."

"Maybe Dominic wasn't all that good a barrister," Mike suggested. "Maybe he only got a job with the law firm because he was family and they couldn't refuse him. Noblesse oblige and all that." His eyes widened. "Maybe he *had* to leave the firm."

"Yeah, you didn't leave your career all that far behind, did you?" Jonathon chuckled. "You still think like a copper, don't you?"

Mike laughed. "Guilty as charged, in possession of an overactive imagination." He sighed. "Sorry. I keep forgetting."

"What—that I've just lost my uncle?" Jonathon gave him a hard stare. "Well, you go on forgetting, okay? Don't handle me with kid gloves, don't treat me with care. I'm twenty-eight. I can handle a death in the family." He stuck out his chin. "Life goes on, right? And soon I'm going to have bigger things to worry about."

"Such as?" Mike frowned.

"The fact that you're looking at the next occupant of de Mountford Hall. If my father gets his way, that is."

Mike stilled. "You… you're the heir?"

"Apparently. But can I ask you not to discuss this with anyone? I only know because my father told me. Let's wait until the will is read. Then I'm guessing all will be revealed."

"Wow." Mike rubbed his chin. "I can see why you'd be less than happy to inherit. Taking on such a responsibility might curtail a career in photography."

"Tell me about it." Jonathon glanced over Mike's shoulder. "You're wanted. Customers."

Mike twisted around to take a look, then returned his attention to Jonathon. "Hey, want to help me behind the bar? It might keep your mind off things."

Jonathon let out a sigh of relief. "And that might be the best thing you've said since I met you. Yes, please."

"Come on, then." Mike grinned. "You can start by collecting the empties."

Jonathon had a feeling he'd just made the wrong decision.

# CHAPTER FOUR

JONATHON OPENED his eyes and blinked groggily. For a moment he had no clue where he was. Then he remembered. He was in a room at the Hare and Hounds pub in Merrychurch, it was Saturday, July 22nd, Uncle Dominic was dead, and for reasons they'd decided upon between themselves, Dominic and Jonathon's father had agreed that Jonathon was to inherit de Mountford Hall—whether he wanted to or not.

Any hopes Jonathon might have had that it had all been some ghastly dream vanished with the sunlight that poured in through the gap in the curtains.

A sharp tap on the door brought his attention back to his surroundings. "Yes?"

"Just wanted to say, the bathroom's free," Mike said through the door. "And I'm making scrambled eggs and bacon for breakfast, if you're interested."

The rumble in Jonathon's belly announced the return of his appetite. "That sounds great. I'll be down shortly."

"Okay. There'll be coffee or tea when you're ready too."

Jonathon stifled his groan. "Coffee would be wonderful."

A loud chuckle erupted. "A man after my own heart. See you down there."

When silence fell once more, Jonathon threw back the covers and climbed out of the bed. He'd anticipated being unable to sleep the whole night through, but to his surprise, the last thing he remembered was his head hitting the pillow. *I must have been out like a light.* The bed was supremely comfortable, which might have accounted for it.

The controls for the shower over the bath took some figuring out, but finally hot water was flowing. The aroma of frying bacon seeped under the bathroom door and into his nostrils, and that was all the impetus Jonathon needed to wash as fast as was humanly possible. By the time he descended the narrow staircase, his mouth was watering.

The center of the large kitchen was dominated by a square wooden table, thick and solid-looking, and Mike had set out plates and cutlery on it. Mike stood with his back to Jonathon, facing the ancient AGA range. "How do you like your eggs? Soft and creamy, or bouncy?"

Jonathon snorted. "You can keep the bouncy variety."

Mike laughed and glanced over his shoulder. "Take a seat. There's toast, butter, jam, and marmalade on the table. Help yourself. And if you really want cereal, I can rustle that up too."

Jonathon pulled out one of the heavy-looking oak chairs and sat down. "You can keep the cereal too."

Mike laughed again. "*Definitely* a man after my own heart. Oh, and the coffee's made. Help yourself." He went back to moving the eggs slowly around the frying pan with a spatula.

Jonathon poured out two mugs of coffee and settled back into his chair. "Mike? Are you doing anything this morning?" He'd been thinking while he showered.

"That sounds suspiciously like you have an activity in mind."

Jonathon helped himself to milk and stirred it into his coffee. "I want to go to the hall."

Mike paused and peered at him. "Any particular reason?"

"Well, firstly, I want to see how the police have left it. Secondly, I want a look around. And thirdly, I want to see if this student has come back yet."

"All good reasons, and I can't fault any of them." Mike shared the eggs between two plates, and then once the pan was soaking in the sink, he brought the plates to the table, along with a foil-covered plate. "Bacon. And if you want ketchup, it's behind you on the countertop."

The smell was heavenly. Jonathon began eating, and the taste was as sublime as its aroma. He nodded, humming appreciatively. For the next ten minutes, neither of them spoke while they got on with the very serious task of devouring breakfast. By the time

Jonathon had finished his second mug of coffee, he felt human again.

Mike helped himself to a third mug and buttered the last piece of toast. "I'll call Constable Billings first, just to verify that the police are actually finished up there. Then we can drive over." He paused, his gaze locked on Jonathon, his brow furrowed. "Look, I'm going to say this now. It's unlikely that they've cleaned up the… the blood, so I want you to be prepared for that."

Jonathon swallowed but nodded. "I understand. I still want to go there, though."

"Fine. If they give us the go-ahead, we'll go right after I've cleared up the breakfast things." The last morsel of toast vanished, and Mike smacked his lips. "That's me done." He got up from the table, fished his phone out of his jeans pocket, and scrolled through. He gave a nod toward the coffee pot. "Have that last bit. I've had enough." He walked out of the kitchen, and pretty soon Jonathon heard him talking in a low tone.

He poured the last of the coffee and stared out of the kitchen window at the sky beyond. It was going to be a beautiful day.

Then he thought about their destination, and the day lost some of its allure.

JONATHON SHIVERED at the sight of the yellow-and-black police tape across the main entrance door.

"Hey, you all right? You sure you want to do this?" Mike asked from beside him.

Jonathon cursed himself for his own weakness and straightened. "I'm fine."

Mike pulled the tape away, and they stepped once more into the hallway. "They've dusted for prints," he called out ahead of him. "Standard procedure. But that means we're free to touch anything." He stood in the middle of the wide hallway. "Hello? Bryan Mayhew?" Mike's cry echoed, rebounding off the walls and high ceiling. There was no response. He glanced across at Jonathon. "Well, unless he's in some far-off part of the hall, it looks like he's not around."

Jonathon gazed at the great staircase that followed the curve of the white marble walls, past the statue of an angel that stood at its foot. He craned his neck up and smiled. "At Christmas, this is where the tree stands... stood. I remember watching one year when it was delivered on the biggest truck I'd ever seen." He straightened his neck and stared at the door to the study, unable to repress the shudder that rippled through him.

"The police said they've been in contact with the servants. Most of the house isn't in use, apparently, and is shut off. There's a cook and a housekeeper. They would normally have been here, but your uncle gave them Thursday and Friday off."

"Why?" Jonathon couldn't see his uncle fending for himself. "He knew I was coming on Friday. Why would he do that?"

"The housekeeper thought it strange too, but Dominic assured her he could manage for two days."

There was no use putting it off any longer. Jonathon pushed open the study door and entered.

Instantly he spotted the residue left by the police. "They really did dust everything," he murmured. He tried not to glance at the floor, but it proved an impossible task. Thankfully the blood had been removed, but it had stained the white marble floor. The rug wasn't present, and he wondered if the police had taken it.

"That's a beautiful desk," Mike remarked. He closed the study door after them and walked over to the french windows, where the desk stood in front of them.

Jonathon had to agree. It was a huge item, covered in veneers that glowed with life and rich color. Its wide top was inlaid with leather, and behind it was the high-backed leather chair where he'd sat with his uncle so many times. On top of the desk was a fat album, bound in dark brown leather.

"What's that doing out?" Jonathon forgot his squeamishness and hurried over. The cover still bore traces of the fingerprint dust, a couple of smears at the edge where it had obviously been held after examination.

"What is it?" Mike joined him at the desk.

Jonathon sat in the chair and lifted the cover. "This was one of my uncle's photo albums. He kept these in one of the cupboards below the bookcases. If it's here, then he must have taken it out before he... before he died." He leafed through, turning the heavy black pages with care.

Mike came around the desk to gaze at the photos. "These look old."

Jonathon nodded. "At the start, yes. Some of these date back to the late eighteen hundreds." He pointed to one of the more formal photos of a family gathering, where each person sat with a rigid back, their gazes focused. "Further on, they begin to be more informal, and I'd guess they were taken by someone in the family. Those date back to the early twentieth century."

"Old family, huh?"

Jonathon glanced at Mike, taking in his rapt expression. "I'm in here too."

"Really? Show me."

Jonathon turned the pages until he reached the end of the album. "There's only the one photo. Dominic showed it to me years ago, when I was very young." He scanned the pages, searching. "Funny. I can't find it." He turned a page and stilled, staring at the small white corners left on an empty page. "Here. It was here."

"Are you sure?"

Jonathon frowned. "I'm positive. It was taken in the early nineties, I think. I was maybe two, just a toddler really. I was sitting on Dominic's knee, and there was a lady sitting next to us. We were at the seaside—an office outing, I think he said—and she was someone who worked with him." He sat back in the chair. "That's odd. Why should it be missing?"

Mike straightened, then froze beside him. "Er, Jonathon?"

Something in his voice caught Jonathon's attention, and he looked up. "What's the matter?"

Mike gestured to the walls of the study. "How do you get out of here? I know we came in, but for the life of me, I can't see a way out. Where's the bloody door?"

Jonathon laughed. "Ah, the mystery of de Mountford Hall." The walls were lined with linenfold panels, and the door wasn't immediately apparent. "See the bosses in the middle of each panel?"

Mike blinked. "Bosses?"

"The carved heads, surrounded by oak leaves, set equidistant apart on the horizontal panel. Well, if you go to the—" He counted with his finger, tapping through the air. "—third one along and slide the head to the right, it opens the door." Then he froze as the head moved, and the door opened.

"Would you mind telling me what you're doing in the middle of my crime scene?"

The owner of the strident voice stood in the doorway, dressed in a dark blue suit, pale blue shirt, and matching tie. He was glaring at Mike.

Jonathon cleared his throat. "We have permission to be here from Constable Billings." He was suddenly aware of how stiffly Mike held himself.

"And it's not a crime scene," Mike added. "This was an accidental death."

The man ignored him and addressed Jonathon. "Constable Billings is no longer in charge of this investigation, and when I see him, I'll be having words about this. Letting civilians loose where they have no right to be." Another glare at Mike. "That's correct, isn't it, Mike? You *are* still a civilian? You haven't rejoined the service and no one thought to mention it to me?" He gave Mike a mocking smile.

Mike took a deep breath. "John. Fancy seeing you here. Must have been something pretty drastic to get you out of Scotland Yard."

"That's *Detective Inspector Gorland* to you. As for me being here, that's down to someone pulling some very long strings." His gaze flickered briefly in Jonathon's direction before he continued. "And as for this not being a crime scene, that's where you're wrong.

Dominic de Mountford's death is no longer being treated as an accident. The coroner's report is in."

Mike gaped. "How? His body was only discovered twenty-four hours ago. There's no way the coroner would move that fast."

DI Gorland nodded. "See what I mean about long strings? The police commissioner got a call first thing yesterday morning. He called the superintendent, who then called me. And the upshot of the report is that there are signs of a struggle. There was bruising to the sternum, indicative of a sharp blow, plus a couple of cracked ribs. So we're looking at murder, or at the very least, manslaughter."

Jonathon gripped the arms of the chair. "Who would kill my uncle?" It didn't seem real.

"That's what I aim to find out, so I can get out of here and back to civilization." DI Gorland gave them both a hard stare. "And the last thing I need is you getting under my feet. So take my advice and stay out of my way."

"What about the hall? Is Jonathon free to visit?" Mike demanded. "Surely the investigation team have documented everything here."

DI Gorland sneered. "It's *Jonathon*, is it? I'll give you this, Mike: you're a fast mover." He regarded Jonathon, his expression cool. "I'll inform you when you are free to return here. I take it neither of you have seen this student, Bryan Mayhew?"

They shook their heads.

"In that case, I must ask you both to leave the premises. Now."

Jonathon got to his feet, feeling dazed. Mike nudged his elbow, guiding him toward the door.

"Come on. They know where to find you if they need you." He led the way past DI Gorland. By the time they reached the car, Jonathon was trembling.

"I don't believe it. Who would want my uncle dead?"

Mike rubbed his back. "Easy now. It doesn't have to be murder. What if there was an argument, someone shoved him, and he fell? It doesn't mean it was deliberate. Let's wait and see what the investigation turns up."

Jonathon glanced toward the house. "I take it you know this DI Gorland?" When there was no response, Jonathon gave him his full attention. "Mike?"

"We worked together in London." Mike's face tightened.

"Is he good at his job?" Jonathon wanted to know.

Mike stiffened as DI Gorland came out of the hall. "Not here. Let's talk about this back at the pub." He got into the 4x4, and Jonathon hurried to get in as well.

As they drove away from the house, Jonathon twisted in his seat to stare out of the rear window. The detective stood by his car, watching them. His gut clenching, Jonathon sat back and stared ahead, his mind awash with questions. The overriding thought in his head was that Mike was hiding something.

"So, TELL me about this Scotland Yard detective." Jonathon wanted to add *who has you so pissed off*, but it wasn't his place. He barely knew Mike, and certainly not well enough to make such a comment.

Mike put down his coffee mug and shook his head. "He's one of those officers who like everything neat and tidy. Nothing wrong with that, but it does mean he goes for the obvious suspects and sticks with them until his theory is proved wrong."

Judging by Mike's furrowed brow, Jonathon got the impression that Gorland's modus operandi worried him.

*There's more to this than simply not liking Gorland's methods.*

"Okay, you can tell me to back off, shut up, whatever," Jonathon began hesitatingly, "but I sort of got the impression that he doesn't like you very much."

Mike snorted. "Not like he hid it, right?" He took a long drink from his mug before continuing. "He's had it in for me ever since I made DI before he did."

"Ah. Hence the pointed remark about his rank."

Mike nodded. "At the time he kicked up quite a fuss. Said I hadn't been promoted because I was good at my job, but for… other reasons." He focused on the tabletop.

Jonathon couldn't miss Mike's body language; it screamed tension. "Other reasons?" When Mike jerked his head up, his eyes wide, Jonathon held up his hands in a placating gesture. "You don't have to tell me. It's none of my business."

Mike sagged into his chair. "Look, I suppose I can tell you. It's not like it's a secret around here. It's just not something I go shouting from the rooftops to every stranger who comes into the pub." His gaze met Jonathon's. "Except, you don't feel like a stranger."

Jonathon waited.

Another drink of coffee. "Gorland claimed I'd been promoted because of… positive discrimination."

Jonathon frowned. "And what's that when it's at home? Discrimination has always had negative connotations in my book."

Mike sighed heavily. "Positive discrimination first reared its head in Manchester in the eighties and nineties. It's a policy whereby an employer makes the decision to appoint certain minorities to their work-force, ahead of others, so that they're seen to be fair. Those who are physically less able, from a racial minority, maybe female, or… LGBT." He paused. "I don't think for one minute that the London Metropolitan Police employs such a policy, but Gorland muddied the waters a few years back by claiming I'd been promoted simply because they needed an… openly gay DI to enhance their LGBT-friendly appearance."

Jonathon fought hard not to let his jaw drop. *Mike's gay?* He let that new information seep in.

Mike apparently took his silence for disapproval. "I'm sorry if I've shocked you."

"You haven't," Jonathon said quickly.

Mike arched his eyebrows. "Really. Tell that to your face."

There was no way he could let Mike think of him in those terms.

"You remember I told you I'd be the next heir of de Mountford Hall if my father gets his way?"

"Yes." Mike smirked. "That was a very recent conversation. I'm hardly likely to have forgotten already."

"Well, he and I have differing opinions on a few subjects. For one thing, he wants me to give up my 'little hobby,' as he calls it, and move into the hall, with all its responsibilities."

"Little hobby?" Mike gaped at him. "You're a bloody marvelous photographer. You're well on your way to becoming the next David Bailey, Lord Snowdon...."

Jonathon's face grew hot. "You're very kind, but he doesn't quite see it like that. And then there's the fact that he expects me to marry and start producing the next generation of de Mountfords, seeing as the line ends with me."

"You don't want to get married just yet? You're twenty-eight, I think you said? People are getting married older these days. Surely he can wait a while."

Jonathon cleared his throat. "That's where we run into certain... complications. He's already putting together a list of extremely eligible women, and I don't want to marry any of them."

Mike nodded sympathetically. "You'd rather find your own wife, rather than having one forced on you. That's understandable."

"Not exactly." Jonathon drained the rest of his coffee. "You see, there's the small but not insignificant detail that if I ever do get married, it would definitely *not* be to a woman." He raised his chin and looked Mike in the eye.

Mike blinked. "Oh." Then his mouth fell open. "*Oh.*" A moment later, he started to laugh.

Jonathon gazed at him, perplexed. "What's so funny?"

Mike grinned. "Gorland's remark about me being a fast worker? He was trying to imply I was going to make a move on you, because, of course, gay men make a move on every guy they meet, right?" He shook his head. "If he finds out you're gay, he'll have apoplexy."

Jonathon couldn't help grinning too. "Couldn't happen to a nicer man. So when do we break the news to him?"

Mike chuckled. "Yeah, I know. Tempting, isn't it? But seriously, I had no idea you were gay."

Jonathon shrugged. "Not something I go shouting from the rooftops either. And it's not going to change anything, is it?"

"Not at all."

Except Jonathon knew he was lying to himself. It had already changed how he viewed Mike, and he was going to have to work hard not to let it show that he found him very attractive.

A glance at Mike stilled him. Mike seemed lost in his own thoughts, and judging by his frown, they weren't pleasant.

Something niggled at the back of Jonathon's mind. That earlier feeling that Mike wasn't being entirely truthful.

"What's bothering you?"

Mike's creased brow smoothed out instantly. "Nothing. Why do you ask?"

Jonathon knew a lie when he heard one. He merely gave Mike a pointed stare.

Mike huffed. "Okay. If you must know, I'm worried about my sister. She's not answering her phone or replying to texts. And she's not at home either."

"When was the last time you heard from her?"

"A couple of days ago?"

Jonathon nodded. "Is it possible she's gone away and just forgotten to tell you?"

"It's possible, I suppose." Mike stared out of the window at the village beyond. "Part of me is hoping to God that her not being around isn't linked to Dominic's death. Not that I think she's capable of murder," he added quickly.

"There's a but coming." Jonathon regarded him keenly. "Why should she have had anything to do with Dominic's death?"

Mike sighed. "Because a week ago, she and Dominic got into a hell of a row, right here in the pub, which ended in her yelling at him that… she was going to kill him."

# CHAPTER FIVE

JONATHON STARED at him, cold spreading over his skin in icy trickles. "You don't really think…." His throat seized up.

"I don't want to think that, obviously." Mike looked haggard. "When I picked you up near the station? I'd been for a drive, trying to find her. I'd gone to her house, but there was no sign of her. Then I thought maybe she'd taken the dog for a long morning walk. She does that a lot. I drove along her usual route, but no sign either."

"She wouldn't have left the dog… would she?" Jonathon loved dogs, and he hated to think of a poor dog, trapped in a house.

Mike shook his head. "If Sherlock had been around when I went to her place, I'd have known. That mutt starts barking as soon as he hears my car engine."

"Sherlock?" In spite of his present mood, Jonathon couldn't help smiling at that.

Mike scowled. "Sue's idea. I gave her the dog when her husband left her. Figured he'd be company for her. She said the name reminded her of me." He rolled his eyes. "Sherlock. I ask you! And wherever Sue's gone, the dog is with her." He stared at Jonathon. "I know. I should ask the rest of the people she cleans for. Maybe one of them has heard from her." He got to his feet and picked up the empty mugs. "And we can start with the vicarage. She cleans there once a week."

The vicarage....

Jonathon caught his breath. "Damn. I forgot to mention. We're expected for tea there, today at four o'clock."

Mike smirked. "*We* are expected? Since when?"

"I met the vicar's wife when I went for a walk last night, and she invited us both."

Mike smiled. "Yeah, that sounds like Melinda. Heart of gold, that one."

"She'd like me to invite the curate for a drink in the pub. I get the impression she thinks he needs to get out more."

"That definitely sounds like Melinda. Everyone's mother."

Jonathon smiled. "That explains Sebastian's comment about waifs and strays. He seemed nice too."

Mike nodded. "Intelligent bloke. Apparently he preaches well too."

"You haven't heard him?"

A derisive snort exploded from Mike's lips. "I'm not one for church. There are too many Christians who believe I'm going to hell because of what goes on in my bedroom—not that it's any of their business." He chuckled. "And not that there's anything going on in my bedroom in the first place. Chance would be a fine thing."

Jonathon coughed. He hadn't expected such a forthright comment.

Mike's face reddened. "Sorry. My mouth gets away from me sometimes." He headed for the kitchen with the mugs but stopped halfway across the pub and turned to face Jonathon. "I meant to apologize, by the way. Gorland shouldn't have spoken to you so rudely."

"I got the feeling his bad manners were directed more toward you."

"True, but he was still bloody rude." Mike tilted his head to one side. "He might have been more polite if he knew he was speaking to the heir of the manor."

Jonathon shook his head. "Not until it's made official, remember?" Maybe a visit to the solicitor's was imminent after all.

"Okay, got it." Mike hesitated. "Look, I really don't think Sue was serious when she yelled she was going to kill Dominic. I think it was one of those moments we all have, when we get carried away and say things we don't mean."

"Want to tell me why they were arguing in the first place?" Then it came to him that he already knew. "The local hunt. Dominic's decision to allow them on his land. That was it, wasn't it?"

Mike nodded glumly. "Dominic was in the pub for a quiet drink. He did that from time to time, a sort of 'meet the locals' kind of thing. Sue marched right

up to him and started yelling her head off. He told her
he wasn't about to change his mind. And… she told
him she'd kill him before the hunt took place."

"And you still think it was just talk?" Because to
Jonathon's way of thinking, it was pretty incriminating talk.

"Absolutely. Sue doesn't… I mean, she
wouldn't…." Mike sighed unhappily. "I know my sister. She isn't capable of this."

Jonathon wanted to believe him. "Go clean the
mugs, Mike."

"Sure." Mike left and headed for the kitchen, his
shoulders hunched over.

Jonathon got up and walked over to the large bay
window. It was a sobering thought that right then, his
uncle's killer was walking around, possibly someone
who lived in the village. It was hard to believe, looking out at the tranquil scene, that such a thing could
happen in such a peaceful, beautiful spot.

He cast his mind back to what they'd seen at the
hall. That photo album, for instance. Its presence on
the desk could be entirely coincidental, but the missing photo made him doubt that assumption. *Where is
it? Has someone taken it? And if so, why?* Jonathon
closed his eyes and pulled the image from his memory. He could see it in his head, clear as anything, even
down to the clothing he wore. He couldn't remember
the photo being taken, but that was hardly surprising.
He'd been barely two years old, according to Dominic.

On impulse Jonathon got out his phone and called
his father. "Hi."

"Have the police been to see you?" As usual, his
father came straight to the point.

"I met the detective inspector who's taken over the case." Jonathon sat back down in his chair.

"Good, good. Glad to know our family name still carries some weight. Then you know it wasn't an accident."

"Yes."

"Let me know if you meet with anything less than complete cooperation. The police commissioner is a personal friend. He assures me everything will be done to find the perpetrator."

No wonder Gorland had mentioned very long strings.

That photo was still on his mind, however.

"Father, I'm trying to locate a photograph that Dominic had in one of his albums. You might know of it."

"What makes you say so?"

"Well, you worked with him, and the photo was taken during an office day trip to the seaside. It was of Dominic, with me sitting on his lap."

Silence followed, lasting a couple of seconds. "Dominic never took you to the seaside." Jonathon could hear the tone of puzzlement.

"Are you sure? There was another figure in the photo, a lady who worked with him."

"Oh? *Ohhhh*. Yes. Now I remember. I'd forgotten all about that. Why are you trying to locate it?"

Some inner sense bade Jonathon hold his tongue. The same inner sense was telling him his father had just lied to him. "Oh, no special reason. I just wanted to see it again. Dominic told me all about it years ago."

"I see. Well, you have more important things to do with your time than to waste it looking for photographs. Dominic's solicitor, Mr. Omerod, has an office in the village. Perhaps you should pay him a visit?"

Jonathon was well acquainted with his father's speech patterns. There was no *perhaps* about it. For all Jonathon knew, Mr. Omerod had already been told to expect him. "Yes, sir." There seemed little point in arguing.

He disconnected the call just as Mike came back into the pub, walking over to him. Before he could speak, however, Jonathon blurted out, "It wasn't me in the photo."

Mike frowned. "But…. What makes you say that?"

"Because I just asked my father about it, and what I got back was pure obfuscation."

Mike sat opposite him. "Who told you it was you in the photo in the first place?"

"Dominic." Jonathon leaned forward, elbows on the table, his fingers steepled. "Why would he tell me the boy was me if it wasn't?"

"You're sure about this photo?"

Jonathon stared at him. "I can tell you what was in the background, what I—what the boy—was wearing, what the—"

"Okay, okay." Mike held up his hands. "I believe you. In which case, it's obvious."

"It is?"

Mike nodded. "The toddler was the woman's child."

"Then what was Dominic doing in the photo? Why was the child on his knee? And why would he lie to me?" None of it made any sense, especially the most puzzling thing of all—the photo was missing.

"Don't think about it now," Mike urged him. "You need to think about more practical matters, such as visiting Dominic's solicitor. I'm assuming that's on the cards, right? For everything to be made official? And I need to think about shopping."

Jonathon had to smile. "Shopping?"

Mike rolled his eyes again. "Yeah, some of us need to do mundane things like shopping, so *other* people," he said, pointing at Jonathon, "can eat bacon and eggs for breakfast, and have silly little things like lunch and dinner."

"Point taken." In that instant the last thing Jonathon wanted was to visit a dusty solicitor's office. "Can I come too?"

Mike chuckled. "Seriously? If you really want to. I could split the list between us and we could get it done in half the time."

"You're on." Anything was better than sitting around, letting his mind come up with all kinds of theories.

That could wait until later.

THE VICARAGE sitting room was exactly how Jonathon had pictured it. The vicarage itself was a tall building constructed in a dark gray stone, and inside it was a maze of large rooms, sloping corridors, and stairs that led off in all directions. The sort of house, he concluded, that would have been wonderful for a child growing up.

Then he gazed around the warm, cozy sitting room, taking in the absence of family photos.

*Maybe that's why Melinda has so many surrogate children. She and the vicar have none of their own.*

The thought saddened him. Melinda would make a great mother.

"Jonathon?"

Her quiet utterance was a nudge back into reality.

Melinda regarded him, her eyes sparkling. "Nice of you to join us. I was just asking if you wanted more fruit cake."

"No, thanks, although it was delicious." He peered at the table, the crisp white cloth barely visible beneath a delicate china cake stand containing three layers of sandwiches and cakes, a plate on which a rich fruit cake stood, a squat teapot, and taller, more elegant coffee pot, plus all the accoutrements of an English tea. "Is there any more carrot cake?"

Mike snickered. "You've already had two pieces."

Melinda gave Mike a mock glare. "And if he wants a third piece, he can *have* a third piece. I didn't hear anyone commenting when *you* helped yourself to virtually all the chicken paste sandwiches."

It was Jonathon's turn to snicker, especially when Mike's expression turned sheepish.

"I'm sorry I didn't recognize your name last night, Jonathon." Sebastian leaned forward to cut himself a thin slice of fruit cake. "I'm a fan of your work."

"Thank you." Jonathon took the plate of carrot cake from Melinda.

"Where will your next trip take you?"

"I'd planned a visit to Vietnam," he told the curate. "I was going to photograph the tunnels, among other things."

Lloyd Talbot peered at him, his brow furrowed. "Forgive me, but your choice of words makes it sound as though you're no longer going there." His voice quavered and cracked.

"Let's just say I may have to put my plans on hold for the time being." Jonathon took a bite of the moist cake. Melinda definitely had a golden touch when it came to baking.

"Speaking of plans…." Melinda poured more tea. "We need to speak to whomever takes over the hall. The village fete is almost upon us, and if it is to be canceled, we need to know sooner rather than later. Your uncle was always so good to us, letting us hold it in the grounds of the hall."

"Melinda has organized the village fete ever since we first came to Merrychurch," Lloyd explained, gazing proudly at his wife. "This will be our thirtieth year."

That made it easier for Jonathon to reach a decision. Thirty years was a huge milestone. "The fete can go ahead." He took another bite of cake as four heads swiveled in his direction.

"Can you make that decision?" Melinda cleared her throat. "I hope that didn't sound ill-mannered. It's just that I'd hate for us to go ahead, only to have the new occupant of the hall refuse us."

"Trust me." Jonathon smiled at her. "I'll see to it that the family is informed. As long as the police are done with their investigating, I don't see any reason why the fete can't go ahead as planned." He wasn't about to reveal his status, not until it had been made official, but he couldn't see why it should be canceled.

"Oh, that's wonderful." Melinda's face glowed. "Thank you so much. And if you're still in the village, you must attend, of course."

Jonathon's stomach clenched. Right then he had no idea what lay in store for him.

"How long do you plan on staying in Merrychurch?" Sebastian asked. "If you don't mind me asking."

"To be honest, I'm not sure at this point. I'll probably be staying until the funeral. I'm assuming my uncle will be buried in the family crypt?" He addressed his question to Lloyd, who nodded.

"Once his body has been released, we can decide on the funeral details." Lloyd's face fell. "I am only sorry that we had to meet under such tragic circumstances."

It was a phrase Jonathon was growing accustomed to hearing.

"Indeed," Sebastian murmured. "I know I've only been here a year, but this village will not be the same without him."

"Will your sister continue to clean up at the hall?" Melinda asked Mike.

His face darkened slightly. "That will be up to the new occupant, I suppose."

"Speaking of Sue, have you heard from her recently?" Lloyd frowned, his already wrinkled brow creasing even more. "She was supposed to clean the vicarage this morning, but for some reason, she didn't appear. That is simply not like her."

"She didn't call or text to say she wouldn't be here?" Mike looked like someone had just kicked him in the stomach.

Lloyd shook his head. "Not a word from her."

Melinda sighed. "I don't like this. I was in the village after lunch today, and I saw police officers going from door to door. When I asked Rachel in the tea shop if she knew what was going on, she told me they were asking questions about Dominic. Strange questions too."

The skin on Jonathon's arms prickled. "What do you mean?" Next to him, Mike stiffened.

"They wanted to know if Dominic had had any arguments or disagreements with villagers. And she distinctly heard Sue's name mentioned." She gave Mike a sharp glance. "Not that I believe for one moment that she's involved in this business. But I think we all know there are those in this village who wouldn't think twice about spreading malicious gossip where Sue is concerned."

Lloyd sighed. "Very un-Christian of them. The Bible says clearly, 'Let he who is without sin, cast the first stone.'"

"An admirable view, vicar," Mike said quietly. "Unfortunately, not a way that many people choose to live by. In this day and age, it's more a case of throw stones first, then put out an apology when you get it wrong. By which time it's usually too late." Jonathon gazed at him in consternation, and Mike shook his head. *Later*, he mouthed.

Jonathon put his half-eaten cake to one side, his appetite dead. It seemed Mike hadn't told him everything. Again.

"Oh!" Sebastian sat straight in his chair, his eyes bright. "What you said about the police being through with their investigating at the hall. I don't think they are."

Jonathon opened his mouth to speak, but Mike got there first. "What makes you say that?"

Sebastian raked his fingers through thick brown hair. "I'm sorry. It completely slipped my mind. This afternoon I paid a visit to old Ben Threadwell. He lives in one of the cottages on the border of the estate," he told Jonathon. "Ben's not been very well lately, and I was taking him some soup, bread, and fruit that Melinda had put together for him. Anyway, we ended up talking about Dominic." Sebastian appeared unhappy at the recollection. "It wasn't a pleasant conversation, and I felt very uncomfortable."

"Why?" Jonathon demanded.

"Well, it seems he'd received a letter from Dominic, regarding the cottage. Apparently so had all the people who rent the cottages. Dominic was informing them that he was selling off the land and that they had three months to vacate. Now that he knew Dominic was dead, Ben seemed almost... jubilant at the news." Sebastian shook his head. "To feel so much pleasure at the passing of another human being is just wrong."

"But what does that have to do with the police?" Mike asked gruffly.

"That's the part I was coming to. When I came out of Ben's cottage, there were two or three police cars heading up the lane toward the hall, followed by a white van. Now, why would they be going there if they were done?"

Jonathon glanced at Mike, who gave a perplexed shrug. Jonathon set his jaw. "That's a very good question. Maybe we should pay the police station a visit and see if they have an answer."

Mike's mouth went down at the corners. "I can't go now. I have to open the pub soon."

"And let's think logically about this." Melinda interjected. "It's nearly five thirty on a Saturday evening. Any investigations will have stopped for today. I doubt there'll be anyone at the station except one constable on duty. You will gain nothing by going there now."

Lloyd nodded in agreement. "And I sincerely doubt there will be any work done tomorrow. Sunday is a day of rest, after all. Best leave this until Monday morning. Jonathon can stay with you, Mike, for the foreseeable future?"

"He can stay as long as he wants." Mike's gaze flickered briefly in Jonathon's direction. "And I'll keep him busy around the pub. Keep his mind off things." He gave Jonathon a half smile. "It would be good to have another pair of hands around the place."

"Fine," Jonathon muttered. "But come Monday morning, I will be at that police station."

"And I'll be right there with you," Mike added. "I want to see where this investigation goes as much as you do."

Something flashed across his eyes, a reminder that Jonathon needed to have a talk with him when they were alone.

*What aren't you telling me, Mike?*

# CHAPTER SIX

MIKE CLOSED the church gate behind them, and they walked slowly toward the pub.

"What haven't you told me about Sue?" Jonathon hated to think that Mike hadn't been honest with him, especially after what they'd shared about their personal lives.

"Hmm?" Mike appeared deep in thought.

"Something Melinda said, about people in the village spreading malicious gossip about Sue. What reason would they have to do that?"

"Oh, God, this is awkward," Mike groaned. He came to a halt and stuck his hands in his jeans pockets, his gaze not on Jonathon but on the pavement. "Okay. After Sue got divorced, she was very… lonely." He fell silent.

"Okay," Jonathon said guardedly. "And?"

"And… when she started work as a cleaner, there were lots of people in the village who were keen to employ her. Lots of women who had better things to do with their time than do housework."

Jonathon blinked. "You're not telling me people are saying she's capable of murder because she's a *bad cleaner*, are you? Because that would be preposterous."

Mike sighed. "No, they're spreading malicious gossip because Sue's had quite a few affairs—with their husbands."

Jonathon couldn't hold back his soft gasp. "No. Really?" He let out a low whistle. "Well, you know what they say. Hell hath no fury, and all that."

Mike nodded, his face tight. "Exactly. So you can see why if Sue is a suspect, they wouldn't be averse to fanning the flames a little."

"Is she still… having affairs?"

"I think all that came to a stop when I moved into the village. I suppose she felt awkward, now that I was on her doorstep, so to speak."

Whatever else Mike had intended to say was lost when a bell chimed six times.

"Damn. I should be opening the pub by now." Mike starting running up the lane, and Jonathon followed him. He knew they'd probably be too busy to talk any more that evening, but Jonathon figured they'd have plenty of time the following day.

JONATHON ROLLED over in bed and peered at the blue LED alarm clock. It was one thirty, and sleep was proving elusive. He'd climbed into bed feeling bodily tired. Mike had been true to his word and had

kept him busy all night. The plus side of working behind the bar was that he'd met a lot of people. By that
point there were few who didn't know who he was,
and everyone offered their sympathies. Mike had in-
troduced him to some of the village's very interesting characters, and although it had been fun meeting
them, in the back of his mind remained that one stubborn thought.

What if one of them had killed Dominic?

It left him with a sour taste in his mouth and a
knotted mass of snakes writhing in his belly. No wonder he'd found it difficult to sleep.

Then he recalled Mike's invitation. A mug of
warm milk, or something similar, might be exactly
what he needed.

Jonathon clambered out of bed, pulled on a T-shirt
over his boxers, and padded barefoot to the door. He
eased it open as quietly as possible and crept down
the stairs, trying not to make a sound on the wooden
treads. Once in the kitchen, he found a saucepan, located the large bottle of milk, and set some to warming
on the AGA. A microwave would have accomplished
the task more quickly, but he didn't want to run the
risk of waking Mike.

Jonathon pulled out a chair and sat down. Outside, the sky was black, the village quiet. The only
sound in the pub was the occasional creak, but Jonathon put that down to the sounds all houses make,
especially if they were as old as the Hare and Hounds.

He leaned on the table and put his head in his
hands. The conversations at the vicarage had only
served to stir his imagination—and provide his overactive brain with suspects. He appreciated that Mike

didn't believe Sue had anything to do with his uncle's death, but the fact that no one had seen her, or even heard from her, was pretty damning. Then there was the old guy who was about to be evicted from his home. Could he have done it? He lived practically on Dominic's doorstep. Easy enough to get there and back without anyone seeing him. Okay, so he was old—but how old? Still vital enough to shove Dominic so hard that he fell over and cracked his head? And what about the student, Bryan, who had suddenly vanished without a trace? Was his absence linked to Dominic's death?

No wonder Jonathon couldn't sleep. His head was about to implode.

"What are you doing up at this hour?" Mike stood in the doorway, scrubbing a hand over his cheek and beard. He wore a pair of shorts and some slippers, and something seemed off about his appearance, until Jonathon realized what was different—Mike wasn't wearing his glasses.

Jonathon gestured toward the AGA, where the pan of milk had begun to steam. "Well, you did say I could. And I could ask you the same thing. I didn't wake you, did I?"

Mike shook his head. "Couldn't sleep. I came down to warm up some—" He smiled. "Sorry. My brain is way too tired. Got enough milk in that pan for two mugs?"

Jonathon got up from the table. "Maybe not, but I can soon solve that." He went over to the AGA and poured out the steaming milk into the waiting mug. "You have this one. I'll put some more on."

Mike took it and added a spoonful of honey. "So, do I need three guesses as to why you couldn't sleep?"

Jonathon snorted. "You don't need to be Einstein to work that out." He sat down again, and Mike joined him. "Is it me, or did the list of people who could have been involved in Dominic's death just… grow?"

Mike sighed. "I sent Sue a text, asking her to get in touch with me. I didn't mention Dominic."

"Why not?" When Mike didn't respond, Jonathon had a flash of insight. Maybe he didn't mention it because there was the possibility he might not like her response. *Ignorance is bliss, right?*

That knot of writhing snakes was back.

Mike was studying him. "You don't look like Dominic," he concluded.

Jonathon smiled, aware of the change of subject. "I look like my father, who looks nothing like Dominic. Father takes after my grandmother, and Dominic my grandfather. Apparently when they were younger, no one believed they were brothers. Then when Dominic started losing his hair way before Father, that made the differences even more obvious. You wouldn't recognize Dominic in some of the older photos. He had a mass of brown hair."

Photos….

"What just went through your mind?" Mike gave him a speculative glance. "That look on your face…. Did you have an epiphany or something?"

Jonathon shook his head. "Nothing so helpful. I was thinking about that missing photo, that's all. Why would someone take it? Was it somehow incriminating?" He sighed. "I just can't shake the feeling that it's important. Especially after Father lied about it."

"Can I ask you something a little bit personal?"

Jonathon got up to take the milk off the heat. "You can ask. I may choose not to answer, depending on just how personal you're getting." He glanced over his shoulder and winked at Mike. "But I think you're fairly safe. Go for it." He went about pouring out his milk.

"Your dad… he's not supportive about you being gay?"

Jonathon huffed. "That's just one of the items on his list, Things Jonathon Does That Piss Me Off. Not that you'd ever catch him saying those exact words."

"There's a list?" Mike sipped his milk.

Jonathon snorted. "Let's see. I'm gay. I refuse to marry and procreate. I didn't go to Cambridge like he and the rest of my family did, to study Law. I showed no inclination to follow in his barrister footsteps. I don't join him in his belief that London is the be-all and end-all. I'm deluded enough to think that photography is a career." He shook his head. "Funnily enough, it was Dominic who encouraged me to follow my dreams. I'm pretty sure Father has no idea about that."

"So what will you do now? If you *have* inherited de Mountford Hall, I mean. Will you move here?"

Jonathon took a long drink of his milk, letting it warm him. "Honestly? I have no idea. There are a few hurdles to climb before I can even think about that. The first one being Dominic's funeral."

"I meant to ask you about that, after the tea at the vicarage. There's a crypt?"

Jonathon nodded. "Below the church. I always thought it was a spooky place. There are all these stone caskets on three sides, lining the walls. Those are for the really important ancestors. Lesser members of the family got a hole in the wall, with a plaque sealing it. Sir John has his own sarcophagus in the middle of the crypt, complete with statue of him in repose." He shivered. "I hated going down there as a child. Father dragged me there one summer, when Grandfather was still alive. He wanted me to see where I was going to end up one day."

"Ooh, nice. Way to go to frighten a little kid."

Jonathon chuckled. "Just pray you never have to meet him. He still scares me." He cocked his head to one side. "How about your parents? Are they anything like mine?"

Mike laughed softly. "Not even remotely, by the sounds of it. They were proud as Punch when I joined the force, and behind me 100 percent when I left it. And as for the being gay part?" He shook his head. "Dad doesn't mention it much, except if there's some-thing negative on the news and he calls me to tell me what idiots people are. Mum always asks if I'm seeing anyone. I think if I called her up and told her I was dating, she'd faint on the spot. *Then* she'd be back on the phone, asking if we'd set a date yet."

Jonathon laughed. "I don't think I'd mind that kind of questioning in the least." He got to his feet. "I think I'm going to take my milk back to my room and see if I can get a few hours' sleep."

Mike copied him. "I think I'll follow your exam-ple." When they reached the kitchen door, he paused. "And don't worry. This will all get sorted out. I feel it in my gut."

Jonathon tilted his head. "Is that your ex-copper's gut? Or the one belonging to Sue's brother?"

Mike huffed. "They're one and the same." He gave Jonathon a brief hug. "We'll get to know the truth eventually," he said quietly into Jonathon's ear. Mike released him and then picked up his mug. "See you in the morning. That is, later this morning. And as it's Sunday, it won't be an early breakfast. Maybe nine o'clock."

Jonathon smiled, still surprised by the hug. "Sounds good. Here's hoping the warm milk does its stuff." He stepped past Mike and headed for the stairs, carrying his mug. By the time he'd drank it all and was once more nestled in his comfortable bed, his eyelids had grown heavy and he let sleep carry him off into darkness. His last thought as a welcome warmth seeped into his bones was that Mike's hug had felt good.

JONATHON PILED the plates and bowls into the dishwasher and switched it on. Outside, the church bells were ringing, a noise so joyful that he had to open a window to let in the beautiful sound. He stood there, eyes closed, drinking it in.

*I could get used to this.* It was a far cry from the rumble of traffic that passed his door every morning.

"I could really disappoint you and tell you that what you're hearing is a recording out of the church tower."

Jonathon spun around and gaped at Mike. "Aw, don't say that. You'll shatter my illusions. I've been listening to those bells since I was little."

Mike grinned. "Now would I do that to you? Yeah, there are bell ringers."

Jonathon glared at him through narrowed eyes. "Bastard."

Mike let out a heady gasp and clutched his chest. "And here was I, thinking you were a polite, upstanding young man."

Jonathon went back to his task of wiping down the sink. "This polite, upstanding young man is now regretting cleaning the kitchen after breakfast."

"Aw, wow. You didn't need to do that." Mike's voice changed instantly. "You're a guest, remember?"

"Well, this guest is restless." Jonathon was waiting to be given the go-ahead to go to the hall. For one thing, he needed to choose clothing for Dominic to be laid out in, a job he wasn't looking forward to in the slightest.

If he could have pinpointed the heart of his inner turbulence, he would probably have put it down to one thing: it felt as though he was waiting for something to happen.

"How about we go for a walk along the river this morning?" Mike peered into the white porcelain bread bin and pulled out what was left of the loaf. "We could feed the ducks."

Jonathon arched his eyebrows. "Feed... the ducks. You *do* know that bread is actually bad for ducks, right?" He grinned.

Mike shrugged and stuffed the bread into a plastic bag. "Hey, it beats sitting around here all day. As for the bread, I've never once had a duck complain about it. And it *is* a gorgeous day out there."

He had a point. Nearly ten o'clock and the sky was a vast canvas of pale blue, no clouds to be seen. When the bells burst into life again, Jonathon inclined his head toward their jubilant sound. "I could always go to the church service and hear Sebastian preach."

Mike peered at him. "Church. Seriously? Where would you rather be on a day like today?"

That did it. "I'll fetch my jacket." Not that Jonathon was sure he'd need it, but with the British weather, it was always best to err on the side of caution, even in the summertime.

Then he amended that thought. *Especially* in the summertime.

They walked out of the pub, past the village green, and headed down to where the old, warm-colored stone bridge crossed the river. Jonathon stood in the center of it, gazing at where the water bubbled over rocks and created little eddies here and there. He jerked his head toward the bank, scanning the ground and the bushes. He grinned as he spied what he was looking for.

"What are you doing?" Mike asked as Jonathon passed him in a rush, heading for a dead shrub, its branches bare in comparison to the verdant foliage of those around it.

Jonathon snapped off a few twigs, before hurrying to join Mike on the bridge. He held up his prize triumphantly.

Mike's brow creased in a faint line. "Sticks," he said in a deadpan voice.

Jonathon did an eye roll. "Oh, come on, you're not *that* dense, and you're certainly old enough to remember poohsticks."

Mike stared at him. "Poohsticks. Winnie-the-Pooh and Piglet?"

Jonathon smiled. "Thank God. I was getting worried for a minute." He examined the twigs, breaking off bits so they were all roughly the same size, then handed half of them to Mike. "Come on. Best out of three buys the coffee and cake at the tea shop."

Mike shook his head, chuckling. "Can't believe I'm even contemplating this. Forty-two years old, and you want me to chuck sticks into the river."

Jonathon stilled, his mouth open. "Chuck… sticks… into the river. God, I'm talking to a philistine."

Mike ignored him and leaned over the low wall, arm outstretched, a twig held between his fingers. "Well, come on if you're playing," he demanded.

Jonathon let out a low growl and muttered under his breath about people who didn't take poohsticks seriously. He stood a few feet away from Mike, his own twig poised for launch. "On the count of three, we drop, okay?"

Mike nodded.

"One, two… three!"

The second they hit the water, Jonathon dashed to the opposite side of the bridge and peered into the shady water to spot whose stick emerged first. He fist-pumped the air when his nosed out ahead of Mike's.

Mike sighed. "And this, ladies and gentlemen, is the next lord of the manor."

Jonathon grinned. "Sore loser?"

Mike was already holding out his next twig. "Two more goes, remember?"

When Mike won two out of three, Jonathon accepted his defeat with good grace. "I was going to buy coffee and cake anyway, to thank you for being there for me since I arrived."

"Walk first, coffee later," Mike said with a smile. He pointed to the towpath that ran alongside the river.

"If we follow the path, there's a pleasant walk that takes you almost to the hall. We won't go that far."

Jonathon nodded. "Sounds good to me." He followed Mike as he stepped off the bridge and turned left, and soon they were strolling along the graveled path.

"There's another bridge farther along," Mike told him. "Have you ever seen it?"

Jonathon racked his brains. "Wooden? Suspended by ropes?" He had vague memories of Sunday walks after lunch at the hall, his father decked out in his country wear, complete with a silver-topped walking stick and heavy walking boots.

"That's the one."

Jonathon spied it in the distance. "There's someone on it."

A tall, thin man was standing in the middle, tossing something off the bridge, beneath which circled at least ten to fifteen ducks, males and females. The males' glossy green heads reflected the sunlight, and there was much flapping of wings as the birds fought to take possession of the food.

Then Jonathon noted another figure, this one seated in a power scooter on the path, watching the proceedings. It was an older woman, her face impassive as she stared at the scene before her.

"Andrew!" Mike called out.

The thin man turned and smiled. "Hey. Nice day for a walk, isn't it?" He nodded toward the bank. "Mum needed some fresh air." His gaze alighted on Jonathon, and for one brief moment, Jonathon caught a flash of some strong emotion in Andrew's eyes.

Then it was gone. "You must be Jonathon de Mount-ford. I'm... sorry for your loss."

"Thank you," Jonathon murmured politely. Andrew looked to be not that much older than him, but there was a tired air about him, something that spoke of world-weariness.

"This is Andrew Prescott, and his mother, Amy," Mike told him. "They've lived in the village for an even shorter time than I have."

"Pleased to meet you, Mrs. Prescott." Jonathon walked over to her, his hand extended. To his surprise she ignored it and glared at him. Jonathon withdrew his hand hastily.

"You'll have to excuse Mum." Andrew hurried off the bridge, setting it moving gently as he did so. He gave Jonathon an apologetic glance. "She's not herself right now." He patted her shoulder. "Time I got you home, eh?" Andrew gave a nod in their direction. "I'm sure I'll see you around," he said to Jonathon as his mother's scooter lurched into life and began to move along the path toward the village.

"Very possibly." Jonathon watched their retreat until the pair had gone around a bend in the river and were no longer in sight. He turned to Mike. "What was that about?"

Mike shrugged. "No idea. She usually doesn't talk a whole lot, but that was the first time I've seen her act like that. She was almost...."

"Hostile," Jonathon finished for him. "Like she hated me."

"Do you always arouse such strong emotions in people when you meet them for the first time?" Mike's warm brown eyes twinkled with good humor behind his glasses.

Jonathon lifted his eyebrows. "Why—what went through *your* mind when we first met?"

Mike bit back a smile. "Thought you were a bossy little shit."

"Bossy little shi—" He broke off and started laughing when he saw Mike's grin. "Fine. You don't get to feed the ducks."

"Hey, I was the one who had the idea!" Mike retorted.

Jonathon gave him a sweet smile. "Yes, but *I'm* the one with the bag of bread." And with that he strolled nonchalantly onto the bridge, reaching into the plastic bag to break off small pieces of bread.

"Er, Jonathon?"

He looked up. Mike was holding on to the ropes and grinning. "Think you can manage to feed the ducks *and* stay on your feet at the same time?"

Jonathon glared at him. "Don't. You. Dare."

Mike let go and stepped onto the bridge with the same degree of nonchalance that Jonathon had just demonstrated. He held out his hand. "Bread, please."

Jonathon sighed and handed him a big chunk. "Okay, you won that round."

Mike shook his head. "Don't forget the poohsticks." Then he turned to face the ducks and began chucking pieces into the river.

Jonathon didn't bother to hide his smile. Mike was definitely growing on him.

# CHAPTER SEVEN

"YOU'RE PRETTY handy behind a bar," Mike commented as he wiped down the bar top. The lunch-time crowd had departed, it was three o'clock, and they had three hours' breathing space before the pub opened again that evening.

Jonathon gave a short bow. "Why, thank you. I'd say I was a really fast learner, but that would be a lie." When Mike gave him a quizzical glance, he flushed. "When I was in Australia, working on my first book of photos, I stayed with a guy who ran a beach bar."

Mike arched his eyebrows. "'Stayed with'? Now *there's* a euphemism if ever I heard one."

Jonathon chuckled. "Okay, yeah, you got me. We dated for about three weeks. When I moved on, things kind of ended organically. Anyhow, he showed me a thing or two."

"I'll just bet he did," Mike murmured.

Jonathon fired him a warning glance. "About bar work. Turns out I was pretty nifty with a cocktail shaker." He preened, buffing his fingernails on his shirt.

Mike's eyes gleamed. "*Now* you've said something very interesting."

Jonathon was suddenly very wary of Mike's grin. "Uh-oh."

Mike held up his hands, palms turned toward Jonathon. "Nothing too onerous. I was just thinking…."

"Mm-hmm?"

"I get the odd request now and then for cocktails, but for most people in this village, they don't stray too far from the path of a beer, cider, or glass of wine. What if I were to put out a sign tonight for… Cocktail Happy Hour?"

Jonathon eyed him levelly. "And are we actually talking an hour?"

Mike snorted. "Not really. I was thinking more along the lines of keeping it going for as long as we could. It would be something different, for one thing. For another, it might catch on. And let's face it, you've seen this place at its busiest. Not exactly packed out, was it?"

Jonathon had to admit Mike had a point. And it might prove entertaining at least.

"Okay, I'll do it." He had visions of being Tom Cruise, tossing a stainless-steel cocktail shaker into the air and catching it with one hand behind his back.

Then reality set in. *Leave the showing off to those who know what they're doing.*

Mike's beaming smile was very gratifying. "Fantastic! I'll put out that chalkboard ASAP."

Jonathon shook his head. "I'm the creative one around here. Just show me where your coloring chalks are and leave the rest to me."

Mike wiped his brow and let out an exaggerated sigh. "Thank God. You've never seen my attempts at art, have you? No one would ever be able to tell what I was drawing." He went off in search of chalk, leaving Jonathon alone in the bar.

The first thing Jonathon did was to do a quick survey of Mike's bar stock. It wasn't as bad as he'd anticipated for a country pub, but it did mean their first forays into providing cocktails might be a bit limited. Then he reconsidered. *I could always create my own concoctions.* That might prove… interesting. Then he gave a snort. Not to mention possibly lethal.

The morning's stroll had been a pleasant diversion, but once they'd returned to the pub, it didn't take long for Jonathon's mind to turn once more to Dominic. He wasn't sure if he was expecting too much. After all, the police had only been on the case since Friday morning, and a little more than forty-eight hours probably wasn't enough time to have found Dominic's assailant. But all the same, he'd thought they'd have found *something*.

"What are you thinking about, as if I need to ask?" Mike was at his side, placing the boxes of chalk on the bar top.

"You'd laugh." Jonathon hardly dared voice what had just come to him. It sounded so ludicrous.

"Try me." Mike folded his arms across his wide chest.

Jonathon sighed. "I can't just sit here and do nothing. I want to…." He hesitated. Mike was an ex-copper, when all was said and done.

"Want to what?" Mike's unexpectedly gentle tone decided him.

"I want to see if I can find out what happened to Dominic." Jonathon stuck out his chin and awaited Mike's predictable verdict.

What he got back knocked the wind out of his sails.

"Okay."

Jonathon blinked several times. "Okay? No arguments? No 'Oh no, you must leave this up to the professionals'?"

Mike huffed. "I'm sure the local police are doing all they can. Plus we now have the best and brightest the Met can offer." He rolled his eyes. "I'm pretty sure that's exactly how Gorland sees himself. But yes, I'm equally sure that there are avenues we can follow that might lead us to the truth."

"We?"

Mike regarded him calmly. "You don't think I'd let you do this on your own, do you? You may be the expert here at taking a photograph or two, or—"

"Or two?"

Mike smirked. "And you may yet prove to be a dab hand at cocktails, though we'll know more about that tonight. But *I'm* the ex-detective, so I may have a few valid ideas on the subject. Agreed?"

"Agreed."

"And on that subject... I've had an idea, which might be a little... illegal."

*Now* he had Jonathon's full attention. "What did you have in mind?"

"I want a look at that coroner's report."

Jonathon stilled. "And how exactly do you pro-
pose doing that? Just call them up and ask to see it?"
He could imagine DI Gorland's reaction.

Mike chuckled. "You're not that far off the mark,
actually. I was going to ask Graham Billings if he
could get us a copy of it."

"Constable Billings?"

Mike nodded. "Trust me. There's a good chance
he'll say yes." He got out his phone and scrolled
through. "Graham. You got a sec? I have a huge favor
to ask." He wandered over to the window, lowering
his voice. Jonathon watched, trying to gauge how the
conversation was going. After a few minutes, Mike
ended the call and rejoined him. "He'll be here in half
an hour."

"Seriously?" Jonathon was astounded.

Mike smiled. "Okay. I may only have lived here
for eleven months, but in that time, there have been *no*
police callouts for drunken or rowdy behavior, which
apparently was not the case with my predecessor."

"Ahh." Now it made sense. "He likes the way you
run the pub. Less work for him."

"Yes. Added to that is the tiny but significant
point that me and his uncle go way back. We worked
together in London when I first started out." Mike
winked and tapped the side of his nose. "It's all about
who you know."

And that made even more sense.

When Constable Billings arrived, however, he
didn't seem completely at ease. He held a large brown
envelope, while gazing furtively around the pub,
as though he expected DI Gorland to leap out from

behind a chair at any moment. "You do know I could get shot for this, right?"

Mike arched his eyebrows. "One, shooting seems a bit excessive. Two, he's not going to find out. Three, you don't even have to leave the copy with us. We just need a peek at it." When the constable bit his lip, his brow furrowed, Mike patted his arm. "And think of it this way. What if _we_ manage to work out who did it, instead of Gorland? It'll make you look good."

Constable Billings gave a startled cough. "What—you'd let me take the credit for the arrest? Providing we make one, of course."

"Well, _I_ couldn't, could I?" Mike's lazy smile made Jonathon's insides do a little flip-flop, and he shoved aside all such thoughts. _Down boy._ There were more important things to occupy his mind now.

After a moment's hesitation, Constable Billings handed Mike the envelope.

"Now we're getting somewhere." Mike slid out the single sheet of paper and perused it carefully.

Jonathon was suddenly aware that his heartbeat had sped up. "Well?"

"Stuff we already know, like the bruising and the cracked ribs. And the—" Mike fell silent.

"What is it?" Jonathon moved closer to peer at the document.

"They've estimated his time of death." Mike gazed up at Jonathon. "Dominic didn't die Friday morning. It was more like Thursday evening." Mike scanned the sheet. "He fell onto the edge of the fire-place and hit the side of his head. Killed almost in-stantly, they reckon."

Jonathon prayed it was so. His chest tightened at the thought of Dominic lying there all that time, his life slowing ebbing away. "Is there anything else? Anything on the body that gives us any clues?"

Constable Billings gave him a faint smile. "You've been watching too much CSI, mate. I mean, sir."

Jonathon chuckled. "I think I preferred mate." He nudged Mike. "Well? Is there anything else?"

"No trace fibers, but there was something odd. They found pollen on Dominic's clothing."

"Pollen? From what?"

"It doesn't say, apart from possibly being lily pollen. They've sent it off to be tested." Mike glanced at Jonathon. "Are there lilies in the gardens up at the hall? Or in the hall, for that matter?"

Jonathon tried to picture the gardens. "Not that I can recall. Maybe we need to go up there and take a look around." Then a thought occurred to him that sent icy fingers trailing over his skin. "We're forgetting about the rug."

"What do you mean?"

"We know now that Dominic received a pretty hard shove to his sternum, right? And that caused him to fall. Someone went to the trouble of making it look like he tripped on the rug." He locked gazes with Mike. "Can we be sure it wasn't an accident?"

Mike's eyes were full of compassion. "We won't know for sure until we have all the facts." He put the sheet back in the envelope and handed it to Constable Billings. "Thanks for that."

"Don't mention it." Constable Billings narrowed his eyes. "Seriously. Don't mention it."

"Got it." Mike saw him to the door. When he returned, Jonathon lifted his chin and looked Mike in the eye.

"I can't sit around, dwelling on this. I'll go crazy." Just looking at the coroner's report had Jonathon's stomach churning all over again.

"Then don't," Mike said shortly. "Why don't you make a list of what you'll need for tonight, and then you can put up a list of which cocktails will be available."

"I've already taken a peek at your shelves." Jonathon pointed to the line of bottles. "We're going to need stuff like limes, lemons, juice, olives...."

"Then let's get out of here." Mike headed for the door.

"Where are we going?"

"The village shop. They're open every day until nine, and they stock everything. Well, nearly everything."

Jonathon smiled. "What are we waiting for?" Anything to keep his mind off reality for a while.

"A VODKA martini? Isn't that what James Bond drinks?"

Jonathon grinned at the attractive woman who was peering at the cocktails list. "Yes, ma'am. Vodka, vermouth, ice, and an olive. Do you want to try one?" He loved Rachel Meadow's facial expression, a mixture of interest and longing, as if drinking cocktails was somehow an illicit act.

"Ooh." She smiled. "Go on, then."

"Coming right up." Jonathon grabbed the bottles and began measuring into the shaker. He winked at her. "And this will definitely be shaken, not stirred." He shook the stainless-steel container vigorously.

Rachel giggled.

"Can't believe you just said that," Mike muttered at his side. He glanced around the pub. Virtually every table was occupied, along with the padded seats in the bay window. "This was a great idea. I've never seen this place so full."

"Ah, but are they here for the drinks or the new bartender?" The man seated on a stool in front of Mike inclined his head in Jonathon's direction. "I suspect the latter. They all want a peek at the latest de Mountford."

Mike huffed. "Maybe, but as long as they're here to have a drink, I'm happy."

Jonathon laughed. "I see. I'm a draw, am I?" He strained the cocktail into a glass, dropped an olive into it, and then added a slice of lemon on the side. "There you are." He placed the concoction in front of Rachel.

The man to her left chuckled. "You wanna watch yerself there, Rachel. How many is that now?"

She gave him a sly smile. "I'm not counting. And if you were any sort of a gentleman, Paul Drake, you wouldn't be counting either. Besides, it's only fair. Jonathon here came and sampled my cakes this morning. I have to reciprocate, right?" Rachel Meadows winked at Jonathon.

"Of course," Jonathon said with wide eyes. "How's the martini?" he asked as she took a cautious sip.

"Ooh, nice." Rachel's eyes shone. "I think I prefer this to the Cuba Libre." The words came out as though she was savoring their taste.

Paul snorted. "Come on, now. That's nothing but a fancy name for a rum and Coke."

"Amazing what adding a wedge of lime can do to a drink, isn't it?" Jonathon was enjoying himself. He peered at Paul's empty pint glass. "Why don't you try one?"

Paul squinted at the chalk-written list. "Uh, don't know about that. They've all got pretty, froufrou names. I mean, look at them. Piña colada, daiquiri, cosmopolitan, tequila sunrise… these are all your basic women's drinks."

Jonathon bit his lip. "I think I have just what you need." He measured spirit into the shaker over ice and added juice. When he'd shaken it for a moment, he poured it into a squat glass and placed it on the beer mat in front of Paul. "There. A man's drink."

"What is it?" Paul lifted the glass and brought it to his lips.

Jonathon grinned. "A screwdriver."

Mike gave a sound that was half laughter, half snort.

Paul laughed. "Fair enough. I guess I walked right into that one." He took a long drink and smacked his lips. "I always was partial to a vodka and orange." He glanced over his shoulder toward a table where a couple sat. "Hey, Trevor. You bought one of these cocktails for the missus yet? I'm sure Sarah would love a cosmo. That's what they call it on *Sex and the City*, right?"

Jonathon burst out laughing. "You're a dark horse. I wouldn't have had you pegged as a *Sex and the City* kind of bloke." Paul seemed more the farmer type, rough around the edges but good-natured with it.

Paul gave a smug smile. "You'd be surprised at what I watch on the ol' gogglebox. I'm an enlightened kind of guy. Ain't that right, Trev?"

Trevor looked across the bar in their direction, and Jonathon could have sworn he flinched. He tugged his wife's arm. "Think it's time we were off home, eh?" He spoke quietly, but Jonathon caught his words.

Sarah blinked. "What? But we've only been here half an hour. And I haven't tried a cocktail yet."

Trevor snapped his hand back. "Fine. Forget I said anything. You go choose a cocktail. I don't want anything."

Sarah raised her eyebrows and got up from the table, leaving Trevor staring into his empty glass.

"Bloody hell," Mike muttered under his breath. "I think the world just stopped on its axis."

"What do you mean?" Jonathon spoke out of the corner of his mouth as he watched Sarah reading the list.

"Trevor Deeping. One of my best customers, in the sense that he drinks more than any other bloke in here." Mike paused for a moment. "Come to think of it, I haven't seen him in here for a few nights."

Jonathon gazed at Trevor with interest. "Wonder why he stayed away?"

Mike chuckled. "And there goes the click of that sleuthing brain of yours."

"What?" Jonathon frowned. "No, I just find it really interesting when people stray from their usual pattern of behavior."

"What's in a mojito?" Sarah asked.

"White rum, Sprite, mint, lime, and sugar." Jonathon gave her a half smile. "Want to try it?"

"Ooh, go on. Sounds exotic."

He laughed and began crushing the mint leaves, lime, and sugar, aware of Sarah watching, clearly fascinated. His mind wasn't on the cocktail, however. *That* was fixed firmly on Trevor, who kept darting distinctly nervous glances in Jonathon's direction.

*Why are you scared of meeting my eyes, Trevor?* Because that much was obvious.

Then he gave himself a mental shake. Mike was right. He was starting to see suspects everywhere.

# CHAPTER EIGHT

JONATHON WAS in the middle of collecting glasses when he happened to glance through the window and stiffened. "Mike? You've got a visitor."

Mike looked across from the bar. "Shit. I wonder what he wants. Go let him in, will you? I've only just bolted the door."

"Sure." Jonathon deposited the glasses on a nearby table and went to unlock the heavy main door of the pub. He pasted on a polite smile as the door swung open. "Detective Inspector Gorland. Is this a social visit, or do you have news for me regarding my uncle?"

DI Gorland regarded him with a neutral expression. "Mr. de Mountford. Still here, I see."

"Until you tell me I'm free to stay at the hall, then, yes."

"Is Mike here?" Gorland stepped past him and into the pub, and Jonathon followed. He could see why Mike didn't like the man.

"John. What can I do for you?" Mike put down his cloth and came around from behind the bar.

"I'll come straight to the point. Where is your sister?"

Mike stilled. "I don't know. I haven't seen her since last weekend, and I haven't heard from her since then either."

DI Gorland arched his eyebrows. "Don't you find that strange that she'd go for over a week without contacting you?"

"Why do you want know where she is?"

"Because she's wanted for questioning. We found emails from her to Dominic on his laptop. Not to mention some anonymous letters we feel certain came from her also."

Mike frowned. "What emails? What anonymous letters?" His gaze flickered briefly toward Jonathon, and Jonathon's throat tightened. There was fear in Mike's warm eyes.

"Emails where she warns him not to go ahead with the hunt. The letters were a different kettle of fish. Nothing remotely subtle about them. Images of a fox torn apart by dogs."

Mike's eyes widened. "They could have been sent by anyone. Let's face it, the whole village knew about Dominic's plans, especially after—" His mouth snapped shut and he swallowed.

DI Gorland's eyes gleamed. "After what, Mike? After she and Dominic got into a blazing row in the middle of your pub? After she was heard by several witnesses to threaten to kill him?" He set his jaw. "The fact that she's not been seen since his death is highly suspicious, you have to admit, but all we want to do is eliminate her from our inquiries."

"Yeah, right, pull the other one." Mike's eyes blazed. "Have you forgotten what I did for a living? You want to pin this on her. Well, she didn't do it."

"Then she has nothing to fear from coming forward and answering our questions, does she? And don't think about concealing her whereabouts. Not unless you want us to do you for obstructing the police in their inquiries."

"I was telling the truth," Mike retorted. "I haven't heard a word from her."

"And while we're on the subject…." DI Gorland got out his notebook. "Where were you on Thursday night?"

"Me?" Mike's eyes bulged.

DI Gorland regarded him calmly. "After Sue argued with Dominic, you were heard warning him off. Telling him to stay away from her." His cool smile made Jonathon ache to wipe it off his face. "Did you think we wouldn't get to hear about that part?"

His words sank in. Jonathon jerked his head toward Mike. *Wait—what?* Mike hadn't once mentioned arguing with Dominic. Dismay filled him at the thought that Mike was still hiding the truth from him. *Is there more to come?* Then the full import of DI Gorland's line of questioning hit him. *He thinks Mike might have done it.* For reasons he couldn't quite fathom, Jonathon found himself holding his breath, praying Mike had an alibi.

"Clutching at straws, aren't you?" Mike's face was impassive. "I was a copper. How many ex-coppers have *you* heard of who go around breaking the law?" His cool demeanor could have been down to two things in Jonathon's mind: either he was innocent, or else he was a bloody good actor.

*Let it be the former?*

DI Gorland shrugged. "You have to admit, it's a good theory. Dominic threatens Sue, so you go up to the manor and warn him again to stay away. Things get out of hand, you two have a fight, you push him, he falls."

"And that's all it is, a theory." Mike froze. "Wait a minute. Thursday night?"

DI Gorland gave a thin smile. "That's right. He died Thursday night, not Friday."

"I was here, serving, until we closed at eleven thirty."

"And after that?"

"Once I'd locked up, I took Trevor Deeping home. He was drunk."

DI Gorland scribbled in his notebook. "Trevor Deeping?"

"He's a local. He was rather the worse for wear on Thursday night, so I made him stay where he was until everyone had gone. When I'd seen off the last of the customers, I helped him into my car and took him back to his house. His wife, Sarah, was still awake when I got there."

"Do you often make a habit of delivering drunken customers to their door?" That supercilious smile hadn't altered.

"When it's the decent, human thing to do, then, yes." Mike stared defiantly at DI Gorland. "Any more questions?"

"Not for the moment." Gorland tucked his note-book into his pocket. "If you should hear from your sister, please tell her to get in contact with us?"

"Of course. Jonathon, would you show the in-spector to the door?"

"Sure." Jonathon walked to the door and waited. He gave Gorland a single nod and then closed and bolted the door. By the time he got back to the bar, Mike was already pacing, scraping his fingers through his hair.

"Did you hear him? He wants to pin this on Sue. That slimy little—"

"Yes, I did. And getting upset about this isn't go-ing to help." Jonathon was doing his best to keep a cool head. He didn't want to believe Mike was involved, not when his senses were telling him otherwise.

Mike let out a heartfelt groan. "Anonymous let-ters? What the hell was she thinking about?"

"You think she did send them, then?"

Mike nodded. "That sounds like something she'd do. You should have seen her bedroom walls when she was a teenager. Greenpeace posters over every inch of available space. But violence like this? I don't think she's capable." He pulled his phone from his pocket, dialed, and pressed it to his ear. "I've got to keep try-ing. She'll have to answer the bloody phone eventual-ly, right?" It was obvious from his expression that she wasn't answering. He banged his phone down on the bar with a sigh of sheer exasperation.

All Jonathon wanted to do was comfort him.

Mike slowly raised his head and met Jonathon's gaze. "Help me."

The look of naked pain and despair in those eyes was enough to convince Jonathon that Mike had no part in Dominic's death. "How? What can I do?"

"Help me to prove it wasn't Sue? You want to know who did it just as much as I do. So... let's work together. Let's prove to that son of a bitch that my sister is totally innocent."

"And if we prove that but find she did break the law?" Jonathon waited for Mike to give the right answer. *Don't let me down now, not when I'm starting to believe in you.*

Mike squared his jaw. "If she broke the law, then she has to accept the consequences."

Jonathon gave an internal sigh of relief. "Then I'm with you. Let's find out who did this."

Mike shuddered. "Thank you." He dashed over to where Jonathon stood and enveloped him in a firm hug. When Mike released him, he stepped back. "Now, let's finish clearing up so we can decide what to do first." He went over to the bar and carried on wiping down the surfaces.

Jonathon returned to the task of collecting glasses, his mind in a whirl.

*Where do we go from here?*

"WHAT, NO cocktails tonight?" Paul Drake gave Jonathon a cheeky grin. "I thought that was gonna be a regular feature."

"Can't have too much of a good thing, y'know," Mike commented. "At least now we know we can do it again, judging by how well it went." If Mike's happy smile when he cashed up that night was anything to go by, it had been a very successful night indeed. Jonathon was pleased he'd been able to do something.

He gazed around the pub at the occupied tables. "No Trevor tonight," he said quietly to Mike, who stood beside him.

"Thought you'd notice that." Mike focused on pulling a pint.

"Well, do you blame me? I got the distinct feeling last night that he was, well... scared of me."

Mike snorted. "Scared of you? Why, for God's sake? There's nothing to you. A strong wind would blow you over."

Jonathon aimed a hopefully withering look in his direction. "Yeah, thanks for that." He shut up when Mike's phone rang. "Here, you answer that. I'll finish this."

Mike smirked. "One night mixing cocktails and suddenly you're Tom Cruise?" He grinned and took out his phone. When he froze, Jonathon's belly clenched.

"Who is it?" he whispered, not even sure why he was doing so.

Mike's gaze met his. *Sue*, he mouthed. He stepped away from the bar and began to talk in low tones. Jonathon knew it was wrong, but he strained to listen.

"Where are you? ... Why not? ... Listen... the police have been here. They want to take you in for questioning. ... Yeah, I know.... Look, just come home. We'll sort it all out, I swear. ... No, no, that's stupid! ... Yeah, I know, but... Sue. Sue. *Sue*! ... Just come home, all right?"

Jonathon hardly dared breathe. When Mike's shoulders sagged, and he expelled a long breath, Jonathon found himself unconsciously mimicking him.

"Great. Come to the pub. You can stay here if you don't want to go home. There's plenty of room." Mike glanced at Jonathon. "I've got a guest staying, but you don't have to worry about him…. Yeah, sure. … Okay, I'll see you when you get here. … Love you too. … Bye." He disconnected the call and peered at Jonathon. "I think that glass is full enough, don't you?"

"Huh?" Jonathon looked down to the pint glass, which was full to overflowing. "Oh shit." He released the tap and set the glass down on the drip tray.

Paul laughed. "I think he still needs a few lessons, Mike."

"Oh, I think he'll improve." Mike's eyes sparkled. "He's a fast learner."

Jonathon poured out a fresh pint, this time paying attention, and was rewarded with a pat on the back from Mike and a happy smile from Paul. Jonathon didn't give a flying fig about the pint.

He wanted to know about the call from Sue.

The chance to talk didn't arrive until after closing time, and as soon as Mike had locked and bolted the door, Jonathon dove right in.

"Well? What did she say? Did she mention Dominic?"

Mike shook his head. "And I didn't either. As soon as I told her the police wanted to question her, she started crying. I've never heard her so upset. But I did get her to agree to come home."

"Well, that's something." Jonathon paused. "Wait a minute. If neither of you spoke about Dominic's death, why was she so upset? Why didn't she want to come home?"

"I don't know!"

The agonized note in Mike's voice was enough to make Jonathon desist his questions.

"Okay," he said softly. "At least she got in touch and she's coming home. That's the important thing, right?"

Mike nodded. He seemed to have aged in the last ten minutes. "And when she gets here, *then* we can talk about Dominic."

"How about I make us some warm milk, and then you can get an early night? We're going to need all our brain power if we're going to solve this."

That seemed to infuse some calm into Mike. "You're right. Things will look different after a good night's sleep. Warm milk it is." He smiled. "After we've cleared up."

Jonathon nodded in agreement. "Then let's get our fingers out."

Sleep was probably the best thing for both of them.


"HEY, MIKE? Where's the bread?" Jonathon had opened every cupboard in the kitchen, but they and the bread bin were equally devoid of a loaf.

Mike entered the kitchen, yawning and scratching himself through his shorts. "Huh?"

Jonathon chuckled. "I see the honeymoon is over."

Mike snorted. "If two guys can't scratch their bollocks in front of each other, then there's something seriously wrong with the world. And there's a reason you can't find the bread."

"Oh?"

Mike grinned. "I ate the last piece."

Jonathon rolled his eyes. "Fine. I'll go to the shop and buy some. While I'm gone, you can put the coffee on." As he left the kitchen, he caught Mike's muttered, "Yeah, the honeymoon is definitely over." It was enough to send him out of the pub with a smile on his face.

It was a glorious morning, the temperature already rising, and Jonathon stood for a moment, breathing in the fresh country air. He felt revitalized, ready for whatever the day had in store for him. A brisk walk to the shop, which was filled with the delicious aroma of freshly baked bread, resulted in his nostrils being tantalized by the smell of the croissants he wasn't able to resist buying. After paying and placing his purchases in a plastic bag, he headed for the exit.

"Excuse me, but… you're Jonathon de Mountford, aren't you?"

Jonathon glanced up from his phone and saw a woman with shoulder-length brown hair, her eyes hidden by sunglasses. He didn't recognize her. "Yes, that's me."

She gave him a hesitant smile and removed her shades. "I've seen photos of you at your uncle's place."

The warm brown eyes regarding him with a hint of trepidation were so like Mike's, it was uncanny. "You're Sue, Mike's sister."

She blinked and stared. "You… you know Mike?"

Jonathon nodded. "I'm staying at the pub. He told you last night on the phone that there was a guest? Here I am."

"I see." She frowned. "But what are you doing staying at the pub? I thought you were going to stay with Dominic?"

Jonathon was stunned into silence.

"Is there something wrong? Are you okay?" Her brow furrowed, and her tone spoke of concern.

Finally he found his voice. "Mike didn't mention Dominic during your call, because you were already upset, but... well, it's fairly obvious that you don't know what's happened."

"Know what?" A hint of a frown creased Sue's brow.

"Mike was going to tell you when you got to his place, so I guess it's okay for me to tell you now." He forced himself to breathe, to be gentle. "Dominic is dead."

Sue blanched. "What the fuck are you talking about?"

Jonathon pushed aside his own feelings of confusion. Right then it seemed like she had enough of her own to deal with. "He had a fall, Thursday evening. He hit his head. But if you didn't know this, why did you stay away? Where have you been? Why do you think the police want to talk to you?"

"Because I thought they knew about—" She pressed her lips together, her eyes wide.

There was something going on here that made no sense, and Jonathon figured the only way to get to the bottom of it was to take her to Mike.

Then the penny apparently dropped. "The police think I had something to do with his death?" Sue's face paled. He nodded, and her jaw fell. "I swear, I had no idea, I—"

"It's okay. Right now, you need to come with me. Mike will be so pleased to see you. We can talk about it at the pub." Jonathon gave a quick glance around them, as though he expected the police to descend on them that instant. It was a fucked-up, illogical feeling, but he couldn't help it.

She nodded. "Okay." Her voice cracked, and she shivered. "Oh my God. Poor Dominic."

"Not here. Not now. Let's get you back to the pub, okay?"

"Okay." Another shiver rippled through her, and instinctively Jonathon walked over to her and put his arm around her shoulders.

"I've got you. Let's go see Mike." He guided her out of the shop, conscious of the stares from passersby.

The sooner he got her to the pub, the better.

# CHAPTER NINE

"OH, THANK God." Mike had his arms around Sue, his eyes closed. To Jonathon it looked like he was afraid to let go of her.

Sue clung to him, sniffing.

"I'll go and fetch us some coffee." Jonathon left them to it, figuring they needed some space. He went into the kitchen and got another mug from the cupboard. From the pub came their muffled voices, but Jonathon wasn't listening. If it was something he needed to hear, he trusted Mike to share it.

By the time he'd poured the coffee, Mike appeared in the kitchen.

"She's gone upstairs to wash her face. When she's ready, I'm going to go with her to the police station."

"She's agreed to go?" Jonathon blinked. After the way she'd spoken in the shop, it was the last thing he'd expected her to do.

Mike scowled. "It's not like I gave her the option. She won't tell me where she's been, and this isn't going to just go away. At least if Gorland asks his questions, he can eliminate her from his inquiries."

"What makes you think she'll talk to him, if she won't talk to you?" Jonathon placed three mugs of coffee on the table.

"I'm hoping he'll prove scarier than her big brother, to be honest."

Jonathon sat down. "I really think she had no idea he was dead." There was no way she could have faked such a reaction.

"I think so too. I just wish she'd tell me—"

From the doorway Sue cleared her throat, then gave Jonathon a bright smile. "Ooh, coffee. Smells good." She sat facing him and reached for a mug.

"Where's Sherlock?" Mike demanded.

"With… a friend." Sue sipped the hot, aromatic brew. "He's okay. Actually, he probably doesn't want to come home. My friend has a golden retriever, and I think Sherlock is in love." She gazed at Jonathon. "I am so, so sorry for your loss. Dominic thought the world of you. Every time one of your photos turned up in a magazine or newspaper, he cut it out and stuck it in a scrapbook. He used to show them to me. So proud, he was."

Jonathon swallowed. "Thanks for sharing that."

"Gorland said something about anonymous letters," Mike blurted out. "He thinks you sent them."

Sue frowned. "Letters? But I only sent one. It was a photo of a fox after the dogs had finished with it. I wanted him to see what he was agreeing to. Oh, I know they *say* it's only hunting with dogs, but are you going to tell me that if those hounds get a whiff of a fox, they won't be off after it? Pull the other one."

"So if you only sent the one...." Jonathon's gut clenched. "Then how many more did he receive, and who sent them?"

"Which is precisely why we're going to the station," Mike declared. "And this time Gorland will be answering some questions. Leave the coffee. That can wait. Let's get this over with." He stared at Sue. "All right?"

She nodded, her face now with slightly more color in it. "All right."

Five minutes later they were out of the pub and climbing into Mike's 4x4.

"Is it a big police station?" Jonathon asked as they sped along the country lanes. He couldn't recall having seen it.

"Not really. And on first sight, it looks nothing like a police station." Mike pointed down the lane. "See what I mean?"

Jonathon followed his finger and saw a delightful house constructed in stone, with a main door to the right, over which was a white-painted archway bearing the word Police. White gables rose to the left, with chimney pots perched on top of the slate-gray roof.

"Really?" It seemed far too quaint for a police station.

Mike pulled the car into the small car park at the rear of the station. They were quiet as they entered the building.

Constable Billings sat behind a wide desk, studying papers. He glanced up as they approached, and his eyes widened when he saw Sue. "Mrs. Bentley. We've been trying to reach you."

"So I hear." Sue appeared calm, but Jonathon saw the way she clutched Mike's hand, his fingers almost white.

"I'll go and find the DI." Constable Billings left them in the sunny reception area, whose walls were adorned with public safety posters.

Mike leaned into her. "It'll be fine," he said in a low voice. "You wait and see."

DI Gorland appeared in the doorway, with Constable Billings behind him. "Mrs. Bentley. So glad you found time to join us. If you'd like to go with Constable Billings, we have a few questions for you."

Sue jerked her head to face Mike. "Don't they have to caution me?"

"They only do that when they arrest you," Mike told her. "This is just questioning. Isn't it, John?" He glared at Gorland.

"For the moment."

Mike and Gorland locked gazes, but then Mike nodded and patted Sue's arm. "Go with Graham, sweetheart. It'll be okay."

She followed Constable Billings, giving Mike one last glance before she disappeared from view.

"You needn't wait for her," Gorland said dismissively. "This might take a while. We'll give you a call when we're done. That's assuming we release her, of course." DI Gorland gave Mike and Jonathon a brisk nod before turning to leave them.

"Can we see your investigation room?" Mike called out.

"Now, why would I let you do that?" Gorland peered at them, his bushy eyebrows arched.

"Because Jonathon here might be able to shed light on some of your investigation. After all, he knows the crime scene better than both of us."

Jonathon had a brainwave. "And besides, I'm sure my father would be pleased to hear you were accommodating our wishes." It was a long shot, but remembering their first conversation, he felt it wouldn't do any harm to remind Gorland of those long strings.

His words appeared to have done the trick. Gorland looked like he'd just sucked on a lemon. "I've commandeered a room. Step this way, gentlemen."

Jonathon and Mike followed him into a large room, empty but for two desks and a large white screen propped against the wall. On one of the desks sat Dominic's laptop. Fastened to the white screen were several photos, and Jonathon wandered over for a closer look. He winced at the sight of Dominic's bare torso, a dark red color all over. Then a thought occurred to him. "How can you tell there was bruising from this photo?"

Gorland huffed. "So now you want a lesson in pathology?"

Mike walked over and nudged Jonathon's arm. "During the autopsy, they'd have found evidence under the skin," he said quietly. "You're right, though. Lividity makes it impossible to see."

"Actually, there is something you could help us with."

Jonathon glanced over his shoulder at Gorland. "Yes?"

"Did your uncle ever do brass rubbings as a hobby?"

Jonathon blinked. "I don't know. I don't think so. He certainly never mentioned doing such a thing. Why do you ask?"

Gorland approached the screen and pointed to a photo. "Do you recognize this?"

Jonathon nodded. It was the photo album from Dominic's desk.

"We found traces of brass polish and brass rubbing wax on the cover and on its pages. Plus, there appears to be a photo missing. We have no idea whether this is recent or if it might have been taken by his attacker." Gorland regarded him closely. "Do you have any knowledge of this?"

For one brief moment, Jonathon was tempted to tell him about the photo. But Gorland's hard features and previous manner were enough to convince him to remain silent. "Sorry, I have no idea."

"I see. In that case I don't think there's anything else we need to ask. If you do think of anything you feel may be relevant, please inform us right away."

"Of course."

Gorland addressed Mike. "Like I said before, if we intend to proceed with charges once we've questioned Mrs. Bentley, we'll make sure you're told. Good day, gentlemen." He gestured toward the door.

There was nothing to do but to leave.

Mike got into the car and sat with his hands balanced on the steering wheel. "Why didn't you tell him?"

"Because I can't see how it's relevant to his inquiries." Even as Jonathon said the words, he knew them to be a lie. There was a mystery here, and he aimed to solve it.

Mike sighed. "I know he said not to wait, but I don't feel like going back to the pub just yet."

"Then let's not. How about a coffee at the tea shop? A change of scenery?"

Mike considered this suggestion for a moment. "Yeah, why not? We can drive straight there." He switched on the engine and backed out of the space. A minute or so later, Mike sighed again. "She'd better answer their questions."

"What if she doesn't?"

"If they think she had something to do with his death, they might arrest her. Especially if she doesn't tell them what they want to hear, like where the hell she's been."

They drove through the village, and Jonathon took a good look around. Monday morning in Merrychurch had none of the hustle and bustle of a larger town. He spied what appeared to be a group of tourists, all armed with cameras and phones, traipsing along the lanes, snapping pictures of the cottages, the gardens, and the small array of shops.

"They'll be off to the church soon," Mike commented, indicating the group with a nod of his head. "It always gets a lot of tourists, especially at the brass rubbing center."

Jonathon stilled. "Brass rubbing?"

"Yeah, I know. When Gorland mentioned the polish and the wax, that was the first place that came to my mind. But there's a lot of brass in this village. Just take a look." He pointed through the windscreen. "The plaque outside the doctor's surgery, for one."

Jonathon rolled his eyes. "Now you're just being silly."

Mike pulled up outside the tea shop. "Come on. I need some coffee." He switched off the engine, and they headed into the pretty tea shop, with its bow windows lined with teapots of all shapes and sizes. A frothy lace curtain hung halfway down each window, obscuring the view of the shop's patrons.

Rachel glanced up as they entered. "Hey, you two. Your timing is excellent. I've just made some scones and they're still warm." Only one other table was occupied, by two elderly ladies chatting over tea and crumpets.

Jonathon's stomach rumbled, and it was then that he recalled he'd had no breakfast. Sue's arrival had sidetracked him.

"You couldn't do some hot buttered toast, could you?" Mike asked.

Rachel beamed. "Coming right up. Take a seat anywhere you like."

Mike pointed to a small round table near the window. "How about here?"

Jonathon took the chair facing him and gazed around the shop. Watercolor paintings adorned the walls, and high up on the wall was a shelf that ran all the way around, on which sat....

"Look." Jonathon grabbed Mike's hand and squeezed it hard. "There's brass everywhere," he whispered. There were teapots, vases, plaques, horses, a pair of peacocks....

Mike chuckled. "You know what this reminds me of? The time I was thinking about changing my car. I'd been looking at a certain make and model, not one

I was familiar with. But damn me, once I started re-searching? I saw them everywhere! And you can bet we're now going to be seeing brass everywhere we look." He sighed. "Not that it brings us any closer to working out how that stuff got on the photo album." He stopped talking when Rachel came out bearing a tray.

"Coffee, guys. The toast will be out shortly. And I'm bringing you some of my homemade orange and ginger marmalade." She smiled at Jonathon. "Dominic loved it."

"Did he come here often?"

"Once a week. He liked to have tea here and talk to people. He talked with everyone." She pointed to a couple of watercolors. "Those are his, by the way."

Jonathon stared at the delicate paintings of the village church and the green. "Seriously?"

Rachel nodded. "He did them years ago. He do-nates one—I mean, he *donated* one—every year as a prize for the village fete raffle." Her smile faltered momentarily. Jonathon got the impression that Rachel had been very fond of Dominic. Then her face bright-ened. "Speaking of which, I hear the fete will still be happening this year. Melinda spread the word around. I'll need to put together a baking schedule. The re-freshment tent will need all the cakes and biscuits it can get, plus I have to work on my recipe for the cake contest." She grinned and pointed to a colorful plaque at the far end of the shop. "My carrot cake won last year, so I have a lot to live up to." She left them and disappeared from sight.

"Dominic seems to have taken his role in the vil-lage very seriously," Mike remarked.

"And apart from Sue, I've met few people who had a reason to dislike him. There's the old guy in the cottages, of course, but I don't think that sounds likely, do you? So if everyone liked him, who was he arguing with?"

"There's only one answer to that, I'm afraid." Mike looked glum.

"And what's that?"

"There has to be someone in this village whose motives we know nothing about. Yet." Mike turned his head and gazed at the windows. "Out there is someone with a secret."

The thought sent a shiver down Jonathon's spine.

JONATHON COLLECTED the last of the glasses and deposited them in the washer. "Anything else I can do?"

Mike shook his head. "I'm all done here." It had been a fairly quiet couple of hours, until ten or so tourists had arrived for a late lunch, and Abi had been busy in the kitchen. There had been no word from Sue, and Jonathon knew it was preying on Mike's mind—the constant glances at his phone were evidence of that. He wished he could say something to give Mike comfort, but nothing came to mind.

"See you tonight, Mike," Abi called out as she left.

"Yeah, and thanks." Mike followed her to rebolt the door. When he returned, he was frowning.

"What's up?"

"Just wondering how long it takes to ask some bloody questions, that's all. We should have heard something by now. She's been down at the station for more than five hours."

Just then, his phone rang, and Mike darted over to where it lay on the bar and snatched it up. "Can I come and pick her up now?" The frown lines deepened. "Why not?" He listened intently, his eyes widening. "Then let *me* talk to her. She might listen, especially if you've just threatened to charge her with obstruction.... Look, you can be in there while I talk to her, all right? Just... let me try." He listened again, and Jonathon was relieved to see the tension ebbing from him a little. "Okay. I'll be right over." He disconnected the call.

"What's going on?"

Mike scowled. "Sue's not cooperating. She won't tell them where she was, the stubborn...." He sucked in a deep breath. "Gorland says I can have five minutes with her, to see if I can get her to change her mind."

"Is that likely?"

Mike's eyes flashed. "Depends on whether I scare her enough to make her see sense and just answer their questions." He grabbed his car keys from behind the bar.

"I'm coming too."

Mike huffed. "Yeah, I expected that. Well, come on, then."

There was silence on the way to the police station. Jonathon figured Mike had enough on his mind, and let him drive in peace. Once there, they hurried into the reception area, where Constable Billings gave Mike a nod.

"The DI will be out in a sec." Constable Billings gestured to the padded bench along one wall. "You can wait here, Mr. de Mountford."

Jonathon had other ideas.

"Mike. Shall we go through?" DI Gorland regarded them impassively.

"I want to come too," Jonathon blurted out.

Gorland arched his eyebrows. "I'm only letting Mike talk to her because he's ex-force and he might be able to get her to cooperate. *You* are a civilian."

"A civilian whose father knows the police commissioner. Who got you here in the first place." Jonathon stuck out his chin. "This is *my uncle* we're talking about. I'm not asking to question her. I just want to be there. I won't say a word."

"You haven't arrested her yet, John," Mike added quietly. "It's just a conversation, right?"

Gorland rolled his eyes heavenward. "Fine. But he so much as *squeaks* out of turn and he's out of there. Okay?"

Mike glanced at Jonathon, who gazed solemnly at Gorland, his chin held high. "Absolutely no squeaking." Out of the corner of his eye, Jonathon saw Mike's shoulders shake just the tiniest bit.

Gorland narrowed his eyes but then straightened. "Follow me."

He led them into a small room at the rear of the station. Inside was a wooden table with four chairs around it, looking more like a social lounge than an interview room. Sue sat on one chair, her hands around a mug of tea. She glanced up when they entered and her eyes widened.

"Mike? What are you doing in here?" It was obvious from her reddened eyes that she'd been crying.

Gorland pointed Jonathon in the direction of a chair against the wall, and he did as instructed. Mike sat facing Sue, his hands clasped together on the table.

"DI Gorland tells me you won't tell him where you were when Dominic died. He seems to think you know something about this."

"I keep telling him, I don't know anything about this. I only found out Dominic was dead this morning."

Mike nodded. "Sweetheart, you could be in serious trouble. You have to tell the police the truth."

Sue swallowed. "Even if... doing that lands me in trouble too?"

Mike sighed. "I think I know what you're hiding, sis, but now's not the time for keeping quiet. I understand you're scared, but if I'm right, you have less to fear by telling the truth."

Sue lowered her gaze to her mug and drew in a deep breath. "Okay." She lifted her head and looked Gorland in the eye. "On Thursday night, I was nowhere near the hall. In fact, I was in.... Reading. I was part of a raid on a laboratory, one we suspected was testing on animals."

Gorland took out his notebook. "That's been banned in this country for a while now."

Sue snorted. "Would you like me to tell you how many tests were carried out on—"

"No," Mike interjected firmly, "because that would *not* help right now. How many people were with you?"

Sue bit her lip. "Three."

"What were your exact movements?"

She sighed. "I drove to Reading first thing Thursday morning. We raided the lab that night, and then

I stayed with one of the team until early this morning. We were just laying low and waiting to see what happened."

"You know you could face prosecution for breaking and entering, plus any damage you caused, if the laboratory presses charges."

Sue gave a short laugh. "I don't think they will. Not if it means bad publicity."

Gorland tapped his notebook with his pen. "I need names."

Sue flashed Mike a glance. When he nodded, there was a moment of hesitation before she recited the names.

Gorland looked up when he'd finished writing. "Is that all of them?"

Another second of hesitation. "Yes."

He closed his notebook. "Right. We'll check your story and see if the lab wants to proceed further. Until we hear from them, you're free to go."

Sue shuddered out a long breath. "Okay." She pushed back her chair and stood. "Mike? Get me out of here."

"No problem." As Sue stepped around the table, Mike met Gorland's gaze. "Looks like you need to look elsewhere, John."

"Don't worry, we'll keep looking." He addressed Jonathon. "We've concluded our investigations up at the hall. I'm sure you'll be wanting to stay there, rather than the pub. Must be a bit of a comedown."

Jonathon gave him a thin smile. "Detective Inspector, the rest of my family may live in properties just as imposing as the hall, but this is one de Mountford who is used to roughing it. Don't make the mistake of thinking you know me." And with that he followed Mike and Sue out of the station to the car.

Only one thing niggled at him. He had the distinct feeling that Sue hadn't told Gorland the whole truth.

# CHAPTER TEN

JONATHON FOLLOWED Sue and Mike into the pub. She sank into one of the more comfortable chairs and gave Mike a hard stare. "Christ, I need a drink."

Mike chuckled. "Why does not that not surprise me?" He grabbed a glass and turned to hold it up to an optic. "What about you, Jonathon? Do you want a drink?"

"Please. Just a Coke."

Sue gestured to the empty chair beside her. "Sit down. Talk to me while we've got a breathing space, because he'll be opening those doors again before long, and if I know Mike, he's already roped you into helping out around here."

Jonathon snickered. "Very astute. He's had me making cocktails."

Mike spun around. "*Had* you making cocktails? And there was I, thinking you were having fun."

Jonathon laughed. "It *was* fun! I'm just wait-ing for you to make puppy-dog eyes at me and say, 'Jon-a-thonnnn, can we do it again?'"

Sue stared at him and promptly burst out laugh-ing. "Okay, what have I missed? Because considering you can't have been here all that long, you two sound like an old married couple." She gave Mike a search-ing glance. "Something I should know?"

Mike flushed. "Get your mind out of the gutter. It's not like that."

"Yet?" she asked with a grin, her eyes sparkling.

It was Jonathon's turn to flush. He felt the heat crawling up his neck and over his cheeks.

Sue peered at him before turning to Mike. "I like him."

"Yeah, I like him too." Mike's voice was gruff. "Now let's talk about something else?"

Thankfully Sue took the hint. "That police in-spector said you could stay at the manor now. Is that what you want?"

Jonathon had been considering that very thing on the way back from the police station. "Right now, I'm not sure. I know my father would be happier if I stayed there, but...."

"It feels too soon after Dominic's death," Mike finished for him.

Jonathon nodded. "I do want to go up there and take a look around, however." There was something he needed to investigate.

Mike reached into his pocket and pulled out his keys. "Here," he said, tossing them across the bar to Jonathon. "Take my car. I'm gonna be busy setting up for the evening anyway." He gave Sue a hard stare.

"And *you're* gonna help me. That way I know you're keeping out of trouble." He set a squat glass on the bar.

"Trouble?" Sue widened her eyes. "I—"

"And don't bother with that 'butter wouldn't melt' look. Don't forget, I just picked you up from the police station."

Jonathon laughed and left them to it.

He drove slowly through the village, taking it all in. There were little lanes that fed off from the main road, where pale, biscuit-colored thatched roofs could be glimpsed above hedges, set against the backdrop of the lush green of summer. As he passed through the gateposts, the afternoon sun lit up the manor house on the hill, and a sense of pride stirred in him. His family home....

Up until that moment, he'd ignored the idea that it would be his home too. It didn't seem a real prospect. Jonathon had his career, even if his father refused to acknowledge it as such, and the thought of leaving it behind to move to Merrychurch was one he hadn't wanted to even consider. But deep down, he knew he wouldn't go against his family's wishes. It would be as futile as trying to swim against the current, where the waves towered above your head.

Better to ride them, to be carried along on them.

Jonathon turned onto the lane that led up to the house, waving to the few people he glimpsed. He had no idea why Dominic had intended selling off the land and evicting his tenants; the financial health of the estate was unknown to him.

*Then maybe I need to find out.*

He pulled up outside the main door, got out, and locked the car. He was there for one reason only: Jonathon was looking for lilies.

His first stop was the study, but no lilies were evident. He then searched the house, entering every room, opening every cupboard, peering into every space he could find. Nothing. Then he went back to the study and opened the french doors. The garden beyond was laid out with well-stocked flower beds, so Jonathon guessed someone had been tending to them. No lilies grew there, however.

After an hour of searching, he gave up. Wherever the pollen that had found its way onto his uncle's clothing had come from, it had not originated at the manor. Wearily, he got into the 4x4 and drove back to the pub.

Mike smiled as he walked through the door. "Hey, just in time. We're about to open." He peered at Jonathon. "Are you all right? You look pissed off."

Sue came out from the kitchen, carrying two steaming mugs. "Nice timing. I just made some tea. Do you want one?"

"A coffee if there's any going."

Sue put down the mugs and came over to him. "Aw, you look fed up." She put her arm around him, and the friendly gesture was just what he needed.

Quickly, he told her and Mike about his lily hunt.

Sue shook her head. "I wish you'd told me before you went. I could have saved you a trip."

"Oh?"

She nodded. "You won't find lilies up at the manor house because Dominic hated them. Said they always reminded him of death."

"In which case that leaves us with two possibilities. Either he went somewhere and came into contact with lilies, or else whoever pushed him brought the pollen with them and it got transferred to Dominic's clothes." It was an answer, but not the one he had hoped for. "Talk about a needle in a haystack."

Mike huffed. "We can search for needles in haystacks some other time. Right now I have a pub to open." He gave Jonathon a beseeching glance. "Want to help out again?"

Jonathon arched his eyebrows. "Well, that depends. Am I going to be collect-the-empties boy, or make-cocktails boy?"

Sue chuckled. "Here, you get behind the bar and do your stuff. I'll do the menial tasks. Besides, I want to watch how you wield a cocktail shaker." Her eyes sparkled. "And you'd better be as good as Tom Cruise." With that, she disappeared into the kitchen.

Mike gave Jonathon a frank stare. "Well? What are you waiting for, 'Tom'? Get your arse behind this bar." He grinned.

Jonathon gave him a mock glare. "Are you going to talk to me like that when I'm lord of the manor?"

Mike shrugged. "Probably, but admit it. You wouldn't want me any other way." Another grin, and then he carried on placing clean glasses onto the shelves.

Jonathon stepped behind the bar and tried his hardest not to stare at the way Mike's arse filled his tight jeans, the way his muscled thighs stretched the denim. *Down boy.* It didn't help matters that it had been months since Jonathon had had so much as a whiff of a sexual encounter.

But, God, it was a tempting thought.

"MIKE, HAVE we got any more lemons?" Jonathon was just about to run out.

"There's some in the kitchen," Sue said as she brought a tray of empty glasses to the washer. "I'll get them for—" Her eyes widened.

Jonathon followed her gaze and saw a guy of about medium height, slim, with reddish-brown hair and a lot of facial scruff. He glanced around the bar, as if he was looking for someone.

Jonathon hurried over to Sue. "Who is that?" he whispered.

"Bryan Mayhew, the student who's been staying up at the manor." She frowned. "And where the hell has he been?"

Bryan walked purposefully up to the bar. "Evening, Mike. A pint of Pride, please."

Around him, people fell silent, all eyes on him.

Mike stared at him. "A pint of Pride? Is that all you have to say, when the police have been wanting to talk to you since Friday?" Murmurs broke out, as several people looked from Mike to Bryan, waiting for his response, before hurriedly glancing into their glasses and whispering.

Jonathon studied Bryan's reactions, unable to miss the way he stiffened, his eyes widening.

"Why should the police wanna talk to me?"

"Because you haven't been seen in the village for a while, and Dominic is dead, that's why." Mike's voice rose loud and clear, and a hush fell on the rest of the pub.

There was no missing the pallor that crept over Bryan's face. "He's… dead?"

Jonathon's main suspect was either telling the truth, or else he was a fantastic actor, because to Jonathon's mind, his reaction appeared genuine.

"Where've you been?" Mike demanded.

The bar's patrons were trying to look like they weren't listening in, and failing miserably.

Bryan swallowed. "I… I was staying with a friend before he went on holiday."

"And when did you leave the village?" Mike leaned on the bar, his expression more watchful than Jonathon had seen it previously.

"Thursday afternoon. I packed a bag and took the bike down to Dorchester, where Andy lives."

"When did you last see my uncle?" Jonathon blurted out, unable to keep silent a second longer. He joined Mike, standing beside him, a lemon clutched in one hand.

"Your uncle?" Bryan gaped. "Oh my God. You're Jonathon. Dominic said you were coming to visit. I… I saw him Thursday afternoon, just before I left. He was in his study, at his desk." He swallowed again. "But he was alive, I swear it. He was about to make a phone call."

Mike hadn't broken eye contact once. "The police will need the name of your friend, along with his address and how to get in touch with him, so he can corroborate your story."

Bryan blinked. "S-story? Mike, I swear to Almighty God, I did *not* kill him." His voice rang out, steadier than before. "As for Andy, he's gone backpacking around Bali, Singapore, and God knows how many other places. He'll be gone for at least a month. Part of the reason I went to see him is because he wants me to keep an eye on his place for him. He's got his phone with him, but fuck knows what signal he'll have." He winced. "Sorry. I don't usually swear in public, but this is kind of a strange situation."

"Did you see anyone else up at the manor that afternoon?" Jonathon asked suddenly.

Bryan jerked his head in Jonathon's direction. "Anyone else?" He took a deep breath. "No, it was just me."

Jonathon locked gazes with him. "You're sure?" He couldn't put his finger on what was giving him that coiling of unease in his belly. Maybe it was the slight hesitation.

Bryan didn't look away. "Positive." He gave Mike a weak smile. "I think the pint had better wait, don't you? At least until I've spoken with the police."

Mike nodded. "There's a DI Gorland who'll want to see you. Make sure you tell him everything, all right?"

It was Bryan's turn to nod. He turned to go, but paused and gazed at Jonathon. "I suppose in the circumstances, you don't want me staying at the manor, right?"

Jonathon hadn't given it a moment's thought until that second. "*I'm* not even staying there." He glanced at Mike. "What do you think?"

Mike rubbed his chin thoughtfully. "You're staying in the annex, aren't you? Not the main hall—the bit that backs onto the stables?" When Bryan nodded, Mike addressed Jonathon. "I don't think he'll cause any problems if he continues staying there. Provided the police are okay with it too. And you," he added pointedly.

Jonathon knew what *that* meant. As the new lord of the manor, the final say-so was his.

*I really do need to see Dominic's solicitor.*

He gave Bryan a half smile. "Sure. That's okay. How much longer did you plan on staying in Merrychurch?"

"Originally Dominic said I could stay just for the summer. Then I'll be back at uni, writing my doctorate." Bryan shivered. "Not sure how I feel about being alone up at the manor, not now that I know he died there."

*Wait a minute.* Jonathon cocked his head. "No one said he died there." He racked his brains, going over everything they'd said.

Bryan stilled. "Yeah, but... you asked me if I'd seen anyone else up at the house, so I kinda assumed...."

"A plausible assumption," Mike agreed. "Okay, you'd best be off to the police station. I can give you a ride there if you like."

Bryan smiled. "Thanks, but I've got the bike outside. And you know what? I don't really feel like drinking now." He gave a nod in Jonathon's direction before heading for the door.

The moment he was no longer in sight, the muttering began, people's voices raised as they discussed what had just happened.

Mike glanced around before regarding Jonathon with obvious concern. "Are you okay? You seem a little... off-color."

Jonathon sighed. "I've suddenly gone off the idea of making cocktails, that's all." His head was pounding, and the questions that had plagued him since the awful discovery were still colliding in his head.

"Would you mind if I just went up to my room for a while?"

Mike's hand was a comforting weight at the small of Jonathon's back. "Of course not," he said softly. "If you need anything—a drink, food, even the TV from my room—just let me know, all right?"

Jonathon gazed at him in gratitude. "Thanks. I'll be sure to do that. Sorry to leave you in the lurch with all those ladies demanding cosmos and martinis. Oh, and Paul and his screwdrivers, of course."

From a nearby barstool, Paul guffawed. "I'll have to manage with me pint, then, won't I, young'un? A good early night, that's what you need. Do you a power of good."

Jonathon had a feeling he could be right. At least when he was asleep, he wasn't thinking. Then he amended that thought.

*I can still dream, can't I?*

"MAYBE WE'RE looking at this from the wrong angle," Mike said suddenly before demolishing the last mouthful of toast.

The kitchen was quiet. Sue was still in her room. Jonathon had padded downstairs at six o'clock to make coffee, only to find Mike had beaten him to it.

Mike's gaze met his. "You look brighter this morning. That sleep did you good."

Jonathon certainly felt like his batteries had been recharged. "I feel better, thanks. What do you mean?"

Mike got up to refill his coffee cup. When he turned, hand outstretched, to find Jonathon already holding out his empty mug, he grinned. "You're getting used to me, aren't you?"

It wasn't exactly a chore. Jonathon felt comfortable around him, like they... fit. He matched Mike's grin. "Let's just say both of us need our coffee to get our brains in gear."

"Now that's the truth." Mike went back to his task of filling the mugs. "You know what we haven't considered yet? Dominic's career. Maybe this was revenge. *Maybe* it was someone who Dominic prosecuted, back in his barrister days, and they got put away. *Maybe* they got out, and they wanted revenge." He handed Jonathon a mug, grinning. "See? That makes sense, doesn't it?"

Jonathon bit his lip. "I hate to burst your bubble, Mr. I-Used-to-Be-a-Copper, but don't you think that if such a person had turned up in the village, Dominic would have recognized them? From what I've been hearing, he was always spending time here—in the pub, the tea shop, at church.... And Merrychurch isn't exactly huge, is it? Even if such a person had moved here but had kept out of sight of Dominic, word would have got around, right?" He sipped his coffee, feeling smug. "Am I right?"

Mike pulled a face. "It was worth a try."

Jonathon's heart went out to him. His sister might have been cleared, but he was still trying to help. "Of course it was. And it was a good idea, one that needs mentioning to Gorland."

Mike arched his eyebrows. "Seriously?"

Jonathon nodded. "Just because I came up with some potential flaws in your reasoning doesn't mean I'm right, does it? So tell Gorland. At least he can look into it. Dominic was a barrister for a few years. There might be more than a couple of disgruntled villains out there who'd want to see him dead."

Mike gave a decisive nod. "You're right. I'll call him." He glanced at the clock on the wall. "Although maybe not now. Can't see him being all that happy about getting phone calls before seven in the morning." He chuckled, and his eyes gleamed. "But it's bloody tempting."

Jonathon gave him a hard stare. "Do I need to confiscate your phone?"

Mike burst out laughing, and the joyful sound went a long way to lightening Jonathon's heart.

*We just need to keep thinking, that's all. If we put our heads together, we can work out who did this.*

He hoped.

# CHAPTER ELEVEN

*IF LOOKS could kill....*

Gorland put his hands on his hips in a stance that was already becoming familiar and glared at Mike. "Keep your nose out of this, Mike. Police business, remember? None of your concern anymore."

Mike gave as good a glare as he got. "It was just an idea, for God's sake. All I said was that you might want to look in—"

"And I repeat—nothing to do with you anymore. Is that clear? And as ideas go, I have to say, I don't think much of it. So leave it alone." With one final glare, Gorland spun around and strode out of the pub.

Jonathon cleared his throat. "That went well," he said brightly.

Mike gave him a pointed look. "Gorland can think what he likes. I'm not so sure that it was such a bad idea after all. In fact…." He fished out his phone and peered at the screen from underneath his glasses.

Jonathon waited, drumming his fingers on the bar top. "Are you going to tell me what you're doing?"

Mike glanced up. "Looking up an ex-colleague of mine who might be able to help us."

Jonathon's belly did a little flip-flop. "But Gorland said—"

"Never mind what Gorland said. Besides, I'm not gonna be the one who's doing a little digging. I'll leave that up to Keith. That man could find your proverbial needle, I'm telling you." He smiled sweetly. "See? All I'm doing is calling an old mate." He went back to his scrolling.

"And I think you're bringing this down to the level of mere semantics." Not that Jonathon was about to stop him, especially if Mike's hunch paid off.

THE LUNCH crowd had come and gone, Abi had already left, and still nothing from Mike's friend Keith. Jonathon was starting to feel like they were wasting their time. It was already four o'clock, and Mike had called him at ten. *Surely if there was anything to be found, it would have surfaced by now?*

When Mike's phone gave a loud ring, Jonathon almost jumped out of his skin.

"You were off in your own little world," Mike observed, grabbing his phone from the bar. When he saw the screen, he grinned. "Aha."

Jonathon put down the cloth with which he'd been wiping down the tables, and walked over to Mike.

"Okay, that sounds interesting. Hang on, Keith, while I put you on speaker."

Jonathon widened his eyes. *Good news?* he mouthed.

Mike nodded. "'Kay, Keith? You've got my friend Jonathon listening in. Repeat what you just told me."

"Hello, friend Jonathon," Keith said quickly. "Now, Mike, as long as we're clear about this. You did *not* get this information from me, all right? I know who's on this case, okay? Word gets around fast, mate."

"I won't breathe a word, I promise."

"Okay." Keith didn't sound too convinced. "There was one case that stood out. Dominic defended a guy charged with sexual offenses. Guy claimed he was innocent but was found guilty. Then he got pretty vociferous, blaming the verdict on Dominic, saying he didn't do that good a job of defending him."

"That sounds like someone who might harbor a grudge," Jonathon acknowledged.

"Agreed, but then it gets complicated."

"In what way?" Mike asked, frowning.

"I'm emailing you all the details now, Mike. Hope it helps."

"Thanks, mate. I owe you one."

Keith chuckled. "Keep your mouth shut and I'll consider it paid. And if I'm ever down your neck of the woods, you can buy me a pint."

"You're on." Mike disconnected, then peered at his phone. "Okay, I've got the email." He fell silent as he read. Finally he scowled. "Now I see what he meant about complications."

"Well, tell me, then."

Mike rolled his eyes. "Keep yer hair on! Okay…. Aidan Prescott was released from prison about ten years ago."

"Seems like an awful long time to bear a grudge. Is it likely that he'd wait this long before acting?"

"Not really, but that's more to do with the fact that he's dead."

Jonathon stared at him in shocked silence. "Dead?"

Mike nodded. "According to Keith, Prescott had a bad time in prison. He was a broken man when he came out, and apparently he couldn't cut it on the outside. So… he killed himself."

"Oh my God." Jonathon didn't know what upset him more—the fact that Aidan Prescott had gone to prison for something he claimed he didn't do, or the fact that they'd just hit a dead end.

"Wait a minute, wait a minute!" Mike was staring at his phone. "Says here Prescott was married, with a kid. Wife's name was Amy, son's name Andrew…." Slowly he lifted his gaze from the screen and locked eyes with Jonathon.

"Why do those names sound familiar?" Then icy fingers crawled over Jonathon's skin when he realized where he'd heard them before. "That guy we met by the river? Didn't you say his name was Andrew Prescott? And his mum is Amy…." Those icy fingers were now skating up and down Jonathon's spine. "Do you think they know Dominic defended him? Is that why they moved to the village, for revenge? What if… what if Andrew killed him?"

"Whoa, hold on a minute." Mike put down his phone and grasped Jonathon's hand tightly. "Don't go leaping into the deep end. We don't know that's what happened, all right? There's this great word you might have heard of. What is it now? Oh yeah—coincidence."

"Coincidence?" Jonathon pulled his hand free of Mike's and lurched to his feet so fast, his stool wobbled and fell over. "Come *on*, Mike. Really?"

"Okay, okay, I understand how it looks, but there's only one way to find out if there's anything to it." Mike's expression was grave. "I'm gonna go over there and talk to him."

"Not without me, you're not." Jonathon folded his arms across his chest.

Mike gazed at him in silence, his face impassive. "Fine," he said at last, "but you're gonna let me do all the talking. Do you understand?"

Jonathon nodded swiftly. "I'll be quiet."

Mike snorted. "Yeah right. Six days I've known you, and even *I* know that's not about to happen." He held his hands defensively. "I've said my piece. Now let's get into the car and go see Andrew."

"And if it turns out he killed Dominic?" Jonathon shivered. "What if he turns violent?"

Mike gave him a stern glance. "When you met him for the first time, what was he doing?"

"Feeding the ducks."

"Mm-hmm. Now, maybe I'm wrong, but feeding little ducks and being violent don't seem to go hand in hand."

Jonathon rolled his eyes. "I'm sure even Jack the Ripper fed ducks at least once in his life," he muttered under his breath. That got him Mike's eyebrows arched so high, they almost disappeared into his hairline.

Mike pointed to the door. "Car. Best behavior. Or else."

Jonathon was pretty sure the "or else" part was a bluff, but he wasn't willing to push it.

ANDREW PRESCOTT'S little cottage was cute, Jonathon had to admit. Tiny, but cute. The two front gardens that sat beneath window boxes were a mass of color.

"They've worked really hard out front," Mike remarked as they walked up the cobbled path. "Someone has a green thumb."

"Someone who grows lilies too," Jonathon added, staring at a clump of tall stemmed flowers that gave off a heady perfume.

"Yeah, I noticed that. I didn't think it would get past you." Mike paused at the front door and gave Jonathon a hard stare. "Now, remember what I said. I'll do all the talking."

Jonathon rolled his eyes. "I'll be good as gold." Mike's explosive snort only went to prove just how well he knew Jonathon. His hands were clammy, and he had no idea why. He reasoned that Mike had plenty of experience. If Andrew had something to do with Dominic's death, Mike would ferret it out.

Mike rang the bell, then took a step back. The door opened, and Andrew stood there, frowning. "I thought it was you when I peeked through the curtains. What can I do for you, Mike?" He gave Jonathon a cursory glance.

"Can we come in? There's something we need to talk about."

Andrew arched his eyebrows. "Well, that sounds… official. Have you suddenly rejoined the police force?"

Mike laughed, but Jonathon's stomach clenched. Maybe it was his imagination, but Andrew appeared uneasy. "Nope, still your local pub landlord, but I wouldn't be here if it wasn't important."

Andrew gazed at him, his brow still furrowed. Then he seemed to relent. "Okay, come on in." He stood aside to let them enter. "First door on the left. Mum's in there too. Is that a problem?"

"Not at all." Mike's easygoing manner was spot on. Jonathon had the impression that he'd been a good copper.

They followed Andrew into a cozy little living room, where his mother sat in a high-backed armchair.

Andrew gestured toward the couch. "Please, have a seat. Would you like some tea or coffee?"

Mike waved his hand. "Nothing, thanks."

"Then how about you tell me why you're here?"

Mike glanced at Jonathon before speaking. "I've been looking into Dominic de Mountford's death, but not in an official capacity, of course. I was doing some research into his career, looking for anyone who might have borne him a grudge. What came to light was… your father."

"Oh?" Andrew blinked, then squared his shoulders. "I can see why you'd think he might have had something to do with Dominic's death, but surely he can't be of interest now. He's dead, for one thing."

Jonathon took a quick look at Andrew's mother, who sat stiffly in her chair, her gaze riveted on Mike.

"Yes, I know. It just seemed highly coincidental that you and your mother came to live in Merrychurch, that's all. I couldn't help wondering if it was because of your father."

"Actually, no. We had no idea that Dominic lived here. It was a total surprise."

"I see." Mike's gaze met Jonathon's, and he could almost read the thought: *this is a dead end.*

"I'm glad he's dead."

The sudden flash of vitriol from Andrew's mother made Jonathon's heartbeat speed up.

"Mum, you know you don't mean that," Andrew said quietly.

She glared at him. "Of course I do. He ruined both our lives. If it hadn't been for his incompetence, your father would never have gone to prison. He was never the same after they let him out, and you know it. You *promised* him, Andrew! Have you forgotten?" Spit flew from her lips, her eyes wild. "We both stood by his bedside and swore to—"

"Mum!" Andrew blanched.

Jonathon's stomach rolled over. *Oh my God, we were right. He killed Dominic because of what happened to his dad.* He wanted to throw up. Right after he punched Andrew's lights out, even if Jonathon *was* a five-foot-six skinny nothing.

Mike regarded Andrew calmly. "Is there somewhere else we can talk?"

Andrew swallowed. "Sure. Come into the kitchen." He addressed his mother. "I'll make you some tea, okay, Mum?" Without waiting for her reply, he led them out of the room and along the tiny hallway. Once they were inside the small, square kitchen, Andrew closed the door softly behind them. "I'm sorry about that. Mum hasn't been herself for a while now." He leaned against the door.

Mike stood with his back to the kitchen sink, his arms folded. He gestured for Jonathon to sit on the stool near the table before returning his attention to

Andrew. "Are you implying that we should disregard what she said? That she didn't know what she was saying? Is that it?"

Andrew's pallor hadn't changed. "I…." He stared at Mike, eyes wide, but then his shoulders sagged, his chest hollowing. "I suppose I should tell you the truth."

"That sounds like a good idea. So…?"

Andrew ran his fingers through his hair. "Okay, so I lied just now. We moved to Merrychurch deliberately. Mum made the decision, but only because Dad got her to swear to do it. When he got out of prison, he tried to find work, but he was a mess, both physically and mentally. Any job he did manage to find never lasted long, and from then on it was a downward spiral. It wasn't long after that time that he began talking about revenge."

"Oh God." Jonathon gazed at Mike, his heartbeat racing.

Mike made a slight gesture with his hand, as if to calm him, before addressing Andrew. "Keep talking. Let it all out. It feels good to be able to talk about this, doesn't it?"

Andrew nodded, the first flush of color reaching his cheeks. "God, yes. It's such a relief."

Warmth flooded through Jonathon on seeing Mike's insightful manner. *He's good with people.* An attribute that made him both an excellent landlord and probably a damn fine detective.

"Dad made Mum and I swear to get revenge." Andrew's face fell. "I think he'd already decided he was going to kill himself at that point. Neither Mum nor I knew things were that bad, of course. But he kept on at her, saying how it was all Dominic's fault, that he had to be made to pay for his failure. I… I didn't really pay much attention to him. I thought what he was suggesting sounded crazy. But when… when he died, Mum didn't let it drop. Except that would be an understatement. It was all she talked about. I think that was what… unhinged her mind. She's mentally unbalanced, Mike. And I don't think for one moment that she was capable of killing Dominic."

"Never mind her—what about you?" Jonathon blurted out. Mike fired him a warning glance, but he couldn't hold it in any longer. "Where were you Thursday night?"

Andrew's face turned ashen. "You… you think I killed him? God, no! I couldn't do that."

"That's not what he asked you," Mike said softly.

Jonathon studied Andrew, noting his hands clenched tight into fists, his aghast expression, and the first shadow of doubt crept into Jonathon's mind. Okay, so he couldn't read people the way Mike could, but Andrew appeared to be a gentle man.

"Thursday night? I… I was here, all night."

"Can you prove that?" Mike spoke calmly, and Jonathon realized he was asking not because he didn't believe Andrew, but because he wanted Andrew to prove his innocence.

"No." Andrew's shoulders sagged once more. "Mum fell asleep early, around six o'clock. She'd been pretty dozy all day. She's spending… a lot of time sleeping these days."

The doorbell rang, making them all jump.

"I'll get that." Andrew left them in the kitchen.

Jonathon regarded Mike keenly. "You don't think he did it, do you?"

Mike shook his head. "My instincts say he didn't. But he doesn't have an alibi, so—" He broke off as voices reached them, one familiar voice in particular. "Shit. That's Gorland." He lurched across the room and through the door, and Jonathon followed.

In the hallway stood Gorland and Constable Billings. Gorland scowled when he saw Mike. "And what the hell are you doing here?"

"Visiting a neighbor and patron of my pub," Mike said, his voice even. "Any law against that?"

Gorland raised his eyebrows. "I see. And the man you're visiting just happens to have a strong motive for killing Dominic. What a coincidence." He sneered. "What did I say about interfering in police business?"

Jonathon's heart sank. Of course. If Mike's friend Keith could come up with Aidan Prescott, then so could Gorland.

"Are you arresting him?" Mike demanded.

"Mr. Prescott is accompanying us to the station to answer a few questions, not that it's anything to do with you."

Andrew jerked his head to meet Mike's gaze. "Mike? Can you get Mrs. Embry next door to sit with Mum? I don't want her to be on her own."

Mike nodded. "Sure. It's not as if you'll be gone all that long." He gave Gorland a pointed stare. "Not when they realize they've got the wrong man."

Gorland's scowl was so deep, his brows knitted together, and his eyes were almost lost in darkness. "You're not a detective anymore, *Mr*. Tattersall. I suggest you work hard on remembering that." With that, he nodded to Constable Billings, who escorted Andrew out of the house. Gorland fired one last glance at Mike before following them out of the house.

Jonathon grabbed Mike's arm. "We have to do something. I don't think Andrew did it."

Mike's eyes were full of compassion. "I don't think he did either, but he doesn't have an alibi."

"And is no alibi enough for them to make a case against him? Surely there has to be physical evidence to link him to the crime scene?" There had to be *something* they could do—something Mike could do. "Please, Mike?"

Mike sighed. "Let's get his mother sorted, and then we'll go back to the pub and get our thinking caps on. Okay?"

It wasn't exactly the response Jonathon wanted, but it would have to do. For now. "Okay."

# CHAPTER TWELVE

WHEN THEY got back to the pub, Sue had the place ready for opening time. "I thought I'd make myself useful."

Mike gave her a hug. "Thanks, love." He peered at Jonathon. "Are you going to help out behind the bar again?"

"Anything to keep my mind off this business."

Sue gave him a sharp glance. "What's happened?"

Mike sighed. "They've taken Andrew Prescott in for questioning."

"What?" Sue gaped. "Why?"

"Turns out Dominic represented his dad, who got sent to prison. He blamed Dominic, and swore Amy and Andrew to seek revenge."

Sue's eyes were huge. "But…. Andrew is such a sweet man. He couldn't hurt a fly."

"He still has to prove where he was on Thursday night."

The silence that followed was so profound that the hair on the back of Jonathon's neck stood on end.

Sue's face was white. "He couldn't have killed Dominic."

Jonathon's scalp prickled. "Why do I get the feeling you know something?"

She swallowed. "It's physically impossible for him to have killed Dominic, because he was nowhere near Merrychurch that night."

"And how do *you* know that?" Mike fixed her with a stern glance. When she didn't respond immediately, he folded his arms. "Susan Elizabeth Bentley...."

She glared at him. "You know how much I hate it when you use my middle name, you sod."

"Then tell me what's going on or I'll keep repeating it." Mike gave her an evil grin.

"Fine!"

Jonathon was torn between dying to know what she was hiding and trying not to laugh at Mike behaving like a little kid.

Sue took a deep breath. "Andrew was in Reading that night."

Mike blinked. "In Reading? Wait—are you saying he was part of that raid? With you?" When she nodded, Mike frowned. "Why would he do that? He doesn't seem the type."

She sighed. "That man would do anything for me. He's totally besotted."

"How long has this been going on?" Mike asked incredulously.

"We've been sort of seeing each other for about six months." Her cheeks regained a little of their previous color.

"And I'm hearing about this now?"

Sue gave him a hard stare. "I don't have to tell you everything, do I? And it's not exactly common knowledge. There are too many people in this village with long memories, if you know what I mean." She straightened up. "Now you have to go to the police station and tell them they have the wrong person—again."

"I don't think Detective Inspector Gorland is about to listen to anything I say."

"Sue's right," Jonathon interjected. "Right now, as far as the police are concerned, he has a powerful motive for killing Dominic, and they obviously have no one else in the frame for it. You *have* to do something."

"I'm not about to go charging off to the police station. I have a pub to run, or have you both forgotten that?" Mike arched his eyebrows.

"Then *I'll* take Sue there." Jonathon set his jaw and held out his hand for Mike's keys.

Mike stared at it for a moment, then huffed and reached into his jeans pocket. He tossed the keys to Jonathon. "You're a stubborn little shit, aren't you?"

Jonathon gave him a sweet smile. "Aw, you know you wouldn't have me any other way." Then the intimacy of the remark struck him, and he marveled at how far they'd come in just six days. Judging by Mike's initial startled glance, then the manner in which his expression morphed into a genuinely warm smile, Jonathon wasn't the only one who felt that way.

*He's a good man. Intelligent, great sense of humor, good-looking, and fiercely protective of his sister.* All qualities that ticked Jonathon's boxes. Of course, the small matter that he was sexy as hell was by no means near the bottom of the list.

"Come on, then, if we're going." Sue tugged at his elbow, pulling him out of his reveries.

Jonathon gave Mike a cheeky grin. "If you play your cards right, I'll make cocktails when I get back."

Mike grinned back. "I'll spread the word. Now go do your knight-on-a-white-charger routine and show Gorland the error of his ways."

Jonathon laughed. "That man doesn't like me already, thanks to my father. This isn't likely to help matters." He held the door open for Sue, then followed her out of the pub to the car.

As they drove through the village, Jonathon gazed at the way the evening sun lit up the treetops, giving added vibrancy to their green foliage. The houses, built in a honey-colored stone, gave off a warm glow. Merrychurch was a beautiful place to live.

"He likes you, you know," Sue murmured at his side, her attention focused on the road ahead.

"Well, I like him too."

She snickered. "I'm not dumb, you know. And I'm not blind either."

Jonathon frowned. "What do you mean?"

"It doesn't take a genius to figure out he's attracted to you. And from what I can see, the feeling's mutual."

*Shit.* If *Sue* could see that….

"And just so you know? I'm happy with that."

"You are?" Concentrating on his driving became that bit more challenging.

"Sure. I haven't seen him this relaxed since he moved to the village. And he's smiling more, for another thing. I think that's due to you."

"Oh." That made him feel good.

"But hurt him and I'll cut your balls off, all right?"

*Fuck.* Jonathon fought to draw air back into his lungs after most of it left him in a startled gasp. "You don't beat around the bush, do you? And who's to say anything will happen between us anyway?"

"Is that your way of saying you *don't* want anything to happen? Because like I said, I'm not blind."

Jonathon wasn't sure how honest he was prepared to be. "Let's just say I'm not going to push things. I have a very organic view of relationships. If it's meant to be, it'll happen all on its own without my help." He glanced across at her. "Or yours, okay?"

Sue sighed. "You can't blame me for wanting Mike to be happy. Being invalided out of the force devastated him. I know he loves living here, loves running the pub, but it's always felt to me like something was missing. I'm not naive, Jonathon. I know he must be… lonely, for want of a better word."

Jonathon snickered. "Oh my, is that you being coy?" Inside, his heart ached at the picture Sue painted of Mike.

She snorted. "Yeah, sorry, but that's as far as I want to go into my brother's sex life. And here we are again."

Jonathon drove into the car park and into an empty bay.

Sue unbuckled her seat belt. "Fingers crossed that they believe me."

They got out of the 4x4 and walked into the quaint police station.

Constable Billings was behind the desk as they entered. "Mrs. Bentley, Mr. de Mountford, what can I help you with?"

Before Jonathon could say a word, Sue launched her verbal assault. "You can stop questioning Andrew Prescott, for one thing. You've got the wrong man, and I can prove it."

Constable Billings blinked. "I see." His gaze flickered in Jonathon's direction before he reached for the phone. "Sir? I have Mrs. Bentley and Mr. de Mountford here. They claim to have evidence to exonerate Andrew Prescott." He paused, listening, but Jonathon couldn't miss the wince he gave. "Yes, sir." He put down the phone and sighed. "DI Gorland will be right out."

Jonathon's heart went out to him. Gorland didn't strike him as a particularly easy person to work under.

Only a few minutes passed before the door behind the constable was flung open and Gorland strode out, his jacket missing, his calm decidedly ruffled. "Well. This is getting to be a habit."

"You need to release Andrew. He had nothing to do with Dominic's death. He was with me in Reading on Thursday night. And if you want more witnesses, just ask the people whose names I gave you." Sue paused to take a breath.

Gorland narrowed his gaze. "So you lied when I asked you how many people took part in the raid."

"Yes." Sue stuck out her chin. "You didn't need to know about him. But if you want a statement now, I'll make one."

He made a sound of sheer exasperation. "Fine. Come with me. Not you, Mr. de Mountford. You can wait right there. I think I've been more than obliging with you so far, and I don't see any reason why you should be present for this."

"I agree entirely." Jonathon gave him a polite smile. "I wasn't about to ask anyway." He glanced around, then sat in a chair facing the desk. "I'll wait for you, Sue."

"Thank you, sweetheart." Sue followed Gorland from the room.

The term of endearment gave him a warm feeling inside.

"Are you still staying at the pub?" Constable Billings asked. "I'd have thought you'd want to be up at the manor." Then his face fell. "Though I can understand why you might not want to do that. Knowing Dominic died there can't be easy for you. I know you and he were close."

Jonathon hadn't expected such an empathetic response. "I didn't realize you knew him so well."

Constable Billings smiled. "You know he used to drink in the pub, right? Well, on my off-duty nights, I go there for a pint and a game of darts, or cards, or whatever. I've lost count of the times Dominic and I played. Dominic handled a mean set of arrows."

"He played darts?" Now *there* was something Jonathon hadn't known.

Constable Billings laughed. "Lord, the times he wiped the floor with me. I was just glad we never bet on the outcome." He smiled. "He was a nice bloke. Bit lonely, maybe. I always thought that was why he used to go to the tea shop and the pub. And there are a lot of people in this village who really liked him."

"Someone didn't." Jonathon shivered.

To his surprise Constable Billings reached across the desk and patted his arm. "We'll get them, whoever they were." He lowered his hand. "Are you going to stick around for the fete?"

Jonathon nodded. "After I talked with Rachel Meadows, I had an idea. It seems my uncle used to donate one of his watercolor paintings as a prize in the fete raffle. That came as a surprise, because I had no idea he painted." He shook his head. "I've learned so much about Dominic. Anyway, I think I'll take a look up at the manor and choose a painting to donate. I'd like to carry on the tradition."

Constable Billings smiled. "Dominic would like that."

"Did Bryan Mayhew come to make a statement?" It had only been just under twenty-four hours, but Jonathon hoped Bryan had done what he'd promised.

"Yes. It wasn't as if he was ever a suspect, to be honest. There was no motive. Your uncle was kind enough to let him stay in the annex, give him access to the family portraits and the crypt, whatever he needed for his dissertation. He basically had the run of the house. It's just a pity he wasn't around when Dominic died. He might have seen something." Constable Billings inclined his head toward the door where Sue and Gorland had gone. "So Andrew Prescott had nothing to do with it? I'm glad about that. He seems like a good bloke, the way he takes care of his mum. I've heard them talking sometimes, in the village or in the tea shop. She doesn't strike me as the easiest person to deal with. Looks like he has his hands full there."

Based on what he'd seen, Jonathon had to agree. He'd wondered briefly if Amy had somehow been able to get up to the hall, but it appeared unlikely, not with the wheelchair at any rate.

A thought occurred to him. "DI Gorland said you'd found brass rubbing wax and polish in my uncle's study. Did Dominic ever do brass rubbings, that you can recall?"

Constable Billings shook his head. "That was a new one on me too."

"I checked the manor for lilies too. None in any of the gardens, or the greenhouses." And based on what he'd learned about Andrew, he wasn't about to mention the lilies growing in his garden. It no longer seemed apt.

The constable's eyes lit up. "Now, I know who might be able to help with that. Melinda Talbot, the vicar's wife."

"Melinda? I've met her. Mike and I had tea at the vicarage just the other day."

Constable Billings nodded. "She'd know about lilies, all right. Hers take Best in Show virtually every year at the village fete. So she'd know who else grows them." He rolled his eyes. "God, I'm stupid. Can't think why she didn't come to mind earlier."

"You've been too busy thinking of possible suspects, not people with local knowledge," Jonathon suggested. "And it's not like Melinda would be a suspect, right?"

Constable Billings laughed. "Melinda? She's more likely to give you the sharp edge of her tongue in public, that one. Put it this way: I wouldn't mess with her."

Jonathon stared at him. "But she seems such a sweet lady."

Constable Billings snorted. "You wouldn't say that if you'd ever got on the wrong side of her in Sunday school."

"Sunday school?" Jonathon chuckled.

The constable shook his head again. "And all I did was ask a few questions, you know, like, why did God create mosquitoes when all they do is bite you? And when it rained, was that God peeing on us? When Jesus walked on water, was that the first time or did he practice first? Oh, and can God read our minds?"

Jonathon burst out laughing. "Oh, my God. I'd love to have seen her face."

"My mum didn't find it amusing when Melinda called her and said maybe she might want to consider keeping me at home on Sundays from then on." Constable Billings stopped talking when the door opened, and Sue came out, closely followed by Andrew Prescott and Gorland. Andrew's face was pale, and Jonathon noted that he and Sue clasped hands.

"Thank you for coming forward, Mrs. Bentley. Imagine how much time and embarrassment you could have saved us if you'd simply told us the truth in the first place." Gorland seemed pissed off, not that Jonathon was surprised by that in the slightest. He had a feeling it was Gorland's natural state.

Sue merely gave Gorland a curt nod, then addressed Jonathon. "Andrew is coming back to the pub with us. His mum will be fine for a while longer. Celia Embry will call if he's needed. But right now he needs a drink and a breather." She gazed at him fondly. "God knows he doesn't get many of those."

Andrew gave her a grateful glance, then squeezed her hand. He met Jonathon's gaze. "If that's okay?"

Jonathon smiled. "I don't think Mike will mind in the least." He glanced in Sue's direction. "In fact, I'm sure he'll have a few questions for both of you."

Sue groaned. "That's what I'm afraid of."

Andrew lifted her hand to his lips and kissed her fingers, in what Jonathon found to be a very sweet gesture. "Nothing to be scared of. I'll be right by your side. No more hiding, okay?"

Sue gazed into his eyes and took a deep breath. "Yeah, okay."

Gorland made a noise at the back of his throat and went back through the door he'd just exited. Constable Billings gave Jonathon a grin, and Jonathon couldn't help but return it.

Jonathon twirled Mike's keys on his index finger. "Home, now." With a last nod in Constable Billings's direction, he led the way out of the police station. He had a feeling there was a very interesting conversation to come, even if they were no nearer to solving the mystery of who Dominic's assailant had been. At least he had another avenue to explore.

He needed to find Melinda Talbot and discuss lilies.

# CHAPTER THIRTEEN

BY THE time they got back to the pub, Mike was already hard at work behind the bar. His face lit up when Jonathon walked in. "Good timing. Get back here and give me a hand? Looks like the world and his wife have decided to come in for a drink tonight." He nodded in the direction of Sue and Andrew. "Have a seat, you two. We'll talk when things quiet down a bit."

"Might've known he wouldn't let me off the hook that easily," Sue mumbled.

Andrew said nothing, but put his arm around her shoulders, his manner almost defiant. Judging by the muted gasps and instant whispers that resulted, Jonathon understood his move completely.

He dashed behind the bar and handed Mike his keys. Only a minute passed before a customer was asking for a cocktail, so he rolled up his sleeves and got to work. "Is it usually like this on a Wednesday night?"

Mike snorted as he pulled a pint into a glass. "Absolutely not. I think word's still getting around, if you ask me. They've come to gawk at you."

"Still? I've been here since the weekend. You'd think they'd seen enough of me by now for the novelty to have worn off." Jonathon poured vodka into a measure before tipping it into the cocktail shaker.

"And how was my delightful ex-colleague?"

Jonathon chuckled. "Pissed off that he's lost a suspect, if you ask me." Gorland's loss was theirs too, however. Jonathon gave a nod to where Andrew and Sue sat at a small table, gazing at each other while they talked quietly, Sue's hand clasped in Andrew's. "And there's one less secret in this village tonight."

Mike sighed. "Yeah. I'm glad she's found someone. I just wish she'd had the guts to tell me about him before this."

"And before he became a murder suspect," Jonathon added. "I'm certain he's thinking that wasn't the best way for you to learn about the two of them."

"Tell me about it."

Jonathon glanced at Mike. "You're not going to give them a hard time, are you? Don't you think they've been through enough?"

Mike smiled at him. "Sue's already got under your skin, hasn't she?"

Jonathon wasn't about to acquaint him with their recent conversation. "I just think she's got enough on her plate. You said it yourself: there are plenty of people in the village who are quite happy to spread malicious gossip about her. This is only going to add fuel to the fire."

Mike gazed at Andrew. "I hope he's got a thick skin."

Jonathon had a feeling Andrew might surprise him. He gave Mike a grin. "Do you think you've filled that glass enough?" Beer was trickling over the rim.

"What? Oh shit!" Mike jerked his head down and groaned. He emptied the glass into the drip tray, then glared at Jonathon. "Haven't you got cocktails to shake, *Tom*?"

Jonathon chuckled, pouring out the martini through a strainer. He was starting to enjoy bar work.

MIKE BADE good night to the last customer, then shut the door. "Thank goodness that's over." He glanced around the bar. "Where's Andrew and my sister?"

"In the kitchen, making us sandwiches. We missed dinner, remember?" Jonathon wiped down the bar and loaded the last of the glasses into the washer. He straightened up and sighed. "Great. Six days since I found Dominic, and what do I have to show for it? I've become good at making cocktails, but we're no closer to discovering who was in that study with him." A wave of frustration rolled over him.

Mike came behind the bar, walked up to Jonathon, and pulled him into a hug. Jonathon stiffened slightly in surprise, but then relaxed into the embrace, his cheek against Mike's scratchy one. Jonathon was at a loss what to do with his hands, but then he put them around Mike, resting them against his back.

"It'll all come right, I know it will," Mike murmured.

Jonathon appreciated the positive comments, but what felt even better was Mike's arms around him, his strong arms supporting him.

A cough had Mike pulling away.

"Oh, sorry. Did I interrupt something?" Sue's voice held amusement. She placed a plate of sandwiches on the bar, grinning.

Supportive or not, Jonathon cursed her timing.

"When you've quite finished enjoying yourself...." Mike cleared his throat. "How did you two get together?"

Andrew gave Sue a swift look, and she nodded. He sighed. "This last year, Mum has become more... demanding. She's needed more looking after, and I've just felt so bloody tired all the time. I'm basically her carer now, so I started looking into getting some respite care, only Mum refused to hear of it. Well, she did when she was in her more lucid moments. In the end I resorted to something that I'm not proud of."

Sue took his hand and squeezed it. "Hey, you did what you had to do to preserve your sanity."

"Are we talking something illegal here?" Mike frowned.

"No, just immoral." Andrew drew in a long breath. "I... crushed up a couple of sleeping tablets and fed them to her in her food. Not something I did often, just now and again, when I needed a break."

"It was one of those times that I came across him sitting in his car by the river, asleep at the wheel." Sue gave Andrew a fond glance. "At first I was scared stiff. I thought he was dead."

"Until I gave a loud snore and woke myself up," Andrew admitted, his face flushed. "She had me drive her home and then invited me in for a coffee."

"I figured he needed waking up," she said with a faint smile. "Anyway, that was how we got talking.

We used to meet up for coffee and a chat, only I had no idea about the sleeping tablets, not until much later. And by then, I was already half in love with him."

Andrew leaned over and kissed her cheek. "Likewise." He glanced at his watch. "I'm sorry, guys, but I really need to get home. Celia says Mum is tucked up in bed asleep, but she's still at the house, bless her, and it's almost midnight. I don't want to piss her off, because she is really good about sitting with Mum now and again."

"Want me to come home with you?" Sue asked.

Andrew's face glowed. "Really?"

Sue flushed. "Well, seeing as we're not hiding anymore, maybe it's time we let your mum in on the secret. Seeing as the rest of the village will know by tomorrow anyway." She chuckled. "Judging by the gossiping that was going on all night. Talk about looks." She did an eye roll.

Andrew chuckled. "In that case, come home with me. I'd love to have you stay."

Sue laid a hand on his arm. "Tomorrow we need to go pick up Sherlock. I miss him, and he must be driving Becca and her three cats crazy, even if he *is* madly in love with Lucy, Becca's golden retriever."

"We can do that. Mum can come too. She'll enjoy the ride. And besides, I'm sure by then we'll have lots to talk about on the way to Reading."

"Yes, we will. Top of my list is the decision I've just come to." Sue squared her jaw. "I'm going to ditch the name Bentley, and go back to being Sue Tattersall. Having that DI call me by that damned name made me realize I don't want to hear it a minute longer."

Andrew's face lit up in a shy smile. "I like that idea." He put out his hand toward Mike. "Thanks for being so understanding, Mike, and for believing me. That meant a lot."

Mike shook it, then gestured toward Jonathon. "He insisted that I had to do something."

Andrew beamed. "Aw. Thank you." He tugged Sue's arm. "Come on, you." He led her to the main door, and Mike followed to let them out. By the time he returned, Jonathon had already wolfed down one sandwich and was attacking a second. He made an appreciative noise that had Mike smiling.

"Sounds like you needed that." Mike picked up a sandwich and began to eat.

Jonathon nodded, finishing his with one bite. "And now I think I'll head for my bed."

"I'll cook us breakfast in the morning, how's that?"

He let out a happy sigh. "That sounds wonderful." Impulsively he gave Mike a firm hug. "Sleep well."

"You too."

Jonathon left him in the bar and climbed the stairs, bodily tired. It was a fatigue he didn't mind, because he'd been busy all night making cocktails. What he needed right then was a night without dreams, a night of deep, velvety sleep.

JONATHON SWITCHED off the water before climbing out of the bath and grabbing his towel. He could already smell bacon cooking downstairs, and the thought of a crisp bacon sandwich on thick slices of bread, with a generous dollop of brown sauce, had him drying himself off rapidly.

By the time he entered the kitchen, the bacon was ready, cooked to perfection, the aroma heavenly. Mike had sliced the bread, and the scent of freshly brewed coffee filled the air.

"I feel spoiled," Jonathon said with a happy sigh as he sat at the heavy wooden table.

Mike laughed. "You need fortifying this morning. You have a visit to make."

Jonathon arched his eyebrows. "I do?" He reached for a plate and began assembling the sand-wich, layering the thick rashers so no trace of bread could be seen.

"Yup. Forgive me if you think I'm butting in, but you really need to see Dominic's solicitor. Not just because you're his heir and you need to see the will, but because there might be a clue in his bequests."

"Such as?"

Mike shrugged. "No idea. It was just a thought. I'm also thinking about people who aren't in it but who maybe should be."

"Ah. Yes." Jonathon held the sauce bottle upside down and whacked it on its bottom. "This stuff doesn't want to come out."

"Careful!" Mike shouted as he landed anoth-er blow. "Sometimes it does that and then it—" His words died as a huge blob of brown sauce landed on the bacon. *Way* too much brown sauce.

Jonathon glared at the bottle as if it was its fault.

Mike chuckled, picked up a knife, and began to scoop up some of the sauce onto its blade. "Oh, look, there's bacon under there! You *did* want bacon with your brown sauce, right?"

Jonathon gave him a look. "You *can* go off people, y'know."

Mike laughed. "Eat up. Then you can call to make an appointment. It's time we had some answers."

Jonathon couldn't agree more, but there was no way he was about to hurry.

Bacon sandwiches were *not* to be rushed.

JONATHON WASN'T really surprised that Mr. Omerod's place of business looked nothing like an office. He lived in a stone cottage, with square windows and white-painted wooden eaves and a sign on the wall beside the glossy black-painted door with its brass lion's head knocker.

He lifted the lion's jaw and rapped against the strike plate. "Hey, Mike. Do you see? Brass," he said quietly.

Mike snickered. "What did I say about seeing brass everywhere?"

The door opened and an elderly, white-haired gentleman stood there, dressed in a black suit with a white shirt and black tie. It took a moment for the thought to register: this was the first person Jonathon had met who appeared to be in mourning.

"Mr. de Mountford. Please, come in." His gaze alighted on Mike, and he arched his eyebrows.

Jonathon gestured toward Mike. "I've invited Mike to join me. I've been staying with him since Friday. That's not a problem, is it?"

"Of course not." Mr. Omerod's tone was dry. He stepped aside to let them enter. "My office is on the left."

Jonathon liked the white walls and black oak beams, the black leather couch beneath the window, and the straight-backed chairs in front of the highly varnished desk. A dark wooden bookcase stood behind it, filled with heavy tomes in dusty shades of black and red.

Mr. Omerod indicated the chairs. "Please, be seated. Would you care for some tea?"

"We're fine, thank you." Jonathon sat down, with Mike taking the chair beside him.

"I was glad to receive your call this morning. Actually, I was going to contact you. I had expected to hear from you sooner."

Jonathon had been expecting the rebuke. No doubt his father had called soon after their conversation. "To be honest the last thing I wanted was to be reminded of Dominic." It was a lame excuse for staying away, but it was the truth. It had taken him until that morning to summon up enough enthusiasm to meet with the solicitor, even after Mike had basically badgered him to do it. Jonathon wasn't quite sure why he'd avoided this meeting. Maybe it was because he associated Mr. Omerod with his family.

Not a welcome association.

Mr. Omerod cleared his throat. "Yes, well, that is understandable in the circumstances. I think Dominic was closer to you than to any other family member, even your father." He opened a thick folder on the desk. "Having spoken recently with your father, I am given to understand that you are already acquainted with the main clause of your uncle's will."

"If you mean that he named me as his heir, then, yes."

Mr. Omerod nodded. "Exactly. You inherit de Mountford Hall, its contents, and its lands. Though I should add that a portion of those lands are in the process of being sold to developers."

"I did hear about that. Do you have any idea why my uncle was selling?"

"I'm afraid not. Whatever Dominic's motivations were for the sale, he kept them to himself. I merely advised him." Mr. Omerod coughed. "At this juncture I feel I should point out that this will has undergone some revisions in recent months."

"Dominic changed his will?" Mike sat up straight, his eyes gleaming as he glanced at Jonathon. "Now we're getting somewhere. What changes did he make?"

Mr. Omerod gave an impatient sigh. "Perhaps I should have expressed myself more clearly. I carried out his instructions regarding the revisions, drew up a new will, which was then signed and witnessed. However, a week later, he called me and asked me to draw up a new will." He coughed again. "I say new, but it was identical to the original. For some reason, Dominic changed his mind and decided to leave the will as it was."

"Then how did Dominic's revised will differ from this one?" Jonathon demanded. Because if the beneficiaries knew about those changes, it might account for some pretty disgruntled people....

Mr. Omerod consulted the document in front of him. "There was only one major change. Dominic intended to leave a large bequest to someone in the village."

"Large can have many connotations," Mike remarked dryly. "Just how large are we talking?"

Mr. Omerod's gaze flickered from Mike to Jonathon, who nodded encouragingly.

"Dominic decided on the sum of fifty thousand pounds to be left to Trevor Deeping of Mill Lane, Merrychurch."

Mike stared at Mr. Omerod. "Trevor? Seriously?"

"Why do I know that name?" Jonathon asked. "Hang on—didn't I meet him in the pub?"

Mike nodded slowly, his eyes shining. "The first night you did the cocktails. In fact, you made cocktails for his wife, Sarah. Trevor's a salesman, does a lot of traveling."

Jonathon tried to picture him. "The guy who wouldn't look me in the eye. The one you took home drunk the night Dominic died."

"Yup. That was Trevor." Mike regarded Mr. Omerod with interest. "Did Dominic ever say if Trevor was aware he'd changed his will?"

"Dominic certainly never mentioned it." Mr. Omerod closed the folder.

"Did he tell you why he wanted to make the bequest?" Jonathon demanded. Maybe there was a plausible explanation. Maybe this Trevor had saved Dominic's life. *But if that was the case, why change his mind and revert back to the original will?*

Jonathon ran out of ideas at that point.

"I have no idea. Whatever the reason, he did not share it with me. And as the will reverted back to its original form, I saw no reason to press the matter further. Apart from small bequests to his staff—which, I might add, includes your sister, Mr. Tattersall—the bulk of his estate goes to you." He gazed keenly at Jonathon. "You have just become a very wealthy man, Jonathon." Mr. Omerod gave him a thin smile. "Congratulations."

Jonathon didn't know how to react. *What the hell are you supposed to say when you're given news like this?* Okay, so he'd known it was coming, but somehow hearing it from Dominic's solicitor made it all the more real. What made the situation surreal, however, was that what interested him most wasn't his inheritance.

He was more intrigued by that large bequest.

*Why on earth would Dominic want to leave fifty thousand pounds to a salesman in his village?* And more intriguing—not give any reason for such a bequest to his solicitor.

There was a mystery here, and Jonathon intended solving it.

# CHAPTER FOURTEEN

"JONATHON!"

He gave a start. "Christ, don't yell at me like that."

Mike smirked. "That was the fourth time I said your name. What planet were you on?"

Jonathon sighed heavily. "Sorry. I was thinking." He glanced at his phone. It was only ten thirty. Mike wouldn't need him to help in the pub for a few hours yet, and Jonathon had a lot going on in his head that needed sorting out.

What was required was a walk.

"Listen, would you mind if I went out for a while? Not too long. I just need some fresh air and a bit of space."

Mike cocked his head to one side. "Actually, you've hit on something I'd meant to mention. Anytime you're ready, I'll take you and your suitcase up to the manor. You don't *have* to stay here, y'know."

The last thing Jonathon wanted right then was to be left alone in that big hall, with only his thoughts for company. Add to that, he was kind of getting used to being around Mike. Maybe *too* used to it, especially if Sue had already noticed his interest in her brother.

He chuckled to himself. *Who wouldn't be interested? I'm not blind either.*

"If it gets to the point where I'm in the way, you have to let me know, all right? And if I'm not? Well, is it okay with you if I stay here? I... like it."

Mike smiled. "You're not in the way, I like having you here, and truth be told, when you leave and go back to wherever you came from, I'm gonna miss you. Now, go for your walk. I'll have fresh coffee waiting for you when you get back, if you want it. And if you have work to do on your laptop, or whatever, then by all means, get on with it. You've done more than enough for me this week."

Impulsively, Jonathon gave Mike a hug. "Thanks." He left Mike in the bar and headed for the door.

Outside, it was a beautiful morning, and he realized August had arrived without him noticing. That meant the fete was only ten days away, on the twelfth. He'd originally planned to stay until after then, but now everything was up in the air. Recalling Melinda's words on the importance of the fete, he decided to stick with his plans. Besides, by then, word would surely have got around about the new lord of the manor.

And there lay the crux of what bothered him.

Jonathon strolled through the quiet leafy lanes, drinking in the quaint atmosphere. It was certainly nothing like Manchester, where he currently resided. He loved the vibrant city, its bars and social life,

the buzz of activity that seemed to permeate everything. Of course, it was also a long way from his family, which was an added bonus. But his inheritance
brought with it a dilemma. *Could* he give up his life
in Manchester for the peace and tranquility of Merrychurch? Granted, he had always loved the village,
even when he was a teenager, but that had been for
limited periods of time. Taking on the responsibility of
the hall, living there permanently… could he do that?

Then there were his father's expectations. Marry,
produce offspring.…

Jonathon knew he had a stubborn streak. It had
been commented upon ad infinitum when he was
growing up. He also knew his refusal to give any
thought to his father's wishes had little to do with being stubborn and more to do with the fact that he was
*not* prepared to deny his sexuality, not even for his
family.

Then it occurred to him.

*If I'm lord of the manor, in Merrychurch, what
can he do to prevent me from living as I want to live?*
In Manchester he'd been free to do just that, away
from the prying eyes of his father. No one gave a shit
that he was Jonathon de Mountford, youngest member of one of the oldest families in England. There, he
was just "that photographer" who lived and worked
in a converted building off Canal Street, occasionally
hooking up with someone when he felt so inclined, but
more often than not keeping to himself.

*Hookups in Merrychurch?* Even with Jonathon's
limited knowledge of the village, that seemed highly
unlikely. Given the demographic of the inhabitants, he
could see how such behavior might alarm or outrage

his new neighbors. And as much as he had no desire to become part of the establishment, he didn't want to fly *that* much in the face of tradition.

"You look like you're deep in thought."

Jonathon dropped back into the present and glanced around him. The tall, bearded man with the shock of dark brown hair was vaguely familiar. Then it came to him. "Hi, Sebastian. Sorry, I didn't hear you approach. You're right, I was in a world of my own."

"I'd hope it was a pleasant world, but I can understand if it wasn't, given the circumstances." He eyed Jonathon keenly. "How are you doing?" At his side, he pushed a bike.

"To be honest, I've kept myself busy." It was only moments like this, when his own thoughts occupied him, that the grief intruded.

Sebastian regarded him with warm brown eyes. "You must allow yourself time to grieve," he said softly. "You may not have spent your whole life with Dominic, but you loved him, that much is obvious. And shedding tears over a loved one is never wrong. We all need to do that sometime." His brow furrowed slightly. "We all have regrets when someone passes. We feel we didn't spend enough time with them. We feel cheated. But we all have to let go. You will always have your memories of him. No one can take those from you."

Jonathon stilled, his mind focused on those times he'd spent with Dominic. "You're right, of course." Sebastian's remark about regrets had struck a sore point. Only now was he realizing just how much he didn't know about Dominic, and yes, he felt cheated. Someone had stolen the years Jonathon had thought he had left to get to know his uncle, the one relative who appeared to understand him, to accept and encourage him.

He gave himself a mental shake. "And what are you up to this morning?"

"Melinda made some soup and bread for Amy Prescott and sent me round to the house with them."

Jonathon grinned. "I didn't realize 'delivery boy' was one of the roles of a curate."

Sebastian laughed. "I have many roles, believe me."

Melinda's words came to mind. "What are you doing tomorrow night?" Jonathon asked suddenly.

Sebastian snickered. "Friday night? Not a lot, but that's normal. I don't tend to do much of an evening, except read, unless I'm working on a sermon, of course. And seeing as Lloyd is preaching on Sunday…. Why do you ask?"

"Would you like to come to the pub and have a drink with me? We could even play darts, if you feel like it. Not that I'm any good. I think I've played maybe twice my entire life."

Sebastian flushed. "Really? I haven't played darts in years." He smiled. "I used to be good at it."

"A pint or two, a couple of games…." Jonathon nudged Sebastian's arm. "Go on, say yes." After what Sebastian had just admitted, it was obvious Melinda was right and he was in need of a night out. Besides, Jonathon was touched that Sebastian had stopped to inquire after his well-being.

Sebastian's eyes gleamed. "Okay. Tomorrow night. Nineish? Or is that too late?"

"Nine sounds good. And if you're really lucky, I might make you a cocktail."

Sebastian snorted. "That might be a step too far for me. I'm more of a beer man myself." He flexed the fingers of his right hand. "But a game or two of darts appeals to me. Prepare to be beaten."

Jonathon laughed. "Oh, *I* get it now. Let's take advantage of the poor nondarts player."

Sebastian hoisted his leg over the bar of his bike and got on the saddle. "Of course. It wouldn't be fun otherwise." And with that, he set off, pedaling slowly at first, a tuneful whistle drifting back toward Jonathon.

Jonathon continued on his walk, choosing the lane that led toward the manor. Around him was the sweet chirping of birds in the hedgerows, and from above came the call of an elusive skylark. People walked toward him, most of them giving a friendly nod. He was beginning to understand why Dominic liked to spend time in the pub or at local events. He might have lived in the manor house up on the hill, but he had also forged connections in the village.

When Jonathon reached the stone posts bearing the de Mountford crest, he stopped at the roadside and gazed up at the white stone house. Since the meeting with Mr. Omerod, the possibility of living there seemed more… real. It was a far cry from his flat in Manchester, located in a busy district, the noise and bustle of traffic always in the background. Yet Jonathon had known quiet. His travels through Australia and India had provided him with a glimpse of spiritual peace, moments when he had cast off the trappings of modern living and embraced the knowledge that he was but a tiny speck in the cosmos. Moments that had humbled him, when he'd reached for his camera to try to capture just the tiniest part of the awe that had welled up inside him.

He could ignore his father's wishes. He could refuse to take on his inheritance. But Jonathon knew that by doing that he would be denying Dominic's wishes too, and he didn't think that would sit happily with him. And that left only one course of action.

It looked like Jonathon was about to move to Merrychurch.

Coming to that realization was sort of cathartic. It was easier to accept that his life was about to change in one important aspect. His address might alter, but he had no intentions of giving up the career he'd begun— there was plenty of room at the manor for setting up a studio. And if he was going to have a fresh start in Merrychurch, then he'd have it on his own terms.

Jonathon wasn't about to initiate a village Pride event or shout about his sexuality from the rooftops, but he'd begin the way he meant to continue—not hiding. And if someone important—*please, God*—came into his life, then the village might see something new for the first time in its history.

A gay wedding.

Jonathon smiled to himself. *Whoa there. Let's not put the cart before the horse, right?* There was a lot of ground to cover before such a momentous occasion could be reached, and it was going to take baby steps to achieve it.

Then it occurred to him that it was arrogant to assume he knew anything about the inhabitants of Merrychurch. For all he knew, half the village comprised of couples on the LBGTQI spectrum. That made him smile. His father would have apoplexy.

Feeling much lighter in spirit, Jonathon turned around and headed back to the pub. As he neared the center of the village, he had an idea. Trevor Deeping lived on Mill Lane, Mr. Omerod had stated. Maybe it was time Jonathon paid him a visit. Nothing heavy, just a little chat concerning a certain bequest. That, added to the odd way Trevor had behaved that night in the pub, led Jonathon to think there was something there that needed investigating.

*Listen to me. I sound like a regular Poirot. And it's not as if this Trevor is a suspect.*

Still, Jonathon wanted answers. And talking to Trevor looked like the only way to get them.

He clicked on Maps on his phone and quickly located Mill Lane. Of course, that didn't help him any; Trevor and his wife, Sarah, could live in any house along the road. Jonathon strolled through the village, noting the tiny lanes that could only accommodate one car's width. Merrychurch had come into existence long before traffic had been a consideration. When he spied the white sign with its black lettering, he turned right onto Mill Lane, which turned out to have seven houses along it, all on one side. On the other was a wooden structure, whose dark green panel declared it to be a water mill, still in operation. A stream ran the length of the lane, ending in a small pond where it was scooped up by the water wheel that turned slowly, spilling the clear waters into a deeper pond. It was undeniably quaint.

But quainter still were the houses. They were all joined together, with a long thatched roof that covered them. Each had tiny windows, some with boxes filled with flowers, the cobbled road surface ending at the front door. At the far end of the lane, Jonathon spied an area for cars—a good idea, since parking in front of the houses would have been an eyesore. He was willing to bet that every last one of them was a Grade II listed building, and he was dying to see what they were like inside.

Jonathon wandered along the cobbled lane, trying not to peer through the windows. What individualized each house was the paintwork: they were done in pastel shades of pink, pale green, pale yellow, and pale blue, reminiscent of the houses he'd once seen on the south coast. Nothing garish, thank goodness.

It was then that he noticed the hand-painted signs attached to the stone walls, each bearing a name. There was the ever-popular *Dun Romin'*, *Rainbow's End*, *The Haven*…. Jonathon thought it a cute touch. When he saw the fourth sign, however, he came to a halt.

*Deepings Den.*

Yeah, that couldn't be a coincidence.

His heartbeat racing a little at his own impetuosity, Jonathon lifted the brass knocker and rapped on the deep blue door.

A woman with long blonde hair opened it, her forehead creased into a frown. Then she smiled. "I remember you. You're the cocktail man."

Jonathon laughed. "A fairly apt description, I suppose. Hi, I'm Jonathon de Mountford, and if my memory serves me, you're Sarah. I was wondering if your husband is home." He kept his tone nonchalant.

Sarah shook her head. "Sorry. He's been away on business this week. He should be back later this afternoon, though." She tilted her head to one side. "De

Mountford? So you *are* Dominic's nephew. I thought when someone said it in the pub that they were joking." She narrowed her gaze. "Why do you want to speak to Trevor?"

It might have been his imagination, but Jonathon was certain a hard edge had crept into her voice.

"I just wanted to have a chat, that's all." He had no idea if Trevor even knew of the existence of the bequest and didn't want to create waves.

"I see. Well, I'll be sure to tell him you called." She gave him a polite smile. "And now if you'll excuse me, I'll go back to my washing. It was nice to see you again." And with that she closed the door.

Jonathon couldn't be sure, but he had the distinct feeling he'd just been lied to. His instincts told him Sarah had no intention of telling Trevor about his visit, and judging by her expression, seeing Jonathon was about as nice an experience as sucking on a lemon.

*So what on earth is going on here?*

Jonathon turned around and strolled back up the lane, heading for the pub. He still had questions, and he wasn't going to be happy until he had answers.

# CHAPTER FIFTEEN

JONATHON POURED himself a mug of coffee,
then sat down at the kitchen table. The increase in
noise from beyond told him Mike had opened the pub,
but Jonathon was in no mood to help out. He'd fetched
a notepad and pen from his room and was making a
list of suspects.

What frustrated him was that every time they
thought they'd found someone with the perfect motive
for hurting Dominic, that person turned out to have an
alibi, or in one case, was dead. He regarded his short
list with a sigh.

*Sue—argued with Dominic, threatened him. BUT
raid in Reading, witnesses.*
*Aidan Prescott—deceased.*
*Andrew Prescott—promised to avenge his dad.
BUT on same raid as Sue.*

*Amy Prescott—promised her husband—see above—BUT in a wheelchair.*

*Melinda Talbot—LILIES. But motive?*

*Bryan Mayhew—staying at the manor. No motive?*

*Ben Threadwell—tenant in cottage near manor— land being sold—about to be evicted.*

*Points to note:*

*Brass rubbing wax / brass polish on photo album.*

*Missing photo—who was in the photo with Dominic?*

*Lily pollen on Dominic's clothing.*

Jonathon was starting to think he wasn't cut out to be a detective. *Damn Poirot. Damn Miss Marple. They made it look easy.* He left the notepad on the table and wandered into the bar.

Mike looked up from his task of pulling a pint, and smiled. "How was the walk?"

"Not as productive as I'd hoped." Jonathon glanced around at the patrons already seated at the bar or at tables. "Abi's not here yet, is she?"

Mike pulled a face. "She called to say she won't be in today. She's had to go to the dentist. I've put up a sign saying no food. Anyone who's hungry will have to go elsewhere or put up with packets of crisps and pork scratchings. Unless…." His eyes gleamed. "I don't suppose you could make a few sandwiches? Rustle up a salad or two?" Mike widened his eyes. "Pretty please?"

Jonathon couldn't stand to see Mike doing puppy-dog eyes. He was already too damn cute. "Fine,

I'll see what's in the fridge, then give you a revised list. How's that?"

Mike grinned. "You're a star."

Jonathon shook his head, chuckling. "I'm a mug, more like." He didn't really mind helping out, not if it kept Mike's customers in the bar for longer. He went into the kitchen and peered into the fridge. Then he checked the bread supplies. A quick shopping trip was called for, but yeah, he could feed a few hungry mouths.

"Just going to the shop," he called out to Mike. "There will be the usual fare on offer when I get back. Just give me forty minutes."

Mike wiped his brow in mock relief, then smiled. "You're wonderful."

Jonathon laughed. "Yeah, yeah." His last thought as he left the pub was that he liked putting that smile on Mike's face.

JONATHON WALKED into the bar to find Mike already wiping down the surfaces. There were only a handful of customers left, and the pub would be closing in five minutes. It had been a busy start to the afternoon for both of them.

"Have I got time for a swift half?" someone called out.

Mike glanced at his watch. "Only if you can drink it in five minutes." He shook his head. "Anyone would think you didn't want to go home. I'll bet Sarah expected you hours ago."

Jonathon jerked up his head at the name and peered into the bar. Sure enough, it was Trevor, sitting in the far corner. Great. Jonathon strode across the bar and up to Trevor's table. "Hey, just the man I was looking for."

Trevor gazed up at him, his brows scrunched up. "Me? Why would you be looking for me?"

"I saw Dominic's solicitor this morning, and your name came up in conversation. I was wondering about your connection to my uncle."

Trevor paled. "Connection? What connection? I didn't even know your uncle. That solicitor fella has made a mistake." He glanced around the pub at the few remaining customers, blinking nervously, and started to rise from his chair.

"Please, wait." Jonathon was not about to let Trevor walk out of the pub, not when there were questions to be answered. "I didn't mean to upset you."

"Who's upset?" Trevor stuck out his chin but sat back down. "You got the wrong man, that's all there is to it."

"Time, gentlemen, please," Mike called out, ringing the small gold bell that hung behind the bar. "You've got a whole two hours to wait until we open again. I'm sure you'll survive."

A couple of men snickered at that.

"Okay, that's me out of here." Trevor got to his feet and grabbed his jacket. "Sarah will be worrying where I've got to."

"She knows you're coming home sometime today, right? Surely five more minutes won't matter?"

"How the—" Trevor's eyes widened. "You've seen Sarah?" He slumped back onto his chair.

Jonathon nodded. "This morning. I went to your house to talk to you."

There was no mistaking the fear in Trevor's eyes. "What… what did you say to her?"

An uneasy roiling started in Jonathon's belly. "Just that I wanted a chat with you. That was all." He caught the solid thump of the bolt being drawn across the pub door. Mike had locked up. It was now or never. "Look," Jonathon said, softening his voice. "I was just curious as to why Dominic changed his will to include a bequest to you."

Trevor narrowed his gaze. "That bastard," he hissed. "He swore to me he'd change it back, that he wouldn't go through with it."

"And how could you know that if you claim not to have known Dominic?" Mike asked, walking across to where they sat.

Trevor's back was rigid, his face still ashen. Jonathon took a moment to really look at him. Trevor was maybe in his late forties, with light brown hair and hazel eyes. Despite the way he glared at them, Jonathon liked his face. He got the feeling Trevor was a kind man.

"Okay." Jonathon made his tone coaxing, hopefully soothing. "It's just us now. And whatever you say will stay between us. I… I'm just looking for answers here."

Mike pulled out a chair and joined them.

Trevor nodded, his expression softening a little. That small step forward gave Jonathon hope.

"Dominic told you he'd changed his will?"

Another nod. "He told me he was leaving me fifty thousand. I… I told him I didn't want it."

"But why? Why would he want to leave you money? And why would you turn it down?"

Trevor sighed. "Because too many questions would have been asked, that's why. Nothing stays secret for long in this village. I'm surprised we lasted as long as we did without someone spotting us."

*Secret.... We lasted....* Jonathon swallowed. "I think you'd better start at the beginning."

Mike went over to the bar and returned with a couple of glasses of brandy. He handed one to Trevor. "I think you might need this." He retook his seat.

Trevor didn't hesitate. He drank it down in one long swallow, then shuddered as he placed the empty glass on the table. "Where to start? I suppose it all boils down to the fact that Dominic and I were having an affair. Last month was our ten-year anniversary." He snorted. "Anniversary. Not that we could tell anyone. Still, we got a night together in a hotel, and as always, he made it special."

Jonathon felt as though he'd taken a step through a door into The Twilight Zone. "Dominic… and you? But…." His brain was having difficulty making the connections.

Trevor regarded him keenly. "You don't appear disgusted. I'd have thought that would have been your first reaction."

Jonathon smiled. "Yeah, well, glad to disappoint you. Firstly, I finally have a reason why Dominic never married. And secondly? Why would it disgust me to learn that Dominic and I were more alike than I imagined?"

Trevor stared at him. "You're… gay? Did Dominic know?"

"I never told him, and I doubt my father would have shared that particular piece of information. He had enough problems digesting it himself." A wave of mingled sorrow and regret washed over him. *Too late now.* Yet again he was conscious of being robbed of time. So much they could have learned about each other and would never get the opportunity to do so.

"I'm not gay, by the way." Trevor regarded them, visibly calmer. "I've always been aware that I'm attracted to both men and women. I love my wife, but Dominic came along when we were going through a bad patch."

"How did this all get started?"

Trevor shook his head. "I was staying in a hotel near London, during one of my sales trips. Dominic was in the same hotel. We ended up sharing a bottle or two of wine, and I guess I let slip more than I'd intended. One thing led to another, and I… spent the night in his room." He sighed. "I think back then it was just sex. I don't believe either of us anticipated how long it would last… or that I'd fall in love with him." Jonathon drew in a sharp breath, and Trevor nodded slowly. "Oh, I loved him. We were careful, though. About once or twice a month, we'd meet up for a night in a hotel in Kent. It was far enough away from Merrychurch that we thought no one would ever spot us." He rubbed his ring finger absently. "We always went there as a married couple. Dominic had bought me a ring that I'd wear." He swallowed. "I know it's a lot to ask, but it must be somewhere at the manor…. If you…?"

Jonathon nodded hurriedly. "If I find it, I'll bring it to you." It was obvious from every word that left Trevor's lips that he spoke from the heart. "I take it your wife didn't know?"

Trevor shook his head vehemently. "And I want it to stay that way. I wouldn't hurt her for anything. I know I've cheated on her, but…. Dominic was a hard man to resist, and when he came along… I guess I just gave up fighting my impulses and went with the flow. I never thought I could love two people, but God help me, I did."

"So when Dominic made that bequest…," Mike said slowly.

"I couldn't let him do that. I know he was only thanking me for my discretion all these years and trying to make my life a little more comfortable. But let's face facts here. If people got to hear about it, tongues would start wagging and everyone would want to know why the lord of the manor was leaving a lowly salesman fifty thousand pounds. Stuff like that? Somebody would have got curious and started digging. And if that happened, you know what would have followed. I'd have been outed in a heartbeat. So I thanked him but refused. I begged him to draw up another will, going back to how it had been."

"He did." Mike pointed toward Jonathon. "He named Jonathon as his heir."

Trevor's face lit up. "Now that feels right. Every time he spoke about you, pride just… shone out of him. And maybe he had an inkling that you were gay. A sense, perhaps? I know he loved you very much." Trevor's face darkened. "But the last few weeks, there was something eating away at him. I don't know what it was, but…. He talked a lot about putting things right. I don't know what he meant by that. I just know that the last time we were… together, it was as if some secret was gnawing at his insides. All I wanted to do was hold him and comfort him. I felt so fucking useless." Trevor bowed his head, but not before Jonathon caught the glint of a tear on his cheek.

"I hate to throw a spanner in the works," Mike said suddenly, "but a thought has just occurred to me. Now that Jonathon has been informed of the contents of Dominic's will, the police might ask to see it too."

"Why?" Jonathon frowned.

"Think about it. We wanted to see it because we wanted to know if Dominic had made any bequests that might have thrown light on his death. If we can think that way, so can the police."

"You think they'll find out about the changes? Even though he didn't go through with it?" Trevor stiffened. "But why would they think I had anything to do with Dominic's death?"

"Maybe there was the possibility that Dominic would out you. Maybe you killed him to make sure that didn't happen. Not that I think you did kill him, all right?" Mike held up his hands. "But look, you have an alibi."

"I do?" Trevor's face was the picture of bewilderment.

Mike nodded. "Thursday night last week. Think about it. Where were you?"

Trevor bit his lip, but then he widened his eyes. "Oh God. That was the night I got really drunk, wasn't it? The night you drove me home?"

Mike nodded again.

"Is that when he died? That night?"

"They say the evening," Jonathon interjected. "They haven't given a more specific estimate. So they could still argue that you killed him before you got to the pub. Where were you before then?"

Trevor's brow furrowed. "I was… driving back from Birmingham. I'd been away for a couple of days. But when I got to the village, I couldn't face going home. I… wanted to see him, only I couldn't, of course. That was our one rule—no contact in the village. I wasn't even to go up to the manor. That way there was nothing to draw attention to us. And as Sarah had no contact with him either, it was an easy rule to stick to." He sighed. "I parked the car a few miles away in a lane near the hall. I just sat there, staring out the window. Then I thought, 'this is stupid,' so I drove to the pub. I didn't intend to drink that much. I guess I was feeling sorry for myself, and… overdid it. You know the rest."

"So the police might think they have a case and you don't have a good alibi." Mike scrubbed his hand across his face. "Okay, at least we know it might be coming. I doubt even Gorland would let this opportunity slip by him. Be prepared, Trevor, okay?"

He nodded. "Though heaven knows how I'll explain all this to Sarah if they do take me in for questioning." His face was still clouded over. "I guess it might finally be time to be honest with her." Trevor stood and grabbed his jacket. "I'd better go home, guys. She'll be worrying."

Jonathon laid a tentative hand on Trevor's arm. "Thank you for telling me. It did answer some questions, but more importantly… I'm glad he had someone. I hated to think of him all alone all these years."

Trevor gave a half smile. "He knew I loved him, and I like to think he loved me too. Dominic was never one for romantic lines, but he showed how he felt in… other ways." His face flushed. "I know I'll never forget the last ten years, that's for sure."

Jonathon withdrew his hand. "Let us know if anything happens, okay?"

"Sure." Trevor followed Mike to the door.

Jonathon picked up his glass of brandy and took a sip before downing all of it, coughing as it hit the back of his throat.

*I certainly didn't see* that *coming.* But Trevor's remarks about Dominic's recent state of mind opened up another avenue to explore. What had Dominic meant about putting things right?

Yet another mystery.

*There can't be any more surprises out there—can there?*

# CHAPTER SIXTEEN

BY THE time Mike returned to the bar after seeing Trevor out, Jonathon had made up his mind. "We're going out."

Mike arched his eyebrows. "We are? And where exactly are we going?"

"To see Melinda, to talk lilies." Jonathon wanted to eliminate suspects from his list. Not that he could really see the sweet-faced vicar's wife brutally shoving Dominic but learning about her lilies made her an important resource.

Mike shrugged. "Why not?" He grinned. "Besides, if we're lucky, she'll have been baking this morning."

Jonathon rolled his eyes. "Do you always think with your stomach?"

Mike huffed. "When it comes to Melinda's or Rachel Meadows's baking? Always." He looked

Jonathon up and down. "Well, come on then. Let's go if we're going."

Shaking his head, Jonathon followed Mike to the back door and out of the building.

The lane leading to the church was in the shade, thanks to the trees that spread out their branches over the cobbles, and the air was cool. August was continuing in the same vein as July; in fact, it looked as though it would be even hotter. The churchyard was deep in shade too, with little light permeating the green canopy.

Jonathon caught a flash of movement over by the stone wall that encircled the church property. Bryan Mayhew was kneeling in front of a gravestone, a piece of white paper laid over it. He was carefully rubbing the surface of the paper with a piece of charcoal. As they approached, he glanced up and smiled.

"Hey. I just made a surprise find." He pointed to the gravestone. "This marks the resting place of Jonathon de Mountford."

Jonathon couldn't help the shiver that rippled up and down his spine. "Seriously?"

Bryan nodded. "He appears to have been born in the late eighteen hundreds, and from what I've discovered, he died soon after birth. Why they buried him out here and not in the crypt, I'm not sure. Maybe because he was only a baby? Still, the name…."

"Did you know you weren't the first?" Mike asked, crouching to peer at the stone. The lettering was almost obliterated.

Jonathon gazed at it in wonder. "I had no idea. Did you find him in your research?"

"Yup." Bryan pulled a notepad from the back pocket of his jeans. "He was born to Elizabeth de Mountford, her firstborn. Subsequently she went on to have six more children." He smiled. "And you're a direct descendant."

"Wow." Seeing the faint remains of his name on the stone still gave Jonathon the shudders. He straightened. "Well, we'll leave you to it."

"Sure." Bryan waved absently, already lost in his notes.

Mike chuckled as they walked back to the path. "Academics."

They walked around the church to the vicarage, and Jonathon gazed in admiration at the beautiful garden with its well-stocked beds and neatly arranged borders. "She's good, isn't she?"

"Melinda? She's amazing. You should see the church at harvest. She puts together arrangements that almost blaze with color."

As Mike finished speaking, the front door opened and Melinda appeared, dressed in linen pants and a cream blouse. "Mike, Jonathon, what a pleasant surprise." Her face crinkled with pleasure.

"I've come to pick your brains." Jonathon saw no point in beating about the bush.

"That sounds interesting. I'm just going into the walled garden to pick some salad for dinner. Why don't you come with me?"

"Great." Jonathon followed her through an arched gate and along a path that led around the house. Ahead of them was a red-bricked wall, with an ornate wrought iron gate set into it. She led them through it, and Jonathon caught his breath. Climbing plants covered the walls, and a heady perfume filled the air. The garden was set out in neat beds, with tiny paths dissecting them. "Did you build this?"

Melinda laughed. "Heavens, no. This garden has existed as long as the vicarage has stood on this spot, which is probably a few centuries." She pointed toward the far wall, where a wooden gate was halfway along it. "Through there is my hothouse. Your uncle built that for me."

"Really?"

She smiled. "I had a tiny little greenhouse, and Dominic wanted to do something to thank me for the church flowers. Such a kind man." She turned to Jonathon. "Now, what did you want to know?"

"Someone told me you're an expert on lilies."

Melinda's face glowed. "Well, I wouldn't say expert, but… I seem to have been lucky with my blooms."

"Now you're being far too modest," Mike said warmly. "I've not been in the village all that long, and even *I've* heard about your collection of first-prize ribbons from past fetes. Sue told me."

"Then step this way, gentlemen, and I'll show you my pride and joy." Melinda walked along the narrow path toward the climber-covered wall.

"Is that honeysuckle I can smell?" The scent reminded Jonathon of his mother's garden.

Melinda nodded. "I have two types, both of which are very fragrant. This is the area where I also grow night-blooming jasmine, and of course, my *lilium regale*. No one else in the village grows this species." She pointed to the tall spikes of green, adorned with white trumpetlike flowers.

"Regal lily, huh?" Mike said casually. When Jonathon flashed him a glance, he shrugged. "So I studied Latin at school."

Jonathon chuckled. "A man of many talents." He walked up to the nearest lily and bent close to inhale its fragrance. "Oh wow. That smells divine."

"I told your uncle I'd grow some for his gardens, but he never took me up on it."

Jonathon already knew the reason why.

Melinda gave him a speculative glance. "I suppose I should congratulate you, Mr. de Mountford, though it doesn't seem proper to congratulate someone who has inherited in such a terrible manner."

"Ah. Word has got around, I see."

She nodded. "I think nearly everyone I met in the village this afternoon was fairly buzzing with the news. So will you be residing at the manor house? Or will Jonathon de Mountford continue on his worldwide adventures, taking photographs to amaze and astound us?"

Jonathon was aware that Mike was watching him closely, as if he too was waiting to learn of Jonathon's plans. "I'm not about to give up my career," he said emphatically.

"Good." Melinda's eyes shone. "That would be a waste of talent, if you ask me."

"Definitely." Mike's voice was gruff.

"But… I *have* decided to move to Merrychurch."

Mike's eyes widened. "When did you decide this?" Then he nodded slowly. "Let me guess. Your morning stroll."

Jonathon bobbed his head in acknowledgment. "I said I had a lot of thinking to do." He turned to

Melinda. "Which leads me to the purpose of our visit. What we want to know is, who else grows lilies in the village?" He grinned. "Put it another way—who's your main competition for the prize at the fete this year?"

"I can't think of why you'd want to know such a thing, but I'm sure you have your reasons for asking. Let me see." She began to count off on her fingers. "Doreen Pointer is often in the running for prizes, as is Les Nugent. Ben Threadwell has produced some gorgeous blooms the last few years. Sarah Deeping usually takes a prize—her *lilium longiflorum* are always spectacular."

Jonathon stilled. "Sarah Deeping?" He briefly met Mike's gaze before returning his attention to Melinda.

"Oh yes. Sarah really does have a green thumb. She helps me out now and again with the flowers for the church. I try to vary the displays, and Sarah often brings flowers from her garden." Melinda sighed. "Poor thing. I feel sorry for her sometimes. She comes and cleans the church when Trevor is away because it gives her something to do. She hates that Trevor has to travel so much for his job, not that she'd ever say such a thing to him. Wouldn't say boo to a goose, that one."

Jonathon wasn't so sure. The Sarah who'd spoken with him that morning hadn't seemed in the least bit timid.

"Now, do you two have time for tea? Once I've picked a nice fat lettuce, that's the next thing on my list. You'd be very welcome to stay." Melinda's eyes twinkled. "Especially as I've just made some fruit scones. They're probably still warm."

Jonathon took one look at Mike and burst out laughing. "Stop it, Melinda, or you'll have Mike drool all over your lilies."

Mike gave him a mock glare. "Drool? What am I, a dog?"

Melinda laughed too. "That does it. Come into the house. Actually, Jonathon, would you go to Sebastian's cottage and tell him it's time for tea? I've hardly seen him all day."

"Sure. And by the way, I did as you suggested. He's going to join me for a drink tomorrow night at the pub."

Melinda beamed. "Good boy. I knew I could count on you." She patted Mike on the back. "And you can make yourself useful and pull up a lettuce for me. Save an old lady's back." She grinned and then pointed to the wooden gate. "Go through there, Jonathon, then turn left. You'll see the cottage at the far end of the garden."

"Okay." Jonathon left them and followed the narrow path to the gate. Pushing it open, he found himself at the edge of a huge lawn, at least one hundred feet in length. On the right stood the vicarage, with french windows that opened out onto a patio, and at the other end stood a tiny thatched cottage. Jonathon strolled across the lawn to the low front door and knocked. To his surprise, it opened.

"Hello? Sebastian?" He stuck his head around the door and peered inside.

It was a cozy little place, with a tiny kitchen to the right, what looked like an even tinier bathroom, then a living room, and finally a door that had to lead to the bedroom. A desk sat against one wall and an old, worn couch against the other. Above the desk were two bookshelves stuffed with books.

Jonathon caught sight of a couple of framed photographs below the shelves and wandered over to take a closer look. They were obviously newspaper cuttings, showing children of all ages in white karate robes, clearly demonstrating moves for the camera. The article next to the photo was about the opening of a karate school for underprivileged kids in London, and—

"Can I help you?"

Jonathon straightened so fast, he bumped his head on the shelf above. "Ouch!" He rubbed it as he turned toward the bedroom door where Sebastian stood, his expression neutral. "I did call out. Sorry, I didn't mean to intrude. Melinda sent me to bring you to tea."

"Ah, I see." Sebastian cocked his head to one side. "Are you all right? That was quite a bump you just got."

"You startled me. My own fault." Jonathon headed toward the door, with Sebastian following. "We came to see Melinda and got invited to tea."

"Yes, she does that a lot." Sebastian chuckled. "Now you understand my comment about waifs and strays."

"Are we still on for a drink and darts tomorrow night?"

"Oh, yes, of course. How's your head?"

"Aching, but it'll pass." Jonathon felt decidedly guilty. Sebastian must have thought he was snooping, and to be truthful, there was no other word for his behavior. He wanted to ask about the karate school, but after being discovered where he had no business being, Jonathon felt it was a subject best left alone.

Besides, he had bigger things to worry about—like how to make sure Mike didn't eat all the scones.

"AREN'T YOU the dark 'orse, then?"

Jonathon poured out a cosmopolitan into a cocktail glass and set it in front of his customer before giving Paul his full attention. "I beg your pardon?"

"I had no idea that the lord of the manor had been making my cocktails." Paul smirked. "You kept that quiet."

"Not really. I only found out myself this morning." Jonathon chuckled. "Things really do get around fast in this village, don't they?"

Paul cackled. "Lad, you have no idea. Do something good around here, and everyone gets to hear about it. Put a foot wrong, and they get to hear about it twice as fast." He raised his pint glass. "Here's to you, then. Good luck and good fortune."

"Thanks, Paul." Jonathon was touched.

Paul waved his hand. "I like to think I'm a good judge of character, an' you strike me as a nice, hardworking lad. Besides, Mike obviously trusts you, and he's got good instincts."

From a few feet away, Mike laughed. "Nah, he's working for free. What's not to like?" Just then his phone rang. Mike glanced at the screen and frowned. "Uh-oh." He picked it up and met Jonathon's gaze, his eyes troubled. "Hi, Graham. What's up?"

*Graham?* Then it came to him. Constable Billings. Jonathon's stomach did a slow flip-flop.

Mike was listening intently, his forehead creased into deep lines. "I see. … Yeah. … Okay, thanks for letting me know. Keep me informed of any new developments, please? … Yeah, yeah, okay. Bye." He placed the phone on the shelf below the bar, moving slowly, his frown still evident.

"Something's happened." Jonathon shifted closer. "What is it?"

"Graham called to say Gorland took Trevor in for questioning two hours ago."

*Shit.* "And?"

Mike sighed heavily. "They just arrested him. He told them the truth, and that was that. No alibi that he can prove. Graham said Gorland thinks they were arguing about the bequest and Trevor tried to kill Dominic so that his secret would die with him."

"But… that doesn't make any sense. Dominic reverted to the terms of the original will. There was no bequest." Jonathon felt sick.

"And right now Gorland's got a man in his cells with no alibi, and what *he* thinks is a strong motive. Now, I don't think Trevor's guilty any more than you do, but I don't know what we can do to help him. Gorland has to be under a lot of pressure. Dominic died a week ago, and he still doesn't have someone in the frame for it. Add to that the phone calls he must be getting from your family, and what do you have?"

"A copper who's making a big mistake," Jonathon ground out.

"Hey." Mike's voice softened. "I don't like it either. But there *is* one thing we can do."

"And what's that?"

"Find out who was really in Dominic's study. Then prove it to Gorland, before he lets this go much further."

"Then we'd better do it fast." Jonathon hated the idea of Trevor in a police cell. He'd just lost the man he loved, and to find himself accused of causing Dominic's death had to be dreadful.

"Right now, you have cocktails to make and I have pints to pull. Neither of us can do anything right this second."

Mike had a point.

Sleuthing would have to wait until the morning.

# Chapter Seventeen

"What was wrong with having coffee in your kitchen?" Jonathon asked as they pushed open the door to the tea shop. "Or is this just your sweet tooth talking?"

Mike swatted him on the backside. "Philistine. There's a reason Rachel wins prizes at the fete for her baking. And if I feel like having a slice of her carrot cake, neither you nor anyone else in this village is gonna stop me."

"Whoa. Far be it from me to come between a man and his sugar fix." Jonathon smiled. "Besides, it's good to get out of the pub now and again." Maybe the change of scenery would help his deductive powers, because they certainly needed it. The lilies research had so far turned up only one name of interest, and Jonathon had added Sarah Deeping to his list, not that there was anything else to link her to Dominic's death.

Still, they only had Trevor's word that she didn't know about the affair. As far as other possible suspects went, Jonathon was beginning to think they'd exhausted every avenue. Unless, of course, there were more skeletons waiting to fall out of Dominic's closet....

Rachel beamed as they entered. "Hey, guys. Good to see you. Have a seat and I'll be over to take your order."

Jonathon pointed to an empty table, and they sat down. The tea shop was already more than half full, and considering it was only ten o'clock, Jonathon wondered if this was normal. From all around them came the buzz of low voices, and judging by the odd word he caught, the topic of conversation was Dominic—and Trevor.

"Looks like the news has already hit the village grapevine," he whispered to Mike. He glanced at the other patrons, conscious of both pointed and less obvious looks in his direction.

"Yeah." Mike didn't look happy. "And you can bet they're really making a meal out of the whole they-were-secret-lovers aspect. Not that it's any of their business."

"I guess you've heard, huh?" Rachel bent over and lowered her voice. "It's all anyone's been talking about since I opened. You'd think the village had never known a bigger scandal." She shook her head. "It's poor Sarah I feel sorry for. What she must be feeling right now, knowing everyone is talking about them. It must have been bad enough knowing it was going on, without Trevor getting arrested."

Jonathon blinked, and his stomach clenched. "But... did she even know about the affair? Trevor says not."

Rachel huffed. "Sorry, but I don't believe that. A woman generally knows if her husband is cheating on her. It's like some sixth sense. And now it all clicks into place."

"What do you mean?" Mike asked.

Rachel took a swift look around the tea shop before lowering her voice to barely above a whisper. "A couple of months ago, maybe April, I was walking through the village, and I saw Dominic's Land Rover parked off Mill Lane. Sarah was with him, and they appeared to be arguing. Okay, so the rain was really lashing down, but I recognized her. I'd never seen her look so... angry. Come to think of it, Dominic looked furious too. Anyway, once the news broke this morning, I got to thinking about that day. I couldn't help but wonder what they were arguing about." She sighed. "Okay, enough gossip. What would you like?"

They ordered coffee and two slices of cake. Once Rachel had walked away from their table, Jonathon edged his chair closer to Mike's. "So much for Trevor saying she had no contact with Dominic," he murmured.

"If Rachel's right," Mike said quietly, "and I don't see any reason to doubt her—then we might have another suspect to add to the list."

Jonathon sighed. "I'd already added her, after we found out about the lilies." His belly felt queasy. "You think Trevor got it wrong? That Sarah did know about the affair?"

"It's possible, isn't it? I mean, ten years? They had to have at least one slipup in ten years. Something that gave the game away. So let's think about it for a minute. Sarah finds out. Does she confront Trevor? Well, we know she didn't, so that leaves confronting Dominic. Maybe they were arguing because she was telling him to put an end to the affair and Dominic was refusing."

"So she goes up to the manor house, gets into a big fight, pushes him, and accidentally kills him?" Jonathon considered the idea. "She'd have to be really strong to shove him hard enough to crack his ribs."

"Hell hath no fury, and all that," Mike said sagely. "And supposing she'd been gardening just before? That would account for the lily pollen, wouldn't it?" Mike shook his head. "That sounds like a long shot to me, but I suppose it could've happened like that. Well, the police can't take her in for questioning without evidence, and I don't think Rachel's memory of seeing them on a rainy day in his Land Rover would be enough."

Jonathon shivered. It was hard to believe that just a week previously, he'd arrived in the village, looking forward to spending time with Dominic, feeling carefree and happy.

"Hey." Mike's hand covered his. "You okay?" Concern laced his voice.

"Just thinking about how everything has changed in the space of one week." Then, he'd been thinking about his Vietnam trip, his next book….

"Did you mean what you said to Melinda? That you're going to live here in Merrychurch?"

Jonathon nodded. "It makes sense. But just because I live in the manor does *not* mean I have to conform to my father's wishes."

Mike chuckled. "I didn't believe for a second that you would. But what about his argument that you're the last of the de Mountfords? Who will inherit after you?"

"Christ, Mike. I'm not even in the hall yet and you're already planning who gets it after I snuff it?" Jonathon snickered. "And as for who inherits… there's this wonderful thing out there called 'adoption.' Ever heard of it?" He grinned. "I'll get married—because heaven forbid there be a scandal touching the family, involving a gay couple living 'out of wedlock'—and then we'll adopt."

Mike laughed. "You've got it all planned out, haven't you? Have you even got a would-be husband waiting in the wings somewhere?"

Jonathon smiled. "I haven't planned *that* far ahead. But I'm not going to hide who I am." Sorrow flowed through him. "Dominic did that, and look where it got him."

"You don't know that's what happened," Mike reasoned, his fingers curling around Jonathon's. The intimate gesture warmed him.

"No, but so far, it's the most likely scenario, isn't it?"

"I can't deny that." Mike's expression seemed to reflect his own sorrow. He straightened, releasing Jonathon's hand as Rachel approached, and Jonathon missed his warm touch instantly. Then he wondered why Mike had severed their connection.

*Is he protecting my reputation, or his?*

Jonathon was more than capable of standing up for himself, and in the light of recent events, he didn't want to hide anymore.

JONATHON LAY on his bed, staring at the ceiling. Mike was downstairs, getting the pub ready to open. It wasn't that Jonathon was feeling lazy; it was just that he'd wanted a little time to himself. Because being around Mike? *Big* distraction....

He knew he'd be lying to himself if he said Mike hadn't entered the equation when it came to his plans to move into the manor. Not that Mike was his primary motivation—*that*, he was sure of—but yeah, he'd thought about the fact that Mike would be his neighbor. His *very attractive* neighbor. And part of him badly wanted Mike to feel the same way.

The sound of feet thudding up the stairs had him sitting up abruptly. The door flung open and Mike came into the room in a hurry.

"The shit has just hit the fan," he said breathlessly.

"What? What's happened?"

"Graham called. They've arrested Sarah Deeping."

Jonathon was off the bed in a heartbeat. "On what evidence?"

"The tech guys going over Dominic's computer found deleted emails—God knows why he deleted them, but there you go—where Sarah threatened him that if he didn't end the affair, she'd out him to the village—and his family."

"Fuck!" Jonathon gaped at him. "So that's it? Has she confessed?"

Mike shook his head. "She says she didn't do it but can't prove where she was when he died. The police think she felt that without Dominic in the picture, Trevor would return to 'normal.'" He air-quoted.

Jonathon huffed. "Yeah, like *that* would work."

"So now they have both her *and* Trevor for the same crime. And get this—Gorland isn't prepared to release Trevor just yet."

Jonathon rolled his eyes. "Well, they couldn't have *both* done it." The sound of the church bell drifted through his open window, and he stared at Mike. "Er, excuse me? Don't you have a pub to open?"

"Bloody hell." Mike dashed out of the room and thundered down the stairs.

Jonathon followed, albeit at a more sedate pace. He wasn't about to get complacent. He'd believe Sarah killed Dominic when a jury sent her down for it, and not before. However, the emails, the lilies, Rachel seeing her arguing with Dominic... Jonathon couldn't deny it was all starting to look more and more likely that she'd done it.

"THIS FOR the game." Sebastian aimed his dart, launched it, and then grinned when it landed firmly on the board. "Ladies and gentlemen, we have a winner."

Jonathon snickered. "Are curates allowed to gloat? Whatever happened to humility?"

Sebastian laughed. "There speaks a sore loser. And speaking of which, the loser buys the next round, correct?" He collected his darts from the board and slipped them into their black case.

Jonathon had to admit, it was the most relaxed evening he'd spent since he'd arrived in the village. Sebastian had arrived at nine, in an obviously good mood, and had been bubbly all night. Maybe that was due to the fact that he'd won *every one* of their five games. Jonathon had no problem acknowledging he'd been outclassed.

"Okay, okay. Another pint of Landlord's?"

Sebastian nodded. "And a packet of cheese and onion crisps, please." His eyes sparkled. "Winning makes me peckish."

Jonathon let out a groan. "You're not gonna let this go, are you? You're going to keep reminding me until Mike throws you out at closing time."

Sebastian laughed. "Yup. Now where's my beer?"

Jonathon shook his head, chuckling, and went over to where Mike was serving.

"Enjoying your night off?" Mike asked with a smile. "He seems to be in a good mood."

"Three guesses why. He's a bloody good darts player. Evidence of a misspent youth, if you ask me," Jonathon grumbled. "Two more pints of Landlord's, please, and a couple of packets of cheese and onion crisps."

"Sure." Mike grabbed clean glasses from above the bar. He nodded in Sebastian's direction. "He seems to have loosened up a lot."

"Yeah, he does, doesn't he?" Maybe Melinda was right all along. All Sebastian needed was someone nearer his own age, someone he could relate to.

He carried the glasses over to where Sebastian sat, the corners of the crisp packets between his teeth. Sebastian chuckled and got to his feet to help him out. When they were both seated, Sebastian took a long drink of beer and let out a sigh.

"Can't remember the last time I did this."

"Then isn't it a good thing that I asked you?" Jonathon raised his glass. "To the winner."

"I'll drink to that." They clinked glasses.

"Did you always want to go into the church?"

Sebastian shook his head. "My father was a vicar, but I never thought I'd follow in his footsteps. Then when he retired, about five years ago, I started thinking about it. I went to Bible college, the same one that he attended. He wanted me to take over his parish, but that was too daunting. I wanted to start somewhere smaller. Then he found out St. Mary's was looking for a curate. And the rest is history." He took a drink from his glass.

"You did it to please him, didn't you?"

Sebastian paused, his eyes wide. "Very percep-tive. Yes, I did. When I was younger, all I wanted was to be a science teacher. Science has always fascinated me. I was your total geek when I was at school."

"I suppose you're still a teacher, of sorts," Jona-thon reasoned.

Sebastian nodded. "True enough. I figured once I'd done a year or two, I'd know if I wanted to con-tinue or not. So far, I'm enjoying it, although I had no idea I'd have to do so many different things."

"Such as?"

Sebastian laughed. "I'm the general dogsbody around there. I get to do everything." He began to count off on his fingers. "Let's start with the obvious bits. I get to preach—only once a month so far, but the work it takes to get a sermon ready is nobody's busi-ness. I visit sick parishioners and those who can't get to the services. Then there's the church building. You name it, I do it—choosing the hymns, arranging the flowers, cleaning the candlesticks on the altar, tidying up the kneelers after the service...."

Jonathon laughed. "Busy man."

"Yes, but you know what? Anything else would be boring, and I'm never bored." He paused, studying Jonathon. "And your life is anything but boring."

"Ah. Are we talking about my travels?"

Sebastian nodded. "You've got a great eye for a fantastic shot. But to have the freedom to do all that—the traveling, the means to do it—I envy that."

Jonathon tut-tutted. "And there you go again, displaying very un-curate-like qualities."

Sebastian smiled. "You're right, of course. Maybe I'm not such a good curate after all."

"What would you do instead?"

Sebastian's eyes gleamed. "Who knows? None of us know exactly what's around the corner, do we? Life is full of surprises."

"Jonathon? You got a minute?"

Sebastian inclined his head in the direction of Mike's voice. "Looks like your night off might be coming to a premature end. Mike's got a lot of customers over there."

Jonathon twisted around to see. "Damn. Where did they all come from?" He got up from his chair. "Sorry to do this, but—"

"No, no, it's okay. Mike obviously needs some help over there. Thanks for the games. I'm going to finish this pint. Then I'll get off home." Sebastian looked at his watch. "Besides, it's nearly eleven o'clock. Already way past my usual bedtime." He grinned.

Jonathon laughed. "Yeah, right. Melinda's told me about you burning the midnight oil, so pull the other one." He held out his hand. "Thanks for this evening. I really enjoyed it."

Sebastian smiled. "You're welcome."

"Jonathon!"

"Oops." Jonathon left him and dove behind the bar. "Okay, I'm here now. What do you want me to do?"

"Three pints for that guy over there, please."
Mike shook his head. "Why do they always descend
just before last orders, as though Prohibition is about
to be declared?"

Jonathon got on with pulling the pints, thankful
that Mike had shown him how to do it properly; the
last thing he wanted was someone getting shitty with
him because the head on their pint was all wrong.

For the next twenty minutes, he poured drinks,
pulled pints, and chatted with the locals that he was already coming to know. Sebastian gave him a friendly
wave as he left, which Jonathon returned. Then it was
right back to serving drinks.

"What're you doin' behind that bar?" the guy in
front of Jonathon slurred.

"Pouring your pint," Jonathon said good-naturedly.

"Yeah, I can see that, but why're *you* doin' it?
You're the fuckin' lord of the manor, ain't ya? Not
like you need the bleedin' work, right?" He looked
around him for support from his fellow drinkers, but
they shied away from him. He glared and returned his
attention to Jonathon. "Bloody de Mountfords. Think
they own the whole bleedin' village. An' then they
turn out to be a bloody poofter. Jus' shows, you can
never tell." He peered at Jonathon, leaning over the
bartop, his breath reeking of alcohol. "Are you one of
'em too?"

Before Jonathon could think of a suitable response,
Mike was around the bar. He grabbed the drunk by the
arms and led him toward the door. "You've had more
than enough for one night, Saul. And if you mouth off
like that again in my pub, I'll bar you. Understood?"
Without waiting for Saul to reply, Mike propelled him

through the door and closed it after him. He walked back into the pub, rubbing his hands together briskly. "Right. Anyone else got anything to add?" He waited for a moment. "What, no more comments? Then I'm calling time." He went to the bar and rang the bell. "Drink up, ladies and gents."

Jonathon gaped. "You didn't have to do that."

Mike gazed at him frankly. "My pub, my rules. Saul Putnam has an axe to grind, by the way. He's one of those tenants who were given eviction notices. So now you know why he was so pissed off."

"Never mind why he was pissed. You don't have to protect me. I've traveled all over the world, Mike. I *can* look after myself." Jonathon didn't know whether he was annoyed or touched.

Mike said nothing but pressed his lips together.

When the final customer had gone, Mike gave the bar one last glance. "I'll clear up in the morning. I'm not in the mood to do it now." And with that he flicked off the lights, leaving Jonathon standing there in the semidarkness while he headed for the stairs.

*What the hell?*

Jonathon followed him, taking two steps at a time. "Mike, wait!"

Mike carried on climbing the stairs, his back stiff. By the time Jonathon reached the top, he was already at his bedroom door.

"Mike, stop!"

Mike paused, his hand on the open door, and looked at him. "Yeah?"

Jonathon walked across the landing to where he stood. "What's wrong?" he asked softly.

Mike regarded him in silence for a moment, then let out a sigh. "What you said a while ago, about not needing me to protect you."

"Yes?" For some reason the hairs on Jonathon's arms were standing on end.

"What if I *want* to protect you?" Mike's voice was low and deep. And before Jonathon could reply, Mike pulled him into his arms and their lips met in a gentle kiss.

Jonathon closed his eyes and molded his body to Mike's, losing himself in the unexpected but totally welcome kiss that made him almost dizzy with its duration.

When they parted, both slightly breathless, Mike cupped Jonathon's chin. "You're sleeping in my bed tonight. Unless you have any objection to that?"

Jonathon gave himself up to the heat that surged through him. "None whatsoever," he said firmly.

Mike smiled. "Thank God." He took Jonathon's hand, led him into his bedroom, and closed the door behind them.

# CHAPTER EIGHTEEN

JONATHON STRETCHED beneath the covers, warm and comfortable. Then he remembered where he was. Only, where Mike had been, there was now a cool spot.

Jonathon sat up and rubbed his eyes. One glance at the clock beside the bed told him it was still early. He scanned the floor for the jeans he'd discarded the previous night, then hopped out of bed and squirmed into them. Everywhere was quiet as he padded barefoot down the narrow staircase and into the pub.

"Mike?"

"In the kitchen."

Jonathon pushed open the door and found him sitting at the table, drinking coffee.

Mike gave him a warm smile. "Well, good morning. There's coffee in the pot."

Jonathon arched his eyebrows. "I have a better idea. Why don't you bring your coffee mug with you and come back to bed?"

Mike's smile widened. "I like that idea. Sounds like the perfect way to spend a Saturday morning."

Jonathon couldn't agree more. He stifled a groan when Mike's phone rang.

Mike gave him an apologetic glance as he reached for it. Frowning, he connected the call. "Lloyd? What's up? This is early, even for you."

It took Jonathon a second or two to register that Lloyd was the vicar. His stomach clenched when Mike froze, his mouth open.

"Have you called the police?" A pause. "Fine, but call them anyway. I'll be right over. And Lloyd? Don't touch anything, do you understand? Keep out of there until I get there." He listened again. "Good man. Yes, you did the right thing." He disconnected the call and stared, wide-eyed, at Jonathon. "You're not gonna believe this. Lloyd Talbot just found a body in the church crypt."

"Body…. A dead body? Who is it?"

"Lloyd doesn't know. Whoever it is, is lying face-down, and Lloyd didn't want to disturb the body." Mike pushed back his chair. "I'll pull on some more clothes and get over to the church."

"I'm coming too." Jonathon stuck out his chin, daring Mike to say no.

Mike sighed. "Like I could stop you anyway. If you're coming, go put some clothes on." He pointed to Jonathon's neck. "And you might want to consider wearing something that, er, covers… *that*." He left the kitchen, his face flushed.

Jonathon turned toward the stainless steel on the oven door and peered intently at his reflection. It wasn't the best of mirrors, but it was enough to reveal the reddish mark at the base of his throat.

Oh. *That*.

He rushed up the stairs, racking his brains as to what was in his suitcase that would do the job.

Five minutes later, Jonathon was safely attired in a shirt, the collar done up. They left the pub and headed along the lane to the church.

Melinda was at the heavy church door, her face pale. "Oh, Mike, this is truly awful."

Mike gave her a brief hug. "Are the police on their way?"

She nodded. "Lloyd spoke with Constable Billings, right after he finished speaking to you. They should be here any minute." She gave a nod toward Jonathon. "This is dreadful. Two deaths in the space of a week."

Jonathon followed her and Mike into the church. The altar sat at the far end, a pulpit off to the left, draped in a gold cloth. Rows of wooden pews lined each side of the aisle, and on the right was a black railing, a gate set into it. Melinda led them toward it.

"Lloyd is already in the crypt." She shivered. "I'm sorry, but I… I can't go down there again."

"That's okay," Mike said soothingly. "Just send Graham straight down there, all right?" She nodded, and then Mike met Jonathon's gaze. "You coming?"

"Yes." Jonathon followed Mike down the worn stone steps that he recalled from his childhood, shivering at the change in air temperature. The crypt was much colder than the church above.

Lloyd stood at the farthest edge of the stone-flagged floor, gazing at the prone, slim body, dressed in jeans, a brown sweater, and scuffed trainers. Jonathon looked at the body's reddish-brown hair. Very familiar hair.

"Oh my God," he said softly. "Mike, it's—"

"Bryan Mayhew, yes." Mike sniffed the air, his nose wrinkling. "Can you smell something?"

Jonathon sniffed and grimaced. "Yes. What is that?"

"No idea, but I've smelled it before someplace." Mike stepped carefully onto the flags, observing where he put his feet. "The floor seems clear of dust, so there don't appear to be any footprints. That doesn't mean they won't find prints of some kind."

"Should you be walking over there?" Jonathon asked.

"No, he shouldn't."

Jonathon froze at the harsh voice from behind him.

DI Gorland glared at Mike. "I can have you arrested for contaminating a crime scene, you know that, right?"

Mike stood still. "I have literally taken two steps. That's it. I gave Lloyd instructions over the phone not to enter here, so your crime scene is preserved, all right? And we've just identified the body."

Gorland blinked. "Oh?"

"Bryan Mayhew," Jonathon volunteered. "The student who is—"

"Yes, yes, I know who he is," Gorland interrupted impatiently. "What I want to know is, what he's doing here."

"The coroner is on her way, sir," Constable Billings called from the top of the stone steps.

"Good." Gorland glanced at the stone sarcophagi surrounding him, the stone plaques that covered the walls. "When was the last time you, or anyone else, was down here?" he asked, addressing Lloyd.

"I rarely come down here," Lloyd commented in his dry, quavering voice. "I'm still not certain why I chose to do so this morning. As for the floor, the crypt is swept clean once a week, usually on a Friday."

"Which is bad timing," Jonathon murmured. "Otherwise there might have been prints."

Gorland swiveled around to stare at him. "Thinking of joining the police force, Mr. de Mountford? As for bad timing, as far as the killer was concerned, it was very opportune timing. He—or she—couldn't have timed it better."

Jonathon suddenly got where Gorland was going. The implication was that the killer was familiar with the church routines.

"Who usually sweeps down here?"

"We have a cleaner." Lloyd cleared his throat. "Sue Bentley."

Gorland's eyes lit up. "Oh, really?"

"Yes, but she didn't sweep it yesterday, because she didn't work yesterday."

Jonathon stared at the clean flags. "Well, *someone* swept it."

Gorland's face darkened. "Who has access to the crypt?"

"Anyone," Lloyd said with a shrug.

"What?" Gorland's eyes were almost out on stalks. "You mean, it isn't locked? What about the church? Can anyone just walk into that too?"

"Of course." Lloyd appeared to have got over his shock. "This is a place of worship, but it is also a place of prayer for those who need it. The door is always open. And as for the crypt, why would we lock it? There is nothing down here to be stolen, unless someone wants to open up a sarcophagus and steal the bones of a member of the de Mountford family." He coughed. "Somehow I don't think that would fetch much, even if one were trying to sell it to a museum."

Jonathon smothered a snicker, and Gorland narrowed his gaze.

Noise from behind them brought all conversation to a standstill, as the coroner entered, carrying her black bag and dressed in pale blue coveralls. "Good morning, gentlemen. Not exactly how I wanted to start my weekend, but still...." She walked over to the body and crouched beside it.

"I think that's our cue to leave," Mike said quietly to Jonathon.

"Not that you should ever have been here in the first place," Gorland hissed.

The coroner raised her head and gazed at him, her eyebrows lifted, before returning to her perusal of the body. "There's been a blow to the back of the head. The hair is matted with blood." She peered at the floor around the body. "No sign of any blood here, though." She opened her bag and took out a thermometer. "Could the body have been here all night?"

"Possibly," Lloyd replied. "I don't think anyone was down here yesterday, so I can't be sure."

She nodded. "Then we'll assume that's the case. It's very cool down here." She rolled the body over.

"Goodbye, Mike."

Mike sighed. "Let's get out of—"

"You might want to take a photo of this," the coroner called out suddenly.

Both Jonathon and Mike gazed at where she was pointing. Under where the body had lain, there were a couple of pieces of broken purple plastic shards—of what, it was impossible to say.

"I believe you were leaving," Gorland said heavily. "Billings, are SOCO here yet?"

"Yes, sir, only I didn't think there was enough room down there for them so—"

"There will be when Mr. Tattersall and his... *friend...* have left."

Jonathon figured Gorland had to be close to snapping by then. "Come on, Mike." He turned and headed for the steps, with Mike behind him. When they reached the gate, Graham Billings gave them an apologetic look.

Mike patted his arm. "Keep in touch," he whispered.

Graham nodded once before directing his attention to the three men in coveralls. "Okay, lads, down you go."

Jonathon walked out of the church, and once outside, he stood for a moment, trying to warm up. When Mike joined him, Jonathon shook his head. "You need to promise me something."

"What?" Mike asked with a frown.

"Do not do *anything else* to piss that man off, do you hear me? Because he is just looking for *any* excuse to throw your arse in a police cell."

Mike gave him a wicked smile. "Aww. Do you care about my arse, then?"

Before he could apply a brake to his mouth, Jonathon blurted out, "I care about all of you. That's what last night was about." Then he smiled too. "Although it is a very nice arse, now that you mention it."

From the left came a cough, and Jonathon stiffened.

"Sorry to interrupt your... conversation." Melinda's cheeks were pink. "But I was going to ask if you would come into the vicarage and have a cup of tea with me. I could use some company right now."

"Of course we will," Mike said quickly.

Jonathon gave him an agonized glance. Having tea with the vicar's wife, who now knew *exactly* what the state of their relationship was, sounded like torture.

IT WAS almost eleven o'clock, and Mike was clearing away the previous night's mess.

"It can't be a coincidence," Jonathon muttered.

Mike straightened up from filling the glass washer and glanced in his direction. "What can't?"

"Two dead bodies, both of them linked to the manor."

Mike leaned against the bar. "Okay," he said deliberately. "But apart from the manor, what else is there to link them?"

That was what had Jonathon stumped.

"I hope Melinda and Lloyd are all right," Mike said in a low voice. As they'd left the vicarage, a police officer had arrived to take statements from them, and Sebastian too.

Jonathon hardly heard him. "Bryan's death has to be linked in some way to Dominic's." He set his jaw. "I'm going to the police station to talk to Gorland."

"Oh no, you're not." Mike came from behind the bar. "You're going to stay as far away from that place as possible. If you want to talk to him, do it over the phone. At least if you annoy him, all he can do is hang up on you."

That made Jonathon laugh. "Good thinking."

Mike got out his phone and scrolled through his contacts. "Here. Try calling Graham first. Might be less explosive that way."

Jonathon copied the number, then hit Call. "Hi, Constable Billings? Jonathon de Mountford here. Have you got a minute?"

Graham laughed. "You *are* kidding, right? After this morning?" A sigh filled Jonathon's ears. "What can I do for you?"

"I think DI Gorland needs to see the path report as soon as possible, to see if Bryan's death is linked to my uncle's."

There was a pause. "The DI doesn't think so," Graham said in a low voice. "Put it this way, he's still got Trevor and Sarah Deeping in custody. He's convinced one of them did it. There's no clue as to who would want Mayhew killed. Look, don't worry. If I hear something, I'll let you know, all right? And I'm only doing this because it's Mike, okay? He's a decent bloke. My uncle said he was a cracking DI. Wish he was still on the force, to be honest."

"I can understand that." Although, after the previous night, Jonathon had a better understanding of what Mike had gone through, once the prosthetic had come off. It had been a shock, but Jonathon had soon realized that what bothered him was not the disability, but the pain that Mike must have suffered, both physical and mental. He'd clearly loved his job. And after a few minutes, Jonathon's empathy had morphed into feelings of an entirely different nature. His face heated up just thinking about their night together.

"Hello? Mr. de Mountford? Are you still there?"

"Sorry, Constable Billings, I... zoned out for a second or two."

Graham chuckled. "Yeah, well, we've all done that. And it's Graham, seeing as you're gonna be my neighbor soon, if what I'm hearing is right. I'll call you, I promise."

"Thank you, Graham," Jonathon said sincerely. He disconnected the call and sat down near the window. Something was niggling away at him, an idea that had only just occurred to him. He fished his notepad from the back pocket of his jeans and flipped it open to his list.

"Do you sleep with that thing?" Mike asked, plainly amused.

Jonathon raised his eyebrows. "I believe you already know the answer to that question." He tapped the page. "I was just thinking about clues."

Mike walked over to where he sat and peered at his list. "Which clue in particular?"

"The missing photo. More importantly, *why* it's missing."

"And what's your theory? Because it's obvious from your expression that you have one."

"What if... what if there's another heir? A real one?"

Mike gazed at him in consternation. "And what does that make you? A fake one?"

Jonathon shook his head impatiently. "No, I'm not expressing myself clearly. What if… the boy in the photo was Dominic's son?"

Mike frowned. "Sounds a bit farfetched, if you ask me. In that case, who was the woman with them?"

"I have no idea. But ever since I found out that the photo had gone, I haven't been able to get it out of my mind. Because someone took it, Mike. Deliberately."

Mike's phone burst into life, making them jump. He answered it. "Well, either you have news or you just can't keep away from me," he joked. After a pause, he smiled. "Thanks for that. Let us know if anything else turns up." Another pause. "That's right, he was. Thanks again." He disconnected. "That was Graham. They've got an approximate time of death for Bryan. Ten o'clock Friday night, or maybe an hour either way. Lloyd and Melinda were alibis for each other, but I doubt even Gorland would seriously suspect either of them. And Sebastian was in the pub with you. I confirmed that."

Jonathon nodded. "Which doesn't help us at all. We're no nearer to knowing why someone would kill him." His phone vibrated on the table, and he glanced at it. "Ah. I'm having all calls to the manor landline forwarded to my phone. Wonder who this is?" He clicked on Answer. "Hello?"

"Mr. de Mountford?"

"Speaking."

"This is Dave Lowther. We spoke a couple of days ago? I'm just calling to confirm that you're still coming for the test-drive tomorrow."

Jonathon was at a loss. "I think you have the wrong person."

"This *is* Jonathon de Mountford, isn't it? You called me on Thursday to arrange a test-drive."

"A test-drive of what?" Jonathon was starting to think the man was cold-calling.

"A Jaguar." He paused. "Lowther Jaguars? On the M3, going toward Winchester, just outside Eastleigh? You called me and asked me to have a top-of-the-line Jag here for you to test-drive this weekend." An exasperated noise. "This wasn't some kind of a windup, was it? This is one very expensive motor we're talking about here."

"Mr. Lowther, I don't know who called you, but it certainly wasn't me. And I definitely did not ask to test-drive a Jaguar. Someone has been playing games."

"Give me the phone," Mike demanded. Surprised, Jonathon handed it over. "Mr. Lowther, my name is Mike Tattersall, and I'm a former DI with the London Met. What number were you given as a contact?" He gestured for Jonathon's notepad, then hurried over to the bar and leaned over it for a pen. "Okay, run that by me again." He scribbled on the pad. "Thank you so much, Mr. Lowther, and I'm sorry your time was wasted. No, Mr. de Mountford will not be requiring a test-drive." He hung up.

Jonathon got up and walked over to him to peer at the notepad. "Okay, that's the number for the manor."

Mike nodded. "He said it was a young man who called. So, therefore, it could only have been...."

"Bryan Mayhew." Jonathon stared at him. "Oh my God."

Mike was still nodding, his eyes shining. "He pretended to be you. It could only have been him, on that number, on that day. And why would Bryan, your typical impoverished student, want to test-drive a very expensive Jaguar that he couldn't possibly afford? Unless his parents were going to buy it for him, of course, but I have a much better theory."

The penny suddenly dropped. "Maybe Bryan thought he was about to come into a lot of money because—"

"Because he was indulging in a little blackmail," Mike concluded with a smile. "And there's our motive. What if Bryan saw something that led him to believe he knew who killed Dominic? He lies to us and to the police, tells us he knows nothing, but in the meantime, he approaches the killer and threatens to reveal all unless the killer meets his demands."

"Only, the killer decides he doesn't like being blackmailed and kills Bryan first." Jonathon beamed. "We're brilliant!"

Mike laughed. "Not yet, we aren't. Right now it's just a theory. *Now* we have to prove it."

Jonathon waved his hand. "We can do that." What amazed him was how confident he felt that they could do it. His feeling that he'd been right, that the two deaths *were* connected, had been vindicated.

Right then, Jonathon felt like he could do anything.

Of course, that might also have had something to do with the man whose bed he'd shared. And in whose bed Jonathon expected to be sleeping that night.

# CHAPTER NINETEEN

THE HARE and Hounds was a very different pub that night. Jonathon noticed the change almost immediately.

There was none of the usual lively chatter, for one thing. Instead, people spoke in hushed tones, and Jonathon grew aware of a great many glances in his direction. The dartboard remained unused, and although Mike had music playing in the background, he kept it low and unobtrusive. Even Paul, who up until that point had been a relatively cheery soul, seemed down.

Mike was quiet too, to the point that Jonathon started to grow concerned.

He put the empties into their tray and walked over to Mike. "Hey, are you okay?"

Mike gazed out at his patrons. "I came here because Merrychurch was exactly what I was looking for—a quiet, almost sleepy little village where people got along with each other. Where the biggest problems were actually tiny, compared to what I'd left behind in London. And now look. The lord of the manor is found dead, and a week later, someone else is murdered." He focused his eyes on Jonathon. "Because Bryan didn't just decide to go for a wander down to the crypt, slip on the steps, and hit his head or something. Not at that time of night."

"I know." Jonathon found it difficult to believe that someone in the village was capable of murder. All afternoon he'd been in kind of a daze, going over the morning again and again. And something had been gnawing away at him since they'd come up with their theory. "You *do* know you need to tell Gorland about the call from the Jaguar guy? Because that's important."

"Already did. I called him half an hour ago."

"What does he think?"

Mike snorted. "That it's unlikely. I swear, if it's not his idea, then it's not feasible. When I was a DI, if someone came to me with a theory, I didn't just dismiss it. I—"

"But you aren't like him. Anyone can see that. And I'm willing to bet that you were a much better copper than he'll ever be."

Mike smiled and shifted closer. "Don't you think you might be a teeny bit biased?"

Jonathon smirked. "Actually? I'd think the same thing even if we hadn't slept together. And speaking of which… where am I sleeping tonight?" He held his breath.

Mike didn't break eye contact. "In my bed, if you want. Especially as it's bigger than yours."

"Hmm, a size queen." Jonathon chuckled, then nodded slowly. "I'd like that."

Paul's voice cut through the quiet. "Okay, I've had it with all the long faces." He met Mike's gaze. "I'd like to buy everyone here a drink, and then we're gonna raise our glasses. Dominic's been dead a week, and no one has had a kind word to say about him in here, an' that includes me. So fill em' up, ladies and gents. We're gonna toast our late lord of the manor."

Murmurs rippled through the assembled villagers, but they left their tables and came up to the bar.

Paul gave Jonathon a smile. "S'only right. He was a good man. But since the news broke about him an' Trevor, it's like that somehow cancels out all the good stuff he did, as though him being gay was wrong. Well, I'm sorry, but that attitude *right there* is what's wrong. I mean, not that I'm gay, you understand, but…."

"Thank you," Jonathon said softly. He seized his courage and leaned forward. "From gay men everywhere."

Paul stilled, his eyes wide. Then he grinned. "Is this something about the de Mountfords that we need to know?"

Jonathon laughed. "Not that I'm aware of."

"Drinks served, Paul," Mike said in a low voice. He placed a squat glass in front of Paul. "And that's on the house."

Paul gave the amber liquid an appreciative glance. "Aw, thanks." He got to his feet, his glass held high. "Ladies and gentlemen, let's raise our glasses to the late Dominic de Mountford. We'll say our proper goodbyes when they finally lay him to rest, but for now let's remember him for the good man he was. He drank with us, talked with us, an' was never too busy to spend time with us. To Dominic."

"To Dominic." The words echoed around the still pub, and tears pricked the corners of Jonathon's eyes as he lifted his glass of Coke to his lips.

"I'd like to make a toast too." Mike's voice rang out in the quiet that followed. "Welcome to Merrychurch, Jonathon de Mountford. May you truly feel at home here and build lasting friendships with all who meet you." His gaze met Jonathon's as he raised his glass.

"Welcome." Voices were raised along with glasses, and Jonathon stood straight, smiling at the faces turned in his direction. The tribute to Dominic had been unexpected, but Mike's toast sent one emotion flooding through him.

Hope.

"Y'KNOW, THE more I think about it," Jonathon murmured drowsily, "the more convinced I become that my father knows more than he's letting on."

Mike shifted behind him, and a solid arm encircled Jonathon's waist as two warm lips were pressed against his shoulder. "Good morning to you too." Mike chuckled. "Do you always wake up like this? And what, exactly, is it that you think your father knows more about? I must have missed something, or else I was still asleep when you said it."

Jonathon wriggled, pushing back against Mike's furry chest. Damn, the man was a great snuggler. "I was thinking about Dominic's possible son and my father's reaction to that photo."

Mike removed his arm and rolled onto his back. "And we're back to this again."

Jonathon turned over and propped his head on his hand. "What don't you like about this theory?"

"I just think it's unlikely that Dominic was in a relationship with a woman, given what we now know about him."

"Who's to say he didn't come out until much later? What if he was bi? And there are plenty of gay dads out there, trust me."

"Okay, okay. So let's say you're right and Dominic has a son somewhere. Why isn't he here? If he was important enough that Dominic kept a photo of him all these years, why isn't he here now? Why wasn't he named in the will?"

"I don't know, all right?" Jonathon sat up, running his fingers through his untidy hair. "But there's one thing I can do to find out." He threw back the covers and got out of bed.

"Gonna share it with me?" Mike called out as he left the bedroom en route to the bathroom.

Jonathon stuck his head back around the door. "I'm going to call my father, right after breakfast."

"Wait—not now? Not striking while the iron is hot?" Mike smirked, sitting up against the pillows, the sheets puddled around his waist.

Jonathon rolled his eyes. "At seven o'clock on a Sunday morning? He'd have a fit. There's such a thing as protocol, you know." He gave Mike a wink and headed for the shower.

The last thing he wanted was to get his father in a bad mood, not when Jonathon needed him to provide some answers.

BREAKFAST WAS over, the dishwasher loaded, and there was fresh coffee in the pot. Jonathon couldn't put off the moment any longer.

He got out his phone and scrolled through to his father's mobile number. He didn't want to call the house phone for fear of getting his mother. She'd only distract him.

"Here." Mike placed a full cup of coffee on the kitchen table in front of him. "You've only had two cups so far."

Jonathon laughed. "You're really getting to know me well, aren't you?" He took a sip of the hot, aromatic brew, then pressed Call. "Here goes."

Mike took the chair facing him, his own cup in his hands.

After three or four rings, his father answered. "Good morning. I was wondering when you'd get around to calling us. I suppose you're up-to-date with the scandal."

"Hardly a scandal. So Dominic was having an affair. So what?"

"With a married man. And I can't think why I'd expect a different response from you, seeing as—"

"We're not going to get into this now," Jonathon said firmly. "I called because I need information."

"About what?"

"Remember I mentioned a missing photo? The one Dominic said was me as a child?"

"Yes." Jonathon couldn't miss the cautious note that had crept into his father's voice.

"Well, I think we both know it wasn't me. My theory is that the boy was Dominic's son."

Silence. Jonathon could almost hear the crickets.

"Father?"

"I don't want to discuss this," his father said tightly.

"I'm afraid what you want doesn't matter, not when there's now another murder investigation going on."

"I beg your pardon?"

"Someone was murdered Friday night, and we think it might be linked to Dominic's death. And knowing who that boy was might be a clue to it all." Jonathon waited, the seconds ticking away as he prayed for his father to relent.

A heavy sigh filled his ears. "Very well. Dominic hadn't been with the firm very long, maybe a year, when they discovered he was having an affair. With a secretary." Disdain dripped from his father's voice.

"How old was Dominic at this point?"

"Twenty-five, I think. I only got to hear about it because I heard your grandfather and your great uncle Frederick discussing it at the house. I was home from Eton at the time. I was seventeen. Anyway, when this secretary revealed she was carrying Dominic's child, your grandfather had her fired."

Jonathon stilled. "This was when—the early eighties? You don't just fire someone because they get pregnant. She could have taken the whole firm to an industrial tribunal for that."

Across the table, Mike widened his eyes.

His father snorted derisively. "As if the family would let her do that. No, she was paid handsomely to keep her silence. Dominic made some noises about marrying her, doing 'the right thing,' but my father soon put him straight on that account. Hmm. Perhaps an unfortunate choice of words, given the circumstances. So, she was paid, and Dominic was told to break all contact with her. No one in the firm was to speak of her again. She left, and that was the last anyone heard of her."

"Except you know that's not true, right? The photo proves that Dominic had some contact with her after the birth."

"If he did," his father remarked dryly, "he did it against the express wishes of the family. Not that I'm surprised by that. Dominic always went against the tide. At least now we know why." He cleared his throat.

"Did she have a name?"

"What? Oh, her. Yes. Let me think for a moment." A pause. "Moira Cunningham. That was it." Another pause. "Do you really think this has something to do with Dominic's death?"

"Let me put it this way. Somewhere out there is Dominic's illegitimate son. He'd be in his thirties by now. What if he discovered who his father was and wanted to claim his inheritance? What if he came looking for Dominic?"

"You're assuming that the child in the photo was in fact Dominic's. We don't know for certain that she had a son."

"Now you're just being obtuse."

His father made an impatient noise at the back of his throat. "Okay, so the odds are favorable that it was Dominic's son. This makes *your* situation somewhat precarious, don't you think? Because if he does turn up and can prove that he is indeed Dominic's son, then by rights the house should be his."

"Fine." That came out more nonchalantly than Jonathon intended. The irony of the situation hadn't escaped him. He'd finally come around to accepting that his future lay in Merrychurch, only to acknowledge that this future might be about to change.

"Yes, you'd like that, wouldn't you? To give up the house, to abdicate all—"

"And that's an end to this conversation. I'll let you know if there are any new developments. Goodbye, Father." Jonathon disconnected the call.

"Is it me, or was that ending a little abrupt?" Mike asked. "And drink your coffee. It's getting cold."

Jonathon put down his phone and picked up his cup. "I don't know why I expect him to change." He drank down half the contents.

"Let's not talk about him. Do we have a name?"

"Moira Cunningham."

Mike nodded. "Then tomorrow morning, I'll go to London. There must be birth records."

"Good idea." Jonathon sighed. "I guess it's true. You can choose your friends, but you can't choose your family." Right then he wanted nothing to do with his.

Mike stood. "Come on. It's a lovely morning. Let's go for a walk and feed the ducks."

Jonathon smiled. "You know what? That sounds perfect."

A stroll along the river, throwing bread to the ducks, watching their antics... and with Mike. Just what Jonathon needed.


AS THEY walked back toward the pub, Mike peered into the shadows against the church wall. "Wait a sec." He hurried over and crouched down. Jonathon followed and saw a black-and-white cat curled up in a ball, nursing its front left paw.

"One of your neighbors?" he joked.

Mike surprised him by scooping the cat up carefully into his arms. "Sort of. This is Jinx. He's Melinda's cat. Well, actually he's more like the church cat. He's a great mouser." Mike held the cat against him. "What did you do to your paw, kitty cat?"

Jonathon looked closer. "Ouch. It's been bleeding."

"He probably climbed over a wall that had glass or wire or something, designed to keep out cats." Mike rubbed his bearded chin on top of Jinx's head. "Let's get you home, eh, Jinx?"

Jonathon smiled. "I didn't know you were a cat person." He liked that Mike could surprise him.

Mike arched his eyebrows. "Good thing or bad thing?"

Jonathon hastened to reassure him. "Oh, definitely a good thing. I love cats."

Mike beamed. "Right answer. Because if you'd said you preferred dogs, that would have been it as far as I was concerned."

Jonathon snickered. "I thought Sherlock goes nuts when he hears you coming?"

Mike gazed at him mildly. "Dogs like me. I never said it was mutual." He went through the arch and up the path toward the church, with Jonathon behind him.

As they reached the vicarage, Melinda approached them from the direction of the garden, her eyes widening when she caught sight of Jinx. "There you are, you bad cat."

"Hey, go easy on him. Jinx has hurt himself."

Melinda's manner changed instantly. "What? Let me see." She eased the cat out of Mike's arms and into her own. "What new trouble have you managed to get yourself into, cat?" She turned around and headed back toward the garden. "Come see what he did."

As they neared the hothouse, Mike shuddered. "You won't catch me going in there."

Jonathon stared at him. "Why not?"

"Greenhouses, hothouses—they all give me the willies. Always have done since I was a kid."

Melinda gazed at him in surprise. "But why?"

"Spiders."

Jonathon did his best to keep a straight face. "Spiders?"

Mike nodded, shivering. "Especially those big fat ones that lurk in the corners, waiting to drop on your head, or run up your leg, or...."

Melinda let out a sigh. "There are no spiders in my hothouse, Mike Tattersall. Jinx sees to that." She shook her head. "Big, strong man, afraid of a teeny tiny spider."

"Hey, they have eight legs. Don't you think that's way too many?"

Jonathon couldn't resist. "Yeah, but it could be worse?"

Mike whirled around and stared at him. "How? How could it be worse?"

Jonathon smiled sweetly. "Imagine if they had wings."

Mike rolled his eyes heavenward. "You had to say that, didn't ya? Now I'll be having nightmares, dreaming about flying spiders, as big as birds...." He paused at the threshold, his nose wrinkling.

"What now?" Jonathon asked in amusement. "Don't tell me—you can smell spiders. It's your superpower."

Mike slowly turned to face him. "That smell."

Melinda made a gruff sound. "That's why Jinx is in trouble. That cat knocked over a brand-new tin of Jeyes Fluid."

"What's Jeyes Fluid?" Jonathon asked.

"It's for cleaning the patio and the paths," Melinda told him.

Mike nodded. "That's the smell I remember from being a kid in my grandma's greenhouse. More importantly, however, that's what I could smell yesterday morning in the crypt."

"What?" Jonathon frowned. "Is it used to clean down there?"

Melinda shook her head. "Not as far as I know." She regarded Mike, her brow furrowed. "In which case, what was it doing down there?"

Now *that* was a very good question.

# CHAPTER TWENTY

THEY STEPPED into the hothouse, and Melinda pointed to the stone flags. "See? That's where the tin landed. See where the fluid stained the stone?" She indicated the shelf above their heads. "I can only think the cat was up there and knocked it off. At least he didn't get any of it on his fur. That stuff really stains."

"When did this happen?" Mike asked.

Melinda frowned. "To be honest, I'm not entirely sure. I bought it on Friday morning. I discovered the mess at lunchtime on Saturday. I wasn't in here between those times, so it could have been anytime within a twenty-four-hour window." She peered at Mike. "Is that important?"

"Possibly."

Jonathon wasn't sure what it meant, but his gut told him Mike's hunch was probably right. "It's lovely and warm in here."

Melinda chuckled. "Sometimes too warm. There have been days when I've forgotten to leave a window or two open, and new plants have literally withered and died in the heat." She tapped the thermometer that was attached to a pane of glass. "The gardener's friend, especially in summer."

Jonathon scanned the floor, looking for anything besides the stain, and his heart raced when he caught sight of something. It was a small shard of purple plastic, molded at one end. He picked it up and held it out for Melinda to see. "Do you know where this came from?"

She peered closely at it. "I have absolutely no idea. Is it important?"

Mike gazed at it, his eyes widening. "Yes, it is." Jonathon could see he'd recognized it from the crypt.

Melinda gently stroked the cat. "I'll take him into the house and bathe that paw. I only came to collect these." She held Jinx in the crook of one arm and pointed to the wooden bench, where some cut lilies lay across it. "I was taking these to the house."

Jonathon walked over to them, bent low, and sniffed. "Such a fantastic scent," he murmured. When he straightened, Mike snickered. "What?"

Melinda wiped her fingers across his shoulder. "You, young man, are dusted with pollen." She held up her fingers, revealing the orange grains. "An occupational hazard, I'm afraid. You should see me every time I use lilies in the church displays." She paused. "I suppose now might be a good time to ask about the fete. I know you said it could go ahead, but that was before we found a dead body in the crypt."

Jonathon had been thinking the same thing. The fete was to take place the following weekend. "Strictly speaking, it might seem odd to hold it, but...."

"You're thinking, what would Dominic have done?" Mike's voice was gentle.

"Yes!" Exactly that. Part of him wanted to say to hell with decorum. This had been why Dominic had chosen August for Jonathon's visit in the first place.

"I was about to ask if you wanted to donate a prize for the raffle. If the fete *is* going ahead as planned." Melinda's eyes were kind. "Maybe something of Dominic's?"

That stirred a memory. Rachel... the tea shop... the watercolors....

"Actually, I'd like to do that. I think I have an idea what I'd like to donate too."

Melinda beamed. "Then it *is* going ahead? Oh, that's wonderful. I'll make sure everyone knows. And whatever you decide to donate will be very gratefully received."

"I look forward to seeing your flowers in the show."

Melinda's cheeks pinked. "About that.... You *do* realize, as the new lord of the manor, that you're one of the judges?"

Jonathon gaped. "Why did no one tell me?" He glared at Mike. "And by no one, I mean you."

"Hey, don't look at me. I wasn't even around for last year's fete, remember?"

Melinda burst into a peal of bright laughter. "Oh my. You two already sound like an old married couple. How sweet."

Both of them regarded her in silence, before Jonathon started laughing too. "Okay, I'll go up to the house tomorrow, while Mike is… out." He wasn't about to mention Mike's trip to London. It would only invite questions that they didn't really want to answer right then. "I'm sure I'll find something suitable."

"Now go take care of Jinx's paw," Mike said suddenly.

Jonathon was getting to love this unexpectedly sweet side to Mike. "And we need to leave. It's nearly time to open the pub." Not that opening time was his main motivation.

Jonathon had a phone call to make.

"HEY, GRAHAM? Sorry to disturb you on a Sunday, but—"

"It's no problem. What can I do for you?"

"I have a few questions about Bryan Mayhew." Jonathon steeled himself for a rejection.

"Well, you can ask. I might not be able to answer."

It was more than Jonathon had anticipated. "Did he have any personal effects on him? You know, a phone, wallet, something like that?"

"His wallet was in the back pocket of his jeans, so robbery clearly wasn't the motive. But no phone. All we found was the remains of a USB drive."

"Remains?"

"Yeah, well, it was pretty smashed up. It was found under the body. Funny thing is, we put it all together, and there's a piece missing."

"This USB drive… was it purple?"

There was a pause. "D'you know, you really had me going for a minute. Then I remembered you were there when the coroner found it. Yes, that was it."

"Okay, then we need to come see you at some point, because I think we found the piece you're missing."

"You... okay, where?"

"In Melinda Talbot's hothouse."

Mike was waving at him.

"Hang on a minute. I think Mike has a question too."

Graham laughed. "So which one of you is Sherlock, and which is Watson? Regular pair of sleuths, you two."

"Ha ha." Jonathon handed the phone over to Mike. "Here you go, *Sherlock*."

Mike rolled his eyes, then spoke into the phone. "Graham? This might sound like a weird question, but... did the coroner notice any pungent chemical notes on the body? Any staining?"

Jonathon frowned. *What the hell?* Then it clicked. Jeyes Fluid.

Mike laughed. "No, I have *not* suddenly developed psychic abilities. ... You did? Interesting. So would that be consistent with something like Jeyes Fluid?" He laughed again. "Yeah, thanks for that, but I am not interested in joining the force again. ... No, I don't think we have any more questions." He gave Jonathon an inquiring glance, and Jonathon shook his head. "Nope, that's all. Thanks again." He disconnected. "Bryan Mayhew had stains on his clothing, consistent with Jeyes Fluid."

"Okay, Sherlock, care to share what's going on in that head of yours?" Jonathon folded his arms. "What did that help you to deduce?"

"That at some point, Bryan Mayhew was in Melinda's hothouse. Maybe the shelf got knocked, the tin fell, and he got splashed in the process."

"Duh." Jonathon gave an eye roll. "That much I was able to work out for myself. But why was he there?"

Mike leaned back on his chair, his hands folded behind his head. "Okay, this might be pushing it a bit, but… what if Bryan didn't die in the crypt?"

Jonathon blinked. "Ok-kay," he said slowly. "Are we suggesting he died in the hothouse?"

Mike shook his head. "Not necessarily. I've been thinking about body temperatures, ambient temperature, algor mortis…."

"Ambient temperature? Algor mortis? I've heard of rigor mortis, but…."

Mike nodded. "Algor mortis is basically the change in body temperature to match the surrounding temperature. Remember the coroner commenting on how cold it was down in the crypt? Well, she used the ambient temperature—the temperature in the immediate vicinity—along with the body temperature, to work out the time of death. Because there are laws of physics that govern at what rate a body cools."

"Still with you."

Mike smiled. "Smart man. Okay, then here's a suggestion for you. What if Bryan died somewhere else but was kept in the hothouse overnight? Then, just before dawn, the body was moved to the crypt."

"What effect would that have?"

"The temperature in the hothouse would keep the body warm, so it would cool at a slower rate, for one thing. So we could be looking at a different time of death."

Jonathon stilled. "Do you think that's why he was moved? To produce a false time of death?"

"Possibly. Maybe the hothouse was just a convenient place to store the body. Or yes, maybe the killer knew exactly what he or she was doing. And we could be looking for either sex at this point. Bryan wasn't a big guy, was he?" Mike got up, went over to the bar, and came back with his order pad and a pen. "Okay, I need to work through some figures. Give me a minute, all right?"

"I'll make sure we're all ready for opening." Jonathon stood.

Mike surprised him by reaching out to grab his arm and pulling him down into a kiss. "Thanks," he said softly.

Jonathon was conscious of a rush of warmth through his body. "My pleasure." He left Mike to his calculations and wandered over to check that the racks were full of clean glasses and that he had the basic fixings for cocktails, should anyone want one.

About ten minutes later, Mike let out a triumphant cry. "Got it!"

Jonathon dashed over to the table. "Well?"

Mike gave him a broad smile. "There's a distinct possibility that the time of death is out, maybe by as much as a couple of hours." He gave a shrug. "It's not the most accurate way to estimate time of death in the first place—too many variables can affect it—but yeah, he could have died any time after eight o'clock.

Ish." In the distance the church bell rang. "And that is our cue to stop talking and get to work." He got up from the table and walked toward the doors.

"What? You're going to leave it there?"

Mike's laughter reached him. "Nothing's going to change in the next few hours. Let's keep ourselves busy, all right? We'll have plenty to do tomorrow, so much that I might not open at lunchtime. Besides, I have no idea how long it will take in London to find out what I need. I only have her name to go on."

It sounded to Jonathon very much like another hunt for that proverbial needle.

"WAKE UP, sleepyhead."

"Huh?" Jonathon struggled to open his eyes. "Wha' time issit?"

Mike leaned over the bed. "Time for me to be out of here. I'm on the early train to London, once I've made my connection. I'll be back as fast as I can. I've put a sign on the door, saying we won't be open until this evening." He kissed Jonathon's forehead. "And you can have a lie-in."

"My, how generous of you," Jonathon quipped. Suddenly he grabbed Mike and pulled him down onto the bed. "Sure you don't want to catch a later train?" he said, coaxingly.

Mike's face was inches from his. "*You* are trouble, mister." His breath was minty.

Jonathon grinned. "And you're only working this out now? Some super sleuth *you* are." He released his grip on Mike's arms with a chuckle.

Mike climbed off the bed and tidied his shirt. "I will see you later."

"If I'm not here, I'll be up at the house."

Mike paused in the doorway. "Sue's Mini is in the car park. Red, 06 plate. She keeps it here because there's no parking space at her place. The keys are hung up in the kitchen. Take it if you don't fancy walking. She won't mind. She hasn't taken it out for a month, anyway. I think it's got fuel." He smiled. "Be good. Don't do anything I wouldn't do." And with that, he was gone.

"Doesn't leave me much, then!" Jonathon called after him.

Mike's laughter was just about audible.

He lay in bed, listening to the 4x4's engine as it burst into life, then faded as Mike drove out of the car park below. He thought about getting up, but a glance at Mike's clock helped him come to a decision. A lie-in, especially one when he could curl up in Mike's bed, surrounded by Mike's scent?

Heaven.

IT WAS almost eleven o'clock before Jonathon reached the conclusion that he was restless. There'd been no word from Mike, but he assumed that was due to the sheer number of documents to go through. He wasn't going to sit around until Mike came back from London—he had a job to do up at the manor. And kind though Mike's offer was, a walk would do Jonathon a lot of good.

He left the pub by the back door, taking a spare key with him, and set off through the village, a bag slung over his shoulder. The sun was already high in the sky, and wispy clouds floated across it, as insubstantial as cobwebs. As he walked, passersby greeted him warmly, and Jonathon returned their greetings. It pleased him that he was already getting to know so many people by sight.

He'd spent the morning rereading his list. A number of items were starting to make sense. Learning that Sarah Deeping sometimes did the flower arrangements, that she grew lilies, cleaned the church…. All of those activities could be linked to Dominic's death. He didn't believe Trevor had anything to do with it, but Sarah? Maybe Mike was right after all and she was indeed "a woman scorned." Only, that didn't explain the missing photo….

At the bridge he paused to look down into the clear waters as they flowed beneath its arch, listening as the current swirled over rocks and around boulders. He smiled to himself as he remembered playing poohsticks with Mike. It seemed such a long time ago. Then he reasoned that an awful lot of water had passed under the metaphorical bridge since then.

"If you're thinking of going swimming, it's not all that deep."

Jonathon turned his head. A dark green Ford Fiesta was parked at the foot of the bridge, and Sebastian leaned out of the driver's window, smiling.

Jonathon laughed. "Damn, and I brought my swimming trunks especially." He walked over to the car. "I thought you had a bike."

"I do—this is Melinda's. I had to take several boxes to the post office for her. Remember? General dogsbody?" He grinned. "Are you on your way to somewhere or from somewhere?"

"I'm walking up to the manor. I need to find a prize to donate for the raffle."

Sebastian's eyes lit up. "Oh. I've never been there. Want a lift?"

Jonathon chuckled. "Sure. Let me show you around the ancestral pile."

"Then get in." Sebastian reached across and unlocked the passenger door, and Jonathon walked around and got in. "I'm glad I ran into you now—not literally, of course." Sebastian pulled away from the bridge and drove down the lane that led to the manor.

"So how come you've never been to the house?" Jonathon asked as they sped along the leafy lanes.

"It was usually Lloyd or Melinda who visited Dominic. I had no reason to." Sebastian turned right onto the long lane that ran past the cottages on the edge of the estate. "I wonder what this would have been like, when it was first built. You can almost picture horse-drawn carriages clip-clopping over the cobbles."

Jonathon smiled. "There speaks someone who likes historical dramas."

"Guilty as charged. You should see my DVD collection." They reached the end of the lane, and Sebastian turned left onto the driveway. "Wow. Look at this." He drove over the gravel, circling the grassy knoll and pulling up outside the entrance. "And it was just Dominic who lived here?"

"Yes." Jonathon had always found that aspect hard to imagine. He'd pictured Dominic, alone, without someone to share his life with. Knowing about Trevor didn't alter that image much; it wasn't as if Dominic could ever have brought him up to the house.

*I'm not going to live like that.* Jonathon knew that in spite of his wanderlust, he wasn't cut out for a solitary life. He was meant for love and family, and he intended to fill the manor with both.

Sebastian switched off the engine, and they got out of the car. Jonathon led him up to the huge front door.

"Welcome to de Mountford Hall," he said, pushing it open. He stood aside to let Sebastian enter.

"This is impressive." Sebastian gazed around him at the marble floor and walls, the beautiful staircase that curved its way upward. "So have you any idea what you want to donate?" He pointed to the statue of an angel. "That, for instance?"

Jonathon snickered. "It's a bit big for a raffle prize, don't you think? I have no idea how old it is, but I doubt my parents would be happy about me raffling off a family heirloom. No, I had something smaller in mind." He walked over to the study door and paused at the threshold. "Just so you know? There's a… blood stain in here." It had proved impossible to remove it all from the marble.

Sebastian's eyes widened. "Is that where… he was found?"

Jonathon nodded. "I had to tell you. Not that you can miss it." He opened the door and entered the room. The air was warm, in spite of the cool marble floor, and light flooded through the french doors. He tried not to look at the fireplace where Dominic had lain. Instead he scanned the walls, studying the paintings, etches, and prints that adorned them.

"So what are you looking for?" Sebastian asked.

"Something created by Dominic. I know he painted, so maybe one of these is his work. And if they were going to be anywhere in the house, it would be in here. This was Dominic's sanctum."

They walked around the room, peering closely at the works of art, searching for a signature. Sebastian stopped in front of a watercolor painting of the manor. "What about this?"

Jonathon walked over and took a closer look. When he saw the familiar DdM, painted with a flourish, he smiled. "Perfect."

Then he nearly jumped out of his skin when someone cleared their throat loudly.

Mike stood in the doorway.

"Christ, Mike, you scared me to death!" Then he remembered his guest's vocation. "Sorry. That sort of slipped out."

Sebastian chuckled. "I've heard worse, believe me."

Jonathon stared at Mike, who hadn't moved or uttered a word. "How did you get in?"

Mike arched his eyebrows. "You left the door open." He gave Sebastian a cautious glance before staring intently at Jonathon. "Are you all right?"

Jonathon frowned. "Yes, of course I am. What's the matter?"

Another gaze flickered in Sebastian's direction. "I was just surprised to find you in here… and not alone."

"Sebastian gave me a ride here in Melinda's car. We've just found a prize for the raffle." There was something unnerving about the glances Mike kept darting toward Sebastian. "Look, you don't have to stay if you don't want. Go back to the pub and we can talk when I get there."

Mike shook his head. "No way am I leaving you alone… with him."

Sebastian stared at him with wide eyes.

"Him?" Jonathon glared at Mike. "Don't you think that was a little rude?"

Mike sighed. "Fine. Allow me to introduce you to your cousin, Sebastian Dominic Cunningham." He paused. "Dominic's son."

Oh... shit.

# CHAPTER TWENTY-ONE

SEBASTIAN GAPED at him. "What on earth are you talking about? I already have a father, and he's very much alive and well."

Mike shook his head. "I'm not talking about your *adoptive* father."

Jonathon stared at him, openmouthed, and Mike nodded.

"I found the birth certificate for Moira's child. Bit of a coincidence that her son and Sebastian Trevellan have the same date of birth—and don't bother denying it, because I have a copy of your birth certificate too."

Jonathon stared at him in amazement. "How were you able to accomplish that in one morning?"

Mike winked. "I met up with an old tech mate from the Met who agreed to do me a favor." Then he straightened his face and returned his attention to Sebastian.

"And then there's your middle name." Mike leveled a firm stare at him. "Still going to deny it?"

Jonathon regarded Sebastian intently, taking in his thick brown hair, the line of his jaw. Was there a resemblance? Possibly. "Are you really my cousin?"

Sebastian ignored him and made an exasperated noise. "Look, this is sheer nonsense."

Mike closed the study door and came fully into the room. "What I'm trying to figure out is if you told Dominic who you were before he died. Because you *were* here that day, weren't you?"

Sebastian's eyes bulged. "No! Of course not! This is the first time I've been in this house."

Mike shook his head slowly. "Sorry. There are way too many things for it to be mere coincidence."

"Such as what?" Sebastian groaned. "Jonathon, what he's saying has no truth in it."

"So you say, but you know what? I'm going to listen to him anyway." Jonathon trusted Mike wholeheartedly. More importantly, he trusted Mike's instincts.

"Let's start with the physical evidence." Mike counted off on his fingers. "Pollen on Dominic's clothing."

Sebastian stilled. "Pollen? How could that be linked to me?"

"It came from the species *lilium regale*, which, by the way, is only grown by one person in the village—Melinda. And you could have come into contact with those lilies any number of ways. In her garden. The church flower displays. You did tell Jonathon that one of the tasks you perform was helping with the flowers, right? What if you got pollen on you, which then

transferred to Dominic's clothing? You wouldn't notice a few grains of pollen, right? And then there's the
brass rubbing wax and brass polish that was found on
the photo album. You even told Jonathon about cleaning the church candlesticks."

"Oh no." Sebastian shook his head. "There are
lots of people who could have handled that stuff. Your
sister, for one. Bryan Mayhew for another. Bryan was
always rubbing brasses in the church as part of his research. *And* he would have handled the photos too."
He set his jaw. "I don't have to stay here and listen to
one more word of this… fairy tale."

"But then we come to the punch that sent Dominic flying. The blow that ultimately caused his death."
Mike's eyes were cool.

"Punch? What punch?" Sebastian swallowed.
"He fell. He got his feet all tangled up in the rug and
he fell. Everyone knows that."

Jonathon stiffened. "I'd have to check, but I don't
remember if the part about the rug was made public.
Something tells me it wasn't." A sinking feeling sent
cold spreading out through his body.

"Dominic received a sharp blow to the sternum.
It was hard enough to crack his ribs. Maybe like…
a karate punch?" Mike didn't break eye contact with
Sebastian. "You know, just the other day, I was watching a documentary on Bruce Lee. A lousy actor, but
a fantastic karate expert. There was this one move, a
blow with the base of the hand. Do it hard enough, and
it can kill a man."

"So what? I don't know karate." Sebastian's chest
rose and fell more rapidly.

Something stirred in Jonathon's memory. "That photo on the wall of your cottage. The one with the kids in karate gear."

Sebastian arched his eyebrows. "Was I in that photo? No, I wasn't."

"No," Mike interjected, "because you were the one taking the photo. It was *your* karate school that you set up for underprivileged kids in London. I phoned them this morning. The guy I chatted with spoke about you in glowing terms. He also talked about your skill in karate."

"How the hell did you find out about the school?" Sebastian demanded incredulously.

"I googled you," Mike said, deadpan.

Jonathon was seriously impressed by Mike's demeanor. He imagined seeing Mike in full detective mode would have been something to behold.

"I've heard enough. I'm out of here." Sebastian strode past Mike, opened the study door, and left them.

It took about two seconds for the full import of what he'd seen to hit Jonathon.

"Wait!" He glared at Mike. "Stop him!"

Mike dashed out of the room, with Jonathon hot on his heels. Sebastian stood by the staircase, staring at them.

"What now?"

Jonathon turned to Mike. "Did you see that?"

Mike frowned. "See what?"

"Sebastian opening the door and leaving the study."

Mike's expression was vaguely amused. "Er, yeah? What about it?"

Sebastian was staring at Jonathon as if he'd lost the plot.

Jonathon sighed. "Remember the first time you came here? How you couldn't open the study door until I told you how to? How you couldn't even see it?"

Mike's eyes widened. "Oh wow."

Jonathon nodded slowly. "And yet Sebastian, who claims never to have been here before, opened it instantly. No hesitation whatsoever." He faced Sebastian. "Don't try to tell me you just worked it out. That door was designed to blend into the wall. The only way you could have known how to open it was if Dominic had shown you."

Sebastian gazed at him, the color seeping from his face. Then he crumpled. There was no other word to describe it. He clutched the banister as if to hold himself upright. "Okay," he said at last. "I *was* here that day. But I didn't kill him, I swear. It was an accident."

The stark silence that followed Sebastian's words was broken by the strident ringing of Mike's phone. Sebastian froze as Mike answered it.

"Hey, morning, Sue. It's not a good time to talk right now. Maybe later?" He paused. "I'm up at the hall with Jonathon." Another pause. "Yes...." He laughed. "Yeah, that would be great.... See you then." He disconnected the call, then addressed Jonathon. "Sue is going to meet us for a drink at the pub later."

"What was so funny?" Sebastian asked.

"Oh, she asked if Jonathon was going to make some of his famous cocktails." Mike's expression grew more serious. "Now, how about we go back into the study and sit down so you can tell us how it wasn't murder? And start at the beginning."

Sebastian regarded him in silence for a moment, then nodded. "Okay." He followed Mike into the study, and Jonathon brought up the rear.

Once inside, Mike wiped his hand across his forehead. "God, it's hot in here. Jonathon, can you fetch us some water? And I'll open the french doors too, to let some air in here." He set his phone down on the desk.

Jonathon nodded and left the room. He hurried to the kitchen, which was down a flight of stairs. He filled a jug with cold water, found three glasses, and once he'd set them on a tray, carried them carefully up the stairs to the study. Sebastian was sitting on the couch, leaning forward, his head in his hands, and Mike had pulled out a chair to sit facing him. A pleasant breeze wafted in through the open door.

Jonathon set down the tray and poured water into the glasses. "Here." He handed them to Mike and Sebastian before grabbing another chair and placing it a few feet from Mike's. His head was buzzing with questions, but one was uppermost. "How did you discover Dominic was your father?"

Sebastian drank half his water, then sagged against the back of the couch. "I was eight when my parents adopted me. Before that, I spent four years either in an orphanage or with foster parents."

"What happened to your birth mother?" To Jonathon's mind it didn't sound like a very happy childhood.

"I didn't find out until I was old enough to track her down. My father gave me what details he had, but it wasn't much. All I had to go on was her name and that she'd been a secretary in a law firm in London. I had no memories of her. When I finally got to see my birth certificate, there was no father listed. I discovered my mother had died in a road accident when I was three."

"Oh, that's awful," Jonathon murmured.

"I just wanted to know more about her, that was all. I found the law firm and asked about her, but no one wanted to talk to me. It was like hitting a brick wall. Eventually I chose a more circuitous route and put an advert in the newspaper, asking if anyone had known her. Only one person replied, but that turned out to be more than enough."

"You found out she was fired from there?" Mike said. "And that she was pregnant?"

Sebastian stilled. "Yes. When did you find out?"

"Yesterday. Jonathon called his father."

Sebastian narrowed his gaze. "Would that be Thomas de Mountford? He wouldn't even see me. Anyway, I met with Tracy, who used to work there too. That was the only reason she gave for meeting me—she'd left the firm. She told me she'd stayed in touch with my mother for a while after they dismissed her. Tracy said my mother received regular sums of money up until she died."

"Did this Tracy say Dominic was your father?" Mike wanted to know.

Sebastian shook his head. "Apparently my mother never said who my father was. But Tracy had a photo of my mother. It seemed that every year the firm had an official photo taken, with all the staff. There was my mother, at the end of a row, only she wasn't looking at the camera. She was staring at a smartly dressed guy on the front row. He turned out to be Dominic de Mountford." Sebastian snickered. "I covered up my beard and looked in the mirror. What I saw was enough to convince me that I'd found my father."

"What did you do next?" Jonathon asked.

"First, I had to find out where Dominic lived. At that point he'd already left the firm. It didn't take much digging to find de Mountford Hall. Then I started talking to my father about maybe working in a smaller parish to start off with. I gave him some story about having traveled through Merrychurch at some point and that I'd fallen in love with the village." Sebastian's eyes misted over. "I knew he'd do anything to make me happy, so it didn't take him long to pull some strings and get Lloyd Talbot to agree to taking on a curate."

"You've been living here a year. Why didn't you just confront him? For all you knew, Dominic might have been happy to finally meet his son." Jonathon's heart ached. Dominic had not been a bad person. He felt sure his uncle would have welcomed Sebastian.

"I knew nothing about him!" Sebastian shouted. "When I first arrived in the village, I bided my time, trying to get a picture of what he was like. He seemed… inoffensive, I suppose. Kind. And that just riled me. If he was such a nice person, then why hadn't he tried to find me? Did he even know that my mother was dead? Or did he simply not care?"

"You could have just gone up to the hall and asked him these questions, you know," Mike suggested.

Sebastian shook his head. "Too easy. He'd abandoned us. If he'd stuck around, maybe I would never have ended up in an orphanage when she died. I wanted to unnerve him, to prick at his conscience, so I sent him anonymous letters. Nothing specific, just vague threats, you know, like, 'Be sure your sins will find you out.' And then I ran out of patience and came up here to see him."

"What did he say?" Jonathon asked quietly.

Sebastian's face fell. "To be honest, I can't remember much of it. I recall being angry, and I think that clouded my judgment. He said stuff about not knowing what had happened, trying to make things right, but all I could think of was how different my life might have been. I was standing in this beautiful house, where he lived a life of privilege, and I'd had to endure some real nightmares before I was finally adopted. Stuff that I didn't even want to think about, and in front of me was the one man who could have changed my entire life, if he hadn't been such a selfish prick. He even got out that photo album and showed me the photo, as if that was proof somehow that he hadn't forgotten me. As if that was a good enough excuse." He sighed heavily and bowed his head. "I just... saw red. I shoved him away from me, and I must have caught him off-balance, because he fell. He tried to turn, but the speed that he fell... his head struck the corner of the fireplace and... he was gone." Sebastian raised his chin and locked gazes with Jonathon. "I swear, it really was an accident."

"So how did the rug become entangled around his feet?" Mike demanded. "That was a deliberate attempt on your part, right?"

"Couldn't you have been honest?" Jonathon said, aghast. "Couldn't you have told the police what happened? Why try to make it look like he tripped?"

Sebastian swallowed hard but said nothing.

"Oh, of course." Mike stared at him, his eyes gleaming. "You couldn't inherit if you'd caused his death, could you?"

"What?" Jonathon blinked.

Mike nodded slowly. "Think about it. Everyone thinks Dominic died as the result of an accident. Sebastian waits until all the fuss has died down, maybe a year, and then he suddenly comes forward with evidence he's just 'discovered' that he's the rightful heir to the manor. He feigns surprise, shock—and then moves you out and him in."

"No!" Sebastian shook his head violently. "I'm telling you, aren't I?"

"Only because we proved you had to have been here," Jonathon flung at him.

"And then everything began to unravel, didn't it?" Mike got to his feet and walked over to the couch to stand in front of Sebastian. "First, the police worked out that it wasn't an accident, but that was okay, because you were sure there was nothing to link you to Dominic. And then things really went pear-shaped, didn't they? Because someone knew what you'd done. Someone who wanted money to keep his mouth shut."

"What on earth are you talking about?" Sebastian's eyes were huge.

"Bryan Mayhew. What did he do when he returned to the village? Did he contact you right away, to tell you what he'd seen?"

"What?" Sebastian's jaw dropped.

"I don't know for sure, but I'm guessing he had evidence that you caused Dominic's death. He probably figured the same thing as you. That once the police investigation was over, as long as you weren't in the frame for it, you'd come into a lot of money once you inherited. He was probably willing to wait, right? That evidence was his bargaining chip. Pay me, or I'll give this to the authorities and you lose everything." Mike nodded. "A much better idea would be to kill Bryan, then take all the evidence. That way you can still come forward, because there's nothing to link you to Bryan's murder."

"That's because I had nothing to do with the murder!" Sebastian's eyes bugged out. "I couldn't have! I was nowhere near the crypt when he died. I was in the pub with you two."

"Great, except he didn't die in the crypt and we can prove it. Not only that, I think we can also prove he died earlier than the official time of death. And apart from that, there's physical evidence to link you to his murder." Mike shifted closer.

"Such as what? You're making this up." Sebastian's face flushed. "How can there be evidence when I had nothing to do with his death?"

"Oh yeah?" Mike's eyes sparkled. "You really shouldn't have bowed your head just now. Because the first thing I spotted was this." Mike darted forward, pushed Sebastian's head down between his knees, and pulled down the collar of his T-shirt roughly to reveal…

…a dark stain on the back of Sebastian's neck.

"Jeyes Fluid is a real bitch to get off the skin. That's if you even knew it was there in the first place."

# CHAPTER TWENTY-TWO

SEBASTIAN PULLED free of Mike's grip and jerked his head up. "Don't touch me! And that could have happened at any time. I'm always in and out of that hothouse, carrying flowers for the church. I do live there, remember?" His eyes blazed.

"Except you're not denying that it's Jeyes Fluid, are you?" Jonathon said thoughtfully, staring at Sebastian's reddening face. "And that's the problem with your theory. It couldn't have happened at any time, like you said. There was only a short window of time when it could have occurred. We know that for a fact."

"Did you bump into the shelf when you were carrying his body into the hothouse? Is that how it happened? Maybe you got some on your clothes too. Those can always be destroyed, right? Not so easy when it's on the skin." Mike was still standing in front of him.

Sebastian glared at him.

"And then there's the test-drive," Jonathon added.

Sebastian jerked his head to stare at him. "Huh?"

Jonathon nodded. "You didn't know about that part, did you? It appears Bryan was an impatient soul. He had to know it was going to be a year at least before you could even think of coming forward to claim your inheritance—and he could get any money out of you—but I guess he couldn't stop thinking about all that cash."

"So he called up a garage and arranged to test-drive a top-of-the-range Jaguar. He didn't give his own name, of course—clever boy. He gave Jonathon's. We know it was Bryan, though, because he called from this number."

"That was what gave us the idea that he was indulging in a little blackmail." Jonathon cocked his head to one side. "He must have shown you some kind of evidence, right? What was it?"

"My guess is either a photo or video that he took on his phone." When Sebastian twisted around to stare at him, Mike gave a slow nod. "Had to be. There was no phone on him when he was found. Did you take it?"

Sebastian pressed his lips together as if to stifle a reply.

"Oh." Jonathon blinked. "*Now* I understand." He met Mike's inquiring gaze. "That purple plastic we found in the hothouse, the missing piece from Bryan's USB drive."

Sebastian froze. "What USB drive?"

"The one that the police have in their evidence locker. Bryan had it on him when he died. What if he copied the photo or video or whatever onto a USB? As a sort of backup?"

Judging from Sebastian's aghast expression, he hadn't thought about that possibility.

"Well, once they manage to open the files on it, the police will have all the evidence they need. Not to mention everything that I just gave them." Mike locked gazes with Sebastian. "That's right. Everything I found on my trip to London this morning. I went to the police station before I came here. Didn't want to run the risk of losing any of it."

"You bastard." Sebastian growled. "He swore to me that video was only on his phone."

"Where was he when he shot it?" Icy fingers crawled over Jonathon's skin. They'd been right about the blackmail.

"Watching through the french windows. He saw me arranging the rug and filmed it. He'd been on his way to speak to Dominic, but he heard raised voices. He heard the whole argument." Sebastian clenched his hands into tight fists. "I had no idea he was even there. Then Thursday, I was getting into Melinda's car after visiting Ben Threadwell when I spotted him standing by the side of the road, leaning against his motorbike. He came to the point really quickly, even going so far as to show me the video footage. Then he said we needed to meet to discuss his terms. Terms! Sounds so much nicer than blackmail, doesn't it?"

"Where did you meet him?"

"He suggested at the rear of the church on Friday evening. The wall goes all the way around the churchyard, and there's a gate at the back. He wanted someplace where we couldn't be seen, I suppose. He didn't seem concerned by the prospect of being alone with me, but then, why should he have? He'd heard us arguing—he knew it was an accident. I guess he felt safe being with me because I was a curate, a man of the cloth."

"Any man who is cornered is apt to make rash decisions, regardless of his occupation," Mike said quietly. "Which you apparently did."

"I didn't think once about the sixth commandment. I just thought about him taking money from me for the rest of my life." Sebastian raised his chin to look Mike in the eye. "I crouched down by the gate, and as soon as he came through it, I hit him with the biggest rock I could find. That was all it took. Then I picked him up over my shoulder and carried him to the hothouse. I knew Melinda wouldn't be around, not at that time. She's a creature of habit. And your description of banging into the shelf was very accurate. I left the tin on the floor, figuring she'd blame the cat—he was always in there."

Jonathon stared at him. "Of course. You put the body in there deliberately. I remember our conversation about you being a science geek." He caught movement out of the corner of his eye and did his best not to react. "And it *was* you who took the photo from the album, wasn't it?"

Sebastian nodded. "Not that I did it to prevent being identified—I was just a little kid, after all—but because it showed my mother. I wanted it for sentimental reasons."

"Maybe Dominic kept it for sentimental reasons too," Jonathon suggested, his heart pounding.

"We'll take things from here," a loud voice declared.

Sebastian lurched to his feet and turned to face the french windows, where Gorland and two uniformed officers stood. Graham was one of them. The officers strode forward, handcuffs dangling from Graham's hand. Sebastian tried to run toward the door, but Mike blocked his path.

"Oh no, you don't."

The officers grabbed Sebastian's arms, and Graham pulled his hands behind his back to cuff them. He grinned at Mike. "Nice one, Mike. We heard everything."

Jonathon frowned. "What? Heard what?"

Mike smiled. "That call from Sue was actually Graham, checking where I was. I didn't disconnect the call. I left my phone on the desk, hoping it would pick up what was said. Why do you think I mentioned opening the french windows? I was telling them how to get in without alerting Sebastian."

Jonathon shook his head. "You sneaky…."

He listened as the second officer read Sebastian his rights. It all seemed so unreal. Sebastian stood there, his eyes cold, and Jonathon got the feeling he wasn't hearing a word of it. He followed the officers as they escorted Sebastian out of the study, through the hall, and out the front door, where four cars were parked—Melinda's Fiesta, Mike's 4x4, and two police cars. Gorland stood with Mike and Jonathon while Graham placed his hand lightly on top of Sebastian's head, helping him to climb into the back seat of one of the cars. The tires crunched over the gravel as the car pulled away from the house, just as a motorbike roared up in the opposite direction. It came to a stop in front of them, and the rider switched off the engine.

The helmet visor was flipped up, and a young man regarded them inquiringly.

"Hey. Is one of you Jonathon de Mountford?"

Jonathon blinked. "Er, yes, that's me."

The young man took off his helmet and rubbed his scruffy hair. "Hi. My name's Andy Wintersgill. I got a call from a police officer about a friend of mine, Bryan Mayhew."

"Weren't you in Bali or Singapore or someplace similar?" Mike asked.

Andy nodded. "When he said Bryan was dead, I caught the first plane back to the UK. I only got back at four this morning. That was when I found this." He reached inside his leather jacket and removed a creased, sealed envelope. It was addressed to Andy, and bore the words, "To be delivered to Jonathon de Mountford, de Mountford Hall, Merrychurch, if anything happens to me." Andy held it out to Jonathon. "I figured it was important, so I rode over right away." His face fell. "Still can't believe he's dead. Only last week we were drinking and laughing, the night before I went away. I'd never seen him in such a good mood."

Jonathon tore open the envelope, with both Mike and Gorland watching him. Into his palm fell a purple USB drive. Jonathon caught his breath. "There's a note in here too." He eased it out and unfolded the single sheet of paper. He read through the two paragraphs, and sighed. "You were right, Mike. Bryan not only took a photo of Sebastian arranging the rug to make it look like an accident—he recorded the conversation too. It's all on the USB."

"Wow." Andy's eyes widened. "Does this help prove who killed Bryan?"

Gorland gazed at him coolly. "Thank you for bringing this to our attention, Mr. Wintersgill. If I could ask you to ride to Merrychurch police station to give a brief statement?"

Andy nodded. "I'll go now, before I head home to get some sleep. I'm still jetlagged." He nodded in Jonathon and Mike's direction, replaced his helmet, climbed back on his bike, and drove down the driveway, sending bits of gravel flying in all directions.

Jonathon shook his head sadly. "I'm not surprised Bryan was in a good mood that night. He'd just seen Sebastian faking Dominic's accident. He was probably already thinking about how he could profit from it."

Mike frowned. "So what was on the USB that was found with the body?"

"Nothing," Gorland said simply. "It was empty. Maybe it was a new one, to replace the one he'd left with Mr. Wintersgill." He held out his hand. "I'll take those, Mr. de Mountford. They're evidence."

Jonathon nodded and put both the sheet and the USB back into the envelope. He handed it over. "So that's it? Case closed?"

Gorland nodded. "You'll both be witnesses, I expect. Not that Mike will mind that—he's an old hand at giving evidence in a trial." He extended a hand to Mike. "Well done. Good to see you haven't lost all your policing skills," he said gruffly.

"So you'll be releasing Trevor and Sarah Deeping?" Mike said suddenly.

"We released Trevor half an hour ago. Sarah will be released as soon as those two get back to the police station." He gave a thin smile. "And then I can go back to London, once I've reported to my superiors that my work here is done." He nodded to Jonathon, then tipped a two-fingered salute in Mike's direction. "Take care of yourself, Mike. And if I might be bold enough to give you a piece of advice? Stick to running your pub, and leave policing to the professionals. You were lucky this time. Next time might not be the same." He got into the car, switched on the engine, and drove away from the hall.

Jonathon stared after him. "*His* work is done? I like that! We did all the work for him. All *he* did was show up to make the arrest! 'Leave policing to the professionals' indeed," he mimicked. "He's got a bloody nerve. I've got a good mind to call—"

Whatever else he'd intended saying was lost when Mike grabbed him and pulled him into his arms. Two warm lips met his, and Jonathon gave up all thought of talking. When he came up for air, Mike stared into his eyes.

"I don't know about *you*, Mr. de Mountford, but *I'm* going back to the pub, locking the door, and going upstairs for a nap. I've had a busy morning, and I want to recharge my batteries before we open this evening."

"Am I invited?" Jonathon asked shyly.

Mike chuckled. "That depends. Are you taking a nap too?"

Jonathon grinned. "Eventually."

# EPILOGUE

JONATHON HAD to admit, it was the perfect day for the fete. Blue skies, sunshine, and not a cloud to be seen. The grounds in front of the hall were covered with stalls and marquees, the village brass band was playing from a makeshift bandstand that they'd set up, and all sorts of delectable odors filled the air. Everywhere he looked, there were people; it seemed like the entire village had turned out.

He stood on the front steps, taking in the vibrant, noisy scene. The only thorn in his side was the imminent arrival of his parents. His father had insisted on attending Jonathon's first public appearance as the new resident of the manor. He had to smile at that. He'd spent all of two nights in the hall, and he hadn't been alone for either of them. Jonathon was hoping that was going to be a common occurrence.

"What was that phone call about?" Mike appeared at his side, looking relaxed and casual in jeans and a white shirt, open at the collar. "It sounded pretty serious."

Jonathon sighed. "Two phone calls, actually. And we finally have an answer as to why Dominic was selling off part of the land."

"Oh?"

Sorrow washed over Jonathon in a slow tide. "He'd hired a private investigator to find his son. That was who called first. He hadn't heard from Dominic in a while, and he was calling to confirm he'd found Sebastian."

Mike stilled. "Dominic was looking for Sebastian?"

Jonathon nodded. "That was what he'd meant by putting things right. I spoke with my father about the whole situation yesterday. He admitted that once my grandfather discovered Dominic had met with Moira against his express instructions, he laid down the law. Dominic was not to make any attempt to contact her. If he did, then my grandfather promised he'd be removed from the firm. Grandfather was old-school. He didn't want Dominic to even consider marrying out of his class."

"So Dominic caved?"

"Yes, apparently. When Moira died, he must have lost all trace of what happened to Sebastian. Dominic could have tried to find him, but to do that might have incurred the family's wrath, so I guess he did nothing. But he never forgot. That must be why he kept the photo, as a reminder that somewhere out there, he had a son. Maybe as the years went by, he felt bad about deserting Moira and her child and decided he had to do something to make amends. Because get this—the private investigator said Dominic wanted to find Sebastian to provide him with a large amount of money."

"Oh wow."

Jonathon's chest tightened. "If Sebastian had just listened to Dominic, had given him time to speak, he'd have learned all this. Instead, he lashed out, all of the pent-up anger and frustration bursting out of him. And that's why Dominic was selling the land—the funds were for Sebastian."

"And Sebastian had no idea his father wanted to know him." Mike shook his head and sighed. "Two men dead, all because he lost his temper and his patience."

"I meant to thank you for yesterday." Having Mike at his side during the funeral had been exactly what Jonathon had needed. Mike had been a rock, a warm presence to rely on. Not that there had been any shortage of mourners. There had to have been at least two hundred people crowded into St. Mary's for the ceremony. Jonathon's parents had sent their regrets, with the promise of attending the fete instead. And when Dominic's ashes were ready to be interred, Jonathon knew Mike would be at his side in the crypt.

"As if I'd let you go through that on your own." Mike sighed. "Anyway, he's at rest now. I hope he's at peace."

That was Jonathon's prayer too.

From across the lawn, the brass band struck up a rendition of "In the Summertime," and Jonathon smiled. "Good choice. By the way I went through Dominic's jewelry, and guess what I found?"

Mike beamed. "Trevor's ring?"

Jonathon nodded and patted his jeans pocket. "I'll find him later and give it to him. It's the least I can do. I'm also going to ask if there's anything of Dominic's that he'd like."

"That's sweet. I'm sure he'll appreciate that." Mike incline his head toward the lawn. "Ready to mingle?"

Jonathon gazed at Mike. "Almost." He reached down and clasped Mike's hand, lacing their fingers. "*Now* I'm ready."

Mike looked at their joined hands. "Are you sure about this?"

Jonathon smiled, his head held high. "Absolutely. Let them see me—see *us*. No hiding." He locked gazes with Mike. "Are you okay with that?"

Mike leaned over and kissed him softly on the lips. "To quote you—absolutely." He grinned. "Let's go meet the neighbors and have some fun."

Jonathon laughed. "Just remember. At some point this afternoon, my father will be here. One, I doubt fun exists in his vocabulary, and two, he is going to give you some very disapproving looks."

Mike set his jaw. "Bring him on. I'm not going anywhere. And I'm going to be a part of your life for a long time to come." He met Jonathon's gaze. "If that's okay with you."

Jonathon's heartbeat sped up and something fluttered deep in his belly. "Absolutely."

They walked down the steps and across the gravel driveway onto the lawn, where friends old and new waited to greet them.

KEEP READING FOR AN EXCERPT FROM

BFF
K.C. WELLS

www. dreamspinnerpress.com

I'm about to do something huge, and it could change... everything.

I met Matt in second grade, and we've been inseparable ever since. We went to the same schools, studied at the same college. When we both got jobs in the same town, we shared an apartment. And when my life took an unexpected turn, Matt was there for me. Every milestone in my life, he was there to share it. And what's really amazing? After all these years, we're still the best of friends.

Which brings me to this fragile, heart-stopping moment: I want to tell him I love him, really love him, but I'm scared to death of what he'll say. If I've got this all wrong, I'll lose him—forever.

# www.dreamspinnerpress.com

# PROLOGUE

I'VE ALWAYS wanted to write a novel.

Even when I was a kid, I loved writing. My mom remembers me handing her my first "book" when I was five or six. I'd taken several pages from a drawing book, written God knows what on them, and then folded them over. Of course, my writing was for shit back then, but apparently I was so proud of myself. I'd even drawn a pretty picture on the cover.

So yeah, I guess the idea stuck with me, although it got shoved to the back burner for a while. Grandpa had a hand in that. He agreed with me that, yes, most people had a book in them somewhere. His view, however, was that for some folks, it should definitely stay there.

When life threw me a curve ball, it made me look at myself in a whole new way. Nothing like staring death in the face to make you reevaluate your existence. So when Matt brought up the topic of

NaNoWriMo, I figured it was fate giving me a shove in the right direction. Get that book out of my system once and for all.

For those of you not in the know, NaNoWriMo is National Novel Writing Month, and it happens every November. The goal is to write fifty thousand words in thirty days. When Matt first mentioned it, I'll be honest: I stared at him and said, "Are you fucking *crazy*? 50K? Yeah, right." Then, when I'd stopped laughing, he tried to put it to me another way. He went on his phone, pulled up his calculator app, and said if I broke it down, that was 1.6K a day. Sixteen hundred words, people! That made a difference. That was a nice, manageable chunk.

Yeah, I could do this.

Only thing was, Matt had to go and ask me a sort of important question: "What are you going to write about?"

Like I had a clue.

I sat around for weeks, tossing ideas back and forth. Matt suggested sci-fi, seeing as I was a die-hard fan of *Star Trek*, *Babylon 5*, *Star Wars*, *Dune*, *Doctor Who*, *Torchwood*, *Battlestar Galactica*.... You name it, I tuned in. Great idea, but scary as hell. I mean, we're talking building *worlds* here, and as much as I loved the idea of being the next Isaac Asimov, Arthur C. Clarke, or Frank Herbert, I didn't think I had it in me. Hell, let's be realistic here! So we scratched that one off the list and got our thinking caps back on.

Historical stories put me to sleep. Thrillers? Yeah, think I'll leave those to John Grisham and James Patterson. Fantasy? Sorry, but J.K. Rowling pretty much gets the prize for that one, and if I couldn't write the next Harry Potter, what was the point?

So one night we were sitting quietly after dinner. Nothing on TV to make it worth switching on. Both of us kinda contemplative. Then Matt looked at me, and I swear I saw a light bulb go on behind his eyes.

"Write what you know."

"Huh?"

"Something I read online today. It was a forum on writing, and that was one of the suggestions. If you write what you know, what you're familiar with, it makes things easier. You can draw on your own experiences, and that will make your writing better."

It made sense, I suppose. I considered the idea. "Okay. So what could I write about?"

He gave me one of those smiles of his that lights up the room. "Us. Write about us."

"Why would people wanna read about us? And would I have enough to write about?"

Matt laughed. "Are you kidding? How old were we when we first met? Seven?"

"I guess."

Matt was nodding, his eyes bright. "That means we've been friends for twenty years, David. Twenty years. Face it, you could write a book based on the last couple of years alone and you'd have a damn sight more than 50K."

He had a point. They sure had been… eventful. "When you put it like that…."

Matt grinned. "See? What did I tell you? Pulitzer Prize winner, right there."

It was my turn to laugh. "Not sure about that part, but…." I had to admit, it was a great idea. There was just one thing. "Where in the hell would I start it?"

Matt was giving me That Smile again. "At the beginning, where else?"

I could see it now.

*Once upon a time, there were these two little boys sitting next to each other in class….*

# CHAPTER ONE

*1996, Van Hise Elementary School, Madison, WI.*

MRS. DELANEY handed me back my test, and I beamed when I saw the gold star.

*All right!*

"Well done, David." She smiled at me. "You're still at the top of the class chart for spelling."

I thanked her and gave Wendy Taylor a sideways glance. Yeah, she looked mad, not that I was surprised. She'd been telling me all week that *she* was going to be top. *Guess it sucks to be her, then.* But soon I pushed mean old Wendy from my thoughts. Mom and Dad were going to be so pleased. Dad had promised that if I got another gold star, that weekend we'd go to the lake. I loved going to Lake Mendota, especially when Dad hired a boat and took us out on the water.

Mrs. Delaney was moving around the class-room, handing back papers and comments with equal measure. The weekly spelling test took place every Monday, and with our results on Tuesday came the slip of paper with twenty more words for the following week's test.

I guess I was lucky. Spelling was never a chore for me, and my favorite subject was English. Listening to Mrs. Delaney read aloud in her quiet voice that still managed to carry around the room was perhaps the highlight of my week. Writing came a close second. Man, I loved writing stories. There were times when I was in my room, sitting on my bed, a pad of paper balanced on my knees and me lost in my writing. Every time I wrote a new story, Mom would listen to me as I read it aloud. Then she'd get me to think about what I'd written.

I'd always remember the time we discussed one of my stories. I'd described this boy, Billy, as being angry.

Mom looked at me for a minute in silence. "David, have you ever seen me really angry?"

I giggled. "Sure. When the mailman brought you a package that was all busted open."

She nodded. "And how did I look?"

I thought for a moment. "Your face was all red and scrunched up, and your nostrils did this funny thing."

"They flared? Like they opened up wide?"

I smiled. "Yeah. That's it."

"Okay, then." Mom pointed to my page. "Well, instead of *telling* me Billy was angry, why don't you *show* me how angry he was?"

I frowned. "But... how do I do that?"

Mom beamed. "You just did it. Write how his face was red, how his nostrils flared. I don't need to see the word 'angry' to know that he is. Your description does that." She sat back in her armchair. "So next time you write a story, think. Is there a way you can describe what your character does or how they look that gives away how they're feeling? Your writing will be better that way."

"I like that. Mrs. Delaney is always telling us to describe things."

Her eyes shone. "There you go. You try it next time you have a story to write, and see what Mrs. Delaney says."

I guess that was the start of my love of writing stories, because after that? Yeah, Mrs. Delaney *loved* my writing.

I have a really cool mom.

And yeah, although English was never that difficult for me, there were other kids who weren't as lucky. Like Matt Thompson, the kid whose family had just moved to Madison and who was now in my second-grade class. Matt sat at the desk next to mine, and I watched him wince every time Mrs. Delaney handed him back a test paper. He usually didn't do so well on tests.

That morning was no different. I glanced across at him, noting how his head was bowed and his hands had clenched into fists. Yeah, Matt was all kinds of miserable.

I took a quick look at Mrs. Delaney, but she was still handing back papers. I leaned across the aisle and whispered, "You okay?"

Matt raised his head and peered at me. "'M fine," he murmured.

He sure didn't *look* fine, but the way he said it sort of made it obvious he didn't want to talk about it. Besides, by then Mrs. Delaney was standing at the front of the class, telling us to make sure we didn't go home without the list for the following week's test. I knew she'd remind us again before we left at the end of the day.

When the bell for recess sounded, I bolted from my chair and made a dash for the door, eager to be out in the sunshine. June had started warm, and I was praying it stayed that way. Only a few weeks to go until the summer vacation started, and I couldn't wait.

"'Snot fair," Wendy whined as I passed her, heading out to the far corner of the yard. "You *always* get gold stars. Just like you do in every subject. It's *so* unfair."

I ignored her. Like I didn't hear the same thing every week. I went on my way, past the group of girls who were jumping rope and the group of seven or eight kids playing tag. I didn't want to play, not that they'd have asked me anyhow. I wanted to find my quiet place by the old tree and sit with my notebook and a pen.

Only when I got there, my usual space was already taken.

Matt sat on the cool grass in the shade of the tree, his back against the wide trunk. His eyes were red, his face puffy, and he was sniffing and wiping at his nose. The sight of him took away my annoyance at finding him there.

"Hey," I said cautiously. "Can I sit with you?"

Matt jerked his head up and stared at me. "Sure." He scrambled to his feet. "I'll leave you alone."

"Hey, no, you can stay." I felt awful, as if my turning up had made him feel even worse than he evidently did.

Matt regarded me, his mouth downturned, his eyes kind of... empty. "Okay," he said carefully, resuming his position. I sat cross-legged on the grass facing him and threw my notepad onto the ground beside me. He studied me for a second or two. "You're David, right?"

I nodded. "Where did you move from?" He'd only joined the class about a month previous.

"Kentucky. My daddy got a new job working for a company that rents out equipment. He's a mechanic."

I liked the way Matt's voice sounded kinda like music when he spoke.

"Cool. Does your mom work?"

Matt shook his head. "She stays home and looks after my baby sister. My brother is in ninth grade." He cocked his head. "What about you? Got any brothers or sisters?"

"Nope, there's just me." I'd always wanted a brother or sister, but so far there had been no sign. I'd resigned myself to it being just me.

Matt nodded and then fell silent, his shoulders hunched over.

Yeah, if he was fine like he said, my name was Mickey Mouse.

I could've kept my mouth shut. I could've... but I didn't. "Wanna tell me what's wrong?"

Matt blinked. "Nothing's wrong."

I huffed. "Yeah, right. Ever since you got your test back, you've looked like you lost a dollar and found a nickel. Didn't you do so well?"

He sighed. "I never do well. I'm… stupid."

It was my turn to blink. "No, you're not."

Matt opened his eyes wide. "Oh yeah? And what would *you* know? Did you see my test paper this morning? My spelling is crap."

"That doesn't mean you're stupid. Besides, I heard you last week when you gave that report about animals in danger of being wiped out. You knew tons about it."

A faint smile crept across Matt's face. "You liked that?"

"Sure!" I hadn't missed a word of it. "You didn't even read it. You just opened your mouth and out it came. Now, that doesn't sound like you're stupid."

He shrugged. "I watched a lot of shows on TV. Plus, my momma found lots of National Geographic magazines, and we talked about it. And I didn't read it because… I don't read so well."

"But that doesn't make you stupid," I protested. "My cousin Donna couldn't read well, but she's as smart as a whip. She's in college now. Turns out she has this thing where she sees words differently." The term escaped me, which irritated me greatly, because words were important.

"Really?"

I nodded. "Her mom and dad got her tested. Then they got her a tutor."

"And… that helped?" Matt bit his lip, his eyes wide and shining.

"Seems so. Hey, maybe you need to get tested too!" I considered the issue. "Do you read at home with your parents?"

Matt shook his head. "Daddy doesn't have time. When he gets home from work, he's usually tired, and on the weekend, he does stuff around the house. Momma… she doesn't read so well either." He gazed at me with interest. "Do you read to your parents?"

"To my mom, yeah. We read together every night before I go to bed, and she always helps me when I'm studying for a test."

"Sounds neat." There was an expression of longing on Matt's face.

"Maybe your parents need to ask school for you to be tested like my cousin. Maybe all you need is a little help." Then it came to me. "*I* could help you."

He frowned. "How?"

"Well, I could read with you. Maybe we could get together on the weekend, or after school. My mom wouldn't mind if you came to the house. She'd probably be really happy about it, come to think of it."

"Why's that?"

I waved a hand in the air. "Oh, she's always asking why I never bring friends home from school, or why I never hang out with them." I grinned. "I can't really tell her most of the kids in my class would be happy talking about playing in the sand pit."

Matt snorted.

"Tell you what. Why don't we start today?"

Matt regarded me keenly. "With what?"

"Well, we have another twenty words to learn for next Monday. We could start with them."

Matt arched one eyebrow. "I can't see us making that much of a difference in a week."

"We're never gonna know until we try," I announced firmly. I really liked the idea.

Matt pursed his lips and fell silent. "Okay," he said at last. "Let's give it a try."

"Excellent. You can go home first, if you like, and then come over later. Where do you live?"

"On South Segoe Road."

I gaped at him. "You're kidding. Me too. What number?"

"Four sixty-five."

I beamed. "I'm at one twenty-five. We're neighbors. You have to pass my house on your way to school."

"Neat." Matt's expression brightened. "I'll go home after school and tell Momma. Then I'll come by your house. You're sure your mom won't mind?"

"Positive." I knew she'd be fine with it, and actually? I was looking forward to it. I had a really good feeling about Matt.

*Maybe I've finally got myself a friend.*

NOTE

JUST READING back through this part and a couple things struck me.

First, there was that whole smart-as-a-whip thing. Okay, so maybe I didn't actually say "smart as a whip." I mean, seriously, what eight-year-old does that? But I did like how it made me sound smarter.

Which brought me to my second point.

That last line…. What prompted that thought? What was it about Matt that made me latch on to him the way I had? I had to sit for a while and think back to that time. What I came up with? I didn't need words to make me sound smarter—I *was* smarter. I don't mean to sound arrogant, but yeah, I was a bright kid. And therein lay the reason why I had so few friends. I was always top of the class, and it turned a lot of them off from wanting me for a friend. Only I *totally* didn't see it back then. I was oblivious to the whole thing. I had no clue why the other kids were so mean to me. I just accepted that it was the way things were in David Lennon's world.

So when Matt walked into it, a kid who needed my help, who didn't resent me because I had something between my ears…. Yeah, you can bet I wanted him for a friend.

# CHAPTER TWO

*July, 1997*

"I'M PRETTY sure we shouldn't be doing this."

It had to be the third time Matt had said it since we told our parents we were going to play soccer before lunch, as we all exited the Covenant Presbyterian Church after the service. Mom had smiled and delivered her usual "Don't be late for lunch" warning, swiftly followed by "And don't get your church clothes dirty," with added eye roll for good measure. Matt's mom had just shrugged and said fine. It wasn't like she didn't care; she just seemed preoccupied. His dad was the same. Darren, Matt's brother, hadn't even bothered to sit with us. He was too busy talking with a girl from his tenth-grade class.

The pair of us had made a run for it before Mom could change her mind and tell me to get changed first.

"I keep telling you, it'll be fine. And besides, can you picture the look on their faces when we come home with a turtle?" It was all I'd thought about for weeks. I'd first had the idea when I'd found a book in the school library all about the painted turtles of Wisconsin. Well, that did it. I was going to find me a turtle.

And Matt was going to help me.

"Do you have a clue where you're going?" Matt sounded less worried and more amused.

"Of course I do," I replied confidently. "I checked on the route last night. We walk up South Segoe until it becomes North Segoe, and then we keep walking until we reach University Avenue." I pulled the folded sheet of paper from my pants pocket and consulted it. "Then we turn left toward Horizon High School, then right, through Indian Hills Park, heading for Merrill Springs Road, and finally Lake Mendota Drive." That would bring us close to the lake.

Matt shook his head, chuckling. "And what makes you think we're gonna find a turtle, just like that?"

I stopped in the middle of the sidewalk. "You don't *have* to come with me, y'know. You can turn around and go home." Of course I didn't mean a word of it, and I was silently praying Matt wouldn't take me seriously. I was banking on him being the best friend I thought he was.

Matt merely arched his eyebrows and did an eye roll. "Like I'm gonna do that." He pointed ahead of us. "Keep going, Christopher Columbus."

I liked that.

Then *he* stopped. "Wait a minute. Do you have any idea how long it's gonna take us to walk that far? Do you even know how far it is?"

Damn. I was hoping he wasn't going to ask that.

"A couple of miles," I muttered under my breath. Okay, so it was closer to three, but he didn't have to know that.

Matt opened his eyes wide. "A couple of *miles*?"

"Look, do you want to help me find a turtle or don't you?" Yeah, I knew it was crazy, two eight-year-old boys on a quest to find a turtle, both of them decked out in their Sunday best.

Total madness.

Matt stood still for a moment, and then he grinned. "You are loony tunes, do you know that?"

The knot in my belly dissolved a little. Matt was still coming with me.

We walked along, the sun beating down on us. Summer vacation had begun a little more than a week ago, and we'd spent that week in each other's company. Granted, Matt still had to see his tutor twice a week, but the rest of the time was ours. My mom joked that she sometimes felt like she'd adopted him, he spent so much time at our house.

"So where are you gonna put this turtle? That's supposing you actually manage to find one."

I glared at him. "Hey. Think positive. We're gonna find one, okay? And how should I know where I'll put it?" I clearly hadn't considered that far ahead. Then I grinned. "How do you think my mom would feel if she found a turtle in the bath?"

Matt dissolved into giggles. "I think you might find yourself grounded. Lord knows how *my* momma would react." He went quiet for a second. "Do you think she might get up onto a chair and scream, you know, like in the Tom and Jerry cartoons?"

I guffawed. "Mice move a lot faster 'n turtles. Why would anyone be scared of a turtle?" Then I reconsidered. Mom had a habit of surprising me. "And who was that girl Darren was talking to after church? She looked kinda familiar."

Matt huffed. "Her name's Melissa, and she has this laugh that goes right through me. You know, like Lawrence Dunn's?"

I shuddered. When Lawrence laughed, you'd have sworn there was a donkey somewhere close by. "Okay, well, apart from her laugh. Is she all right?"

"I suppose. Darren's been seeing her for a couple of weeks." Then Matt chuckled. "Momma was real mad at him yesterday, 'cause Melissa came over, and he wanted to take her into his room. When Momma said no, Darren got all moody, saying how he was fifteen now and didn't she trust him? That was when Momma blew up. She took him into the yard, and she was telling him how he knew better than to ask, and did Melissa's parents let him go into her room when he went over there? Darren said no, and Momma just folded her arms and nodded."

"Wait a minute. How do you know all this?"

Matt grinned. "I was in my bedroom at the time, and my window was open. Anyhow, Darren got into a snit, and he said he was taking Melissa home. After he'd left, Momma and Daddy were talking quietly." He shrugged. "I think girls are more trouble than they're worth. All the girls I know are just plain annoying. Why would you want to be friends with someone like that?"

It beat me too.

"Is everything okay with your parents?" I asked as South Segoe became North Segoe. "They seemed to have a lot on their minds this morning."

Matt sighed. "I'm not sure. They've been doing an awful lot of talking lately. I was scared for a while back there that maybe they were, you know...."

"What?"

"Thinking about getting a divorce." The words came out in a whisper, almost as if he was too afraid to speak any louder for fear of them coming true. "But Darren told me I was just being stupid and that they're fine, so I guess that wasn't it." Matt shuddered. "Good, because that would be too awful for words."

I knew what he meant. Sarah Bannerman's parents were getting a divorce, and Sarah never seemed to stop crying. "So if it's not a divorce...." The skin around Matt's mouth tightened. Maybe it was time to change the subject. "Where are you all going on vacation?" Mom had informed me we were going to spend a week at my grandparents' house in North Carolina. I liked it there. The mountains were just beautiful.

"We're not." Matt's breathing hitched.

"Not going on vacation?" I glanced at him. Matt looked plain miserable all of a sudden. "Hey, don't think about it. We can find all kinds of fun things to do together, I'm sure."

Matt huffed out a breath. "All Momma said was that we couldn't afford it this year and that we had to 'tighten our belts.' I was gonna ask what she meant, but then Daddy told her to hush, and that was the end of the conversation." He stared at our surroundings. "Hey, look at those kids over there."

It felt like he'd deliberately brought an end to the conversation, and I got the message. Matt did not want to discuss this any further.

To our left was a huge parking lot. Usually it was full, but being Sunday, it was empty, and a group of seven or eight boys had set up a couple of ramps and were skateboarding all over the place. They seemed like maybe they were Darren's age. I watched as one boy zipped along, aiming for a steep ramp, but at the last minute, he veered off. His friends started flapping their arms and making chicken noises. Matt was chuckling, and I hissed at him.

"Shh. We don't want them to notice us, all right?" When he gave me a blank stare, I rolled my eyes. "How do Darren and his friends treat you when they're all hanging out together?"

His eyes widened, and I knew he'd gotten it. Older boys could be real assholes.

We walked along, the traffic beginning to pick up beside us, getting noisier. Ahead was a busy intersection, and we stopped at the curb.

"Hey, we're at University Avenue." Matt gave me a half smile. "Maybe if we talk less, we'll walk faster. After all, we've got a turtle to catch." He cocked his head. "Maybe we should have brought something to feed them with, you know, like bait."

"Like what?" I might have been reading up on turtles, but I had no idea what to bring to tempt a turtle.

Matt scratched his head. "Candy?"

I burst into giggles. "I'm pretty sure they don't eat candy."

"There you are," he said triumphantly. "We give 'em candy, and they'll be following us home."

I had to smile at the image in my mind: me and Matt, walking along South Segoe, a couple of turtles trotting behind us. Except turtles don't trot, of course. The more I thought about it, the more decided I became. I was *not* going home without a turtle.

"I sure am glad school's out, though," Matt said a couple minutes later.

"Ugh, me too." It seemed as if I'd spent the last five or six weeks with my eyes glued to the calendar on the kitchen wall. Not that I didn't like school—I was just impatient for summer to really get going. I didn't count June as summer, not when I spent most of it in a classroom. No, summer was what happened when there were no more school bells for several long sunny weeks. Matt and I had made lots of plans. We were going to build a castle in my backyard. Okay, so it would be made of boxes and whatever else we could lay our hands on, but it was going to look like a castle. Mom had mentioned our two families going on a camping weekend together at the lake. Apparently she and Dad had been discussing it with Matt's parents, but I wasn't allowed to say anything until they definitely gave it the go-ahead.

That was fine by me. I wanted to see the expression of total surprise on his face when they told him. He was gonna flip out.

"You know, I can still picture Deke Fletcher's face when we won the science prize." Deke had gaped at us, jaw dropped, eyes bugging out. He'd made a maze, and then he'd put his pet mouse, Daisy, in it at one end and let her run around it to locate the cheese he'd placed at the other end. He timed how long it took her and wrote it down on a chart. Then he did the same thing again and again, only he kept moving the cheese. I thought it was plain mean. Poor little Daisy.

That final Friday morning, he'd carried the maze into the third-grade classroom, beaming and strutting, his chest all puffed out. Yeah, he obviously thought he had the winning project right there. The look on his face when he caught sight of the volcanic island Matt and I had made told me he'd just realized he had some serious competition. The volcano towered over the little island, and we'd made it so that a side of it could be removed to show the magma inside. Except it wasn't *real* magma, but oatmeal that we'd colored with red food dye. It had taken us weeks, involving a lot of time in my dad's garage with newspaper, water, and glue, to get the shape of the island right. Matt had drawn it out first, and his mom put all his sketches together and made them into a notebook. We had pictures of real live volcanoes, magma flows, and those dense clouds of dust and ash that had probably killed all the people in Pompeii.

When Miss Prince read out mine and Matt's name, we high-fived, both of us grinning like idiots. And when the principal, Mrs. Travis, asked if she could put the island in the glass cabinet where they kept the school trophies and cups and press clippings, we were so proud and stunned that neither of us could get a word out. I'd just nodded, and Matt's smile was so wide, his face must have ached.

Matt snorted. "Serves him right. He was so full of himself the last few weeks."

I knew there was more to Matt's reaction than he was telling. "He's been teasing you, hasn't he?"

Matt's startled hiccup was answer enough. "How… how did you know about that?"

I kept my eyes on the road ahead. "I overheard him in the cafeteria. He was bragging to Dylan Levon and Pete Myres about how he 'put you in your place,' as he told it. Something about your tutoring?" That was the scaled-down version of what I'd heard. Matt didn't need to know the rest. God, some kids could be vicious.

"Yeah." The flat tone of Matt's voice told me plenty.

"Well, don't you worry. One, so what if you have a tutor for your dyslexia? He's helping, isn't he? You read so much better than you did a year ago."

"I'm not sure how much progress is because of my tutor, or you, reading with me every day after school." Matt chuckled. "Maybe my folks should pay you instead of Johnny."

I laughed. "No argument from me. I could do with a raise in my allowance."

Matt laughed right along with me. Then he stopped. "Wait a moment. You said, one. That kinda implies there's at least a two to follow it." He paused. "Well? 'Don't you worry,' you said. Keep going."

Crap. "I… might have told Deke to leave you alone."

A sudden silence fell so heavily that I had to stop and turn toward him.

Matt stood there, rooted to the spot, his cheeks pale, squinting in the bright sunlight. "You told him? What exactly did you tell him? And when was this?"

Something about the way he was looking at me made my stomach churn.

"About… about a week before vacation began."

Matt's eyes widened. "Did you… was it you who hit him?"

"I didn't hit him!" I flung back at him. "My dad is always telling me, fists don't solve anything."

Matt arched one eyebrow, the way he did with his expression that said *Oh really*? "Mm-hmm. Then what gave him that bruise on his cheek, if it wasn't one of your fists?" His gaze grew thoughtful. "He wouldn't tell anyone what had happened." He started walking again.

That didn't surprise me in the slightest. I sighed. "Okay. I found him in the boy's bathroom. I told him to leave you alone. When he told me to—" I glanced around and lowered my voice. "—fuck off, I lost my temper and told him that if he didn't back off, I was gonna tell everyone what he was doing in the bathroom."

Matt's eyes were huge. "He said… that?"

I nodded.

"And what *was* he doing?"

"Looking at a magazine full of pictures of girls… who had no clothes on."

Matt whistled. "Really?" He paused. "What was it like?"

I shrugged. "How do I know? I only caught a quick look at one page as I came into the bathroom. But that and the cover were enough."

"That doesn't explain how Deke ended up with a bruise."

"Well, that happened because he came at me, slipped on the wet floor, and banged his face against the sink."

Matt stared at me for a minute and then bit back a smile. "I shouldn't laugh."

"No, we shouldn't," I agreed. Seconds later both of us were laughing our asses off. When we'd regained our composure, I felt the need to ask a question. "So, are we good?"

Matt shook his head and crossed his arms. "No, we aren't. You don't need to stand up to anyone for me. I can do that myself." He stuck out his chin.

"I know you can," I said earnestly, "but you weren't there, and I didn't want him to think he could get away with it. He had to know. If anyone says something to hurt my best friend, I'm not gonna take it lying down." I clenched my teeth.

Matt grinned, his eyes sparkling. "Your best friend, huh?"

I rolled my eyes. "Well, duh. Who else would I have as my best friend? Wendy?"

Matt guffawed. "Good point." We carried on walking, the sun beating down even more strongly. By the time we reached the lake, I'd need to dip my head in it, just to cool off. Not that I'd be venturing out too far. Unlike Matt, I hadn't managed to perfect the art of swimming yet, despite the best intentions of Mr. Hinton, the swim teacher from the Y.

I was going to stick to wading through the water's edge, hoping a turtle would cross my path. I mean, it could happen, right? And I definitely would not be thinking about the fact that we were already late for lunch. Mom would understand when she saw the turtle.

I hoped.

"ANY SIGN?" I called out to Matt, who was farther along the shore, peering at rocks and into pools. I was doing the same, my pants rolled up to my knees, my jacket, shoes, and socks safely out of the reach of the water, lying on the ground beneath the trees that lined the lake.

"Nope, nothing."

I was starting to worry. I had no idea what time it was, but the uneasy feeling in my belly, which might have been hunger but was more likely to have been fear of what Mom was going to say, blossomed into something much bigger. Never mind my previous thoughts that Mom would understand.

Mom was going to be pissed.

"Hey… wait."

I jerked my head up to find Matt pointing excitedly to a boulder a few feet away from me. "There's a turtle sunning itself on this rock." He kept his voice to an agonized whisper.

*Finally!* I launched myself through water that came halfway up my calves, perilously close to my pants.

"Slow down, you'll scare it off!" Matt was staring at me, his eyes wide.

*But it's a turtle!* I wanted to yell. I strode toward it, my feet alternately slipping on the algae-covered rocks under the water or squelching in the soft mud that lay between them. I watched, horrified, as I got closer and the turtle poked its head out and began to crawl toward the water.

"No!" I screamed and dove forward, waving my arms, as if that would surely stop the turtle in its tracks and make it wait for me to catch it.

Okay, so I was dumb sometimes.

My arms flailing like some demented windmill, I lurched through the water, lost my footing, and fell face-first into it. Man, it was cold. Thankfully, my face missed the rocks. Unfortunately, my clothes didn't miss the mud. I struggled to my feet and stood there, my clothes soaked and my ego bruised.

Matt guardedly waded across to me, and I could tell he was doing his best not to laugh. "You okay?"

I glared at him. "Well, do I look okay?"

That did it. He burst into a peal of bright laughter that sent all the birds in the nearby trees rising into the air with much flapping of wings. I took a glance at the rock. Yeah, no turtle. I trudged to the edge of the lake and clambered out onto the grass. Matt followed, making sympathetic noises interspersed with giggles.

It was a good thing we were best friends; that's all I could say.

Then it began, the gnawing in my belly that said we'd been an awful long time getting there and heaven knew how long looking for the blasted turtles. I got that sinking feeling that we were going to be in real trouble.

"We'd better head home," I said quietly.

Matt sobered instantly. "Oh. Yeah." We picked up our shoes and jackets and headed back through the trees toward Lake Mendota Drive. Matt glanced at a sign as we reached the road, and his eyes widened. "Hey, did you see this?"

I peered at the sign, reading aloud. "Wally Bauman and Tent Colony Woods. What about it?"

Matt gave me a panicked look. "Maybe we shouldn't have been in there. Someone could've seen us and—"

"But no one did," I reminded him. "So quit worrying. We're gonna go home. My clothes will have dried off by the time we get there, so Mom will never know—"

"David Stephen Lennon, you get over here right this minute, mister!"

I froze. Our car was a few feet away, my mom leaning out of the open window. Shit. She looked mad. I knew better than to tangle with Mom when she was in a snit, so I hurried over the grass toward the car, Matt keeping up with me.

Mom looked me up and down, her eyes bulging. "What have you done to your clothes? For God's sake, you're soaking wet. Get out of those clothes right now. You'll catch your death."

I wanted to tell her that they'd dry off pretty quickly in the heat, but one glance at her expression told me to keep my mouth shut. "Yes, ma'am." I stood beside the car, squirming out of wet pants and a shirt that clung to my body. Mom held out her hands for the soggy items and then put them in the back of the car.

"Matt, you can get in the front. David, in the back."

We weren't about to waste time arguing. I climbed onto the seat and fastened the seat belt across my chest, shivering a little.

"Mrs. Lennon, how did you know where we were?" Matt voiced the question I'd been too scared to ask.

Mom huffed as she drove through the streets. "It wasn't until I looked in David's room and saw his books open that I realized what you two were up to. Turtle hunting, hmm? I figured you'd head for the lake. I've been driving up and down this road for the past half hour, trying to catch sight of you. Two hours!

You've been gone for two hours! I was going crazy, thinking that something had happened to you." She glanced over her shoulder at me. "And if you think I'm going to be letting you out of the house anytime soon, you can think—"

"It was my fault," Matt blurted out.

I stilled. What?

Mom gave him a smile. "Matt, I know you two are friends, but—"

"No, really. We were playing around in the water, and I… I pushed him. It's my fault he ended up in the lake, ma'am. Honestly."

I couldn't believe what I was hearing. Not that I could let him do that, though. "Matt, it's—"

He twisted around and glared at me. "I'm sorry I pushed you. And I should never have put the idea in your mind about finding a turtle." I could almost read the words he was holding back in his eyes. *Play along.*

Mom said nothing for a moment. Finally she sighed as she pulled into our driveway.

Ten minutes. It had taken us all that time to get there, and she'd brought us home in ten lousy minutes. Somehow that made it seem less of an adventure.

She switched off the engine and turned to look at us both. "What am I to do with you two, hmm? I suppose boys will get up to this sort of thing."

"And I promise we won't do anything like this ever again," Matt said earnestly, his gaze locked on hers. "I mean, if you still think you need to ground David, then—"

Mom smiled. "By the look of him, David's had enough punishment for one day. But you two need to promise me you won't go off again without telling us where you're going." She peered at Matt. "I imagine your mom will have a few words to say to you when you get home."

"Yes, ma'am." Matt's shoulders sagged, his tone glum.

"Then you'd best get off home. I'll call her, though, to tell her how you spoke up and told the truth. Maybe she won't go so hard on you." Her gaze met mine. "And you need to get into the house and have a bath."

"A bath?" Well, that sure sounded like punishment.

Mom's eyes suddenly had steel in them. "You fell into the lake. Heaven knows what you might have picked up in that water. So you will have a bath. No arguments."

I sighed. "No, ma'am."

See, I really did know when to keep my mouth shut.

NOTE

OF COURSE, that was when Matt decided it was time he taught me to swim. God knows why he thought he'd have more success than the swimming teacher, but he was determined.

I'll always remember the day we hunted for turtles. Matt didn't need to do that, but he did it anyway, to save me from the trouble he knew was coming my way. And that was the day I knew he was truly my best friend.

# CHAPTER THREE

*August, 1997*

"THIS IS great!" Matt stared out over the lake, where people were out in canoes and kayaks, or roaring past on water skis that followed speedboats. It was a perfect summer morning, and I couldn't agree with him more.

Apparently our misdemeanor was forgiven, although definitely not forgotten. Mom had announced a week ago that it was all arranged for both our families to go camping for a weekend. I think they felt sorry for Matt's family. I was just pleased to spend time with him. His older brother, Darren, had declined to join us—he was at a friend's house for a sleepover. Matt's parents were in one tent with his little sister, and mine were in another. The really great part was that they put me and Matt in a tent together. We'd packed flashlights and snacks and had planned to stay up real late when everyone else had gone to sleep.

Of course, Friday night when we arrived at the campsite, we were so worn out that we fell asleep instantly. So much for that idea.

"Why don't you two boys go for a swim?" his mom suggested. She was sitting on one of the camping chairs my parents had brought, with Matt's sister, Paula, curled up against her.

Okay, yeah, my cheeks grew hot. Matt gave me a sympathetic glance.

"That sounds like a good idea," my dad said with a kind smile, "except that I foresee a slight problem. David hasn't learned to swim yet."

"Really?" Matt's mom stared at me. "I had no idea. Matt swims like a little minnow, has ever since he was four years old."

Matt set his jaw, and I knew what was coming.

"I'm gonna teach David to swim this weekend." His tone was firm.

Yep. Just like I'd thought. Then Mom disappeared into their tent and returned a minute later with a pair of bright orange water wings. I groaned inwardly at the sight of them. I was eight, for heaven's sake! I did *not* want to be seen wearing objects that I considered were for little kids.

"Aw, that's great." Matt grinned at me. "Just what we need." He took them from her.

I glared at him, wondering if he'd be so pleased if *he* was the one who had to wear them.

Then Matt leaned closer. "Think of it this way. The sooner I get you to swim, the less time you need to wear these."

Now *that* was incentive.

The pair of us went into our tent and changed into our swim trunks. I glanced down at the sky-blue shorts, covered with little sailing boats and gulls, and tried not to groan. "I can't wait till I'm old enough to shop for my own clothes."

Matt cocked his head. "Are those new?" When I nodded, he said, "Think I'd rather have those than have to wear Darren's old ones." His were dark gray, a bit on the long side, and I spied a pin securing them at the waistband.

One look at Matt's glum expression told me it was time to change the subject.

"Okay, time for you to teach me to drown—I mean, swim." I winked at him, and thankfully my words did the trick. He laughed and held up the water wings.

"Arms out."

I did as instructed, waiting patiently while he blew air into them and secured the little rubber stoppers. Then it was time to leave the haven of our tent.

"If anyone giggles…," I muttered as Matt held up the flap of the tent for us to exit.

"No one will do that," Matt assured me. "Your folks are nice people, and that sounds kinda mean."

He was right, of course. No one said a word as I followed Matt to the water's edge.

"Stay where we can see you!" my mom called, her book in her lap. She and Dad were sitting in chairs in front of their tent, with Matt's parents a few feet away in front of theirs.

I nodded and waved at her before kicking off my sandals and stepping carefully into the cool water. I shivered.

Matt must have seen me. "We're gonna walk out a ways, to where it's sunny. The water will be warmer there."

"Not too deep, right?" I gazed out, trying to fathom just how deep it was.

Matt rolled his eyes. "I can't teach you to swim in a couple of inches of water. It needs to be at least up to your waist."

What I liked was the confident way in which he spoke, like it was a foregone conclusion that I'd be swimming before the day was out. Such confidence was contagious.

I squared my shoulders and lifted my chin. "Okay, then. Let's do this." I tried not to look at the orange monstrosities around my biceps. The mud was soft and oozy beneath my feet, squeezing up between my toes. Strange thing was, it didn't feel gross.

When we were several feet from the shore, though still able to see our parents, Matt came to a halt. "This is far enough." The water lapped at our ribs. "I want you to lean forward, as if you're going to lie down on the water. You won't sink, because of the water wings, and I'm gonna put my hands under you to hold you up."

It was my turn to roll my eyes. "I *have* had swimming lessons, y'know."

Matt regarded me steadily, his lips twitching. "Yeah, and they were so successful, right?"

I had no comeback. And before I could think of something, Matt gave me a hard stare.

"Do it. Now."

I obeyed without thinking, surprised by this very different Matt. I kept my chin out of the water, arms outstretched in front of me, and Matt held me up, his arms under my waist.

"Now kick," he said.

I did as I was told, my heart hammering. "You're not gonna let go, are you?" It felt safe, knowing he held me.

"I promise. We're gonna stay like this until we get you used to it." He smiled. "This is better than your swimming lessons, right? We have lots of time. No one is watching. There's no coach breathing down your neck, yelling at you. It's just you and me."

Now I knew why he'd been determined to teach me. This was *so* much better than my swimming lessons, for all the reasons he'd just voiced. "Yeah," I said quietly.

By the time Mom was calling us to get out of the water, my fingers were beginning to prune, but I felt great. I was starting to enjoy the feel of the water, holding me up. I pulled back against the water with cupped hands, and Matt walked slowly with me as I moved. I liked it when Matt got me to close my eyes. I listened to the sounds all around us: the shouts of people farther out on the lake, the dull roar of speedboats, the cries of gulls high in the air above us, and the splash of my feet as they broke the surface of the water.

After a lunch of burgers that Dad cooked on a camping stove, Matt met my gaze. "Ready for more?"

I nodded eagerly, and we dashed out toward the lake. This time I launched myself into the water with no hesitation, Matt's arms around my waist once more.

"I have an idea," Matt said after a few minutes.

I chuckled. "Why am I thinking this is not good?"

"I want to let a little air out of your water wings."

Just like that, my heartbeat sped up. "Really?"

"It'll be fine," he assured me. "You won't even notice, honest."

I wanted to tell him that *hell, yeah*, I'd notice, but there was also the knowledge that I couldn't keep doing this all day. I stood for a moment while Matt fiddled with the stoppers on the water wings.

"I've not let out all that much. See if it feels any different."

I did as before, stretching out on top of the water. To my surprise, he was right. I felt just the same. "You must only have let out a tiny amount." We went back to our earlier activity, me confidently sculling with my hands and kicking my legs, Matt holding me up. A little while later, he repeated the action, and that was the course of our afternoon, right up to the moment when Matt stopped and stared at me.

"You really don't need the water wings anymore," he said earnestly. "There's hardly any air left in them anyway."

"Seriously?" Okay, the idea scared me to death, but there was also an excitement thrumming through me. Was I about to swim, really swim? I stood up in the water, and Matt removed the water wings, folded them, and shoved them into the waistband of his shorts.

"I'll hold you, all right?" he promised. "Until you're ready to try it alone. Only this time, start paddling as soon as you can."

Nodding, I launched myself at the surface of the water and began to paddle, feet kicking strongly. I could feel Matt's arms supporting me.

"Shall I take away one arm?"

There was that excitement again. "Go for it."

I barely felt him remove his arm, I was so intently focused on what my own arms and legs were doing, my head held high. Matt guided me toward the shore, turning my body slowly. "Ready to swim on your own?"

*Holy hell.* "Yes!" I shouted, my pulse racing. I took a deep breath and paddled for all I was worth, not letting up for a second. Matt was beside me the whole time, yelling encouragements and letting out whoops of delight.

"That's it! You're swimming! You're doing great!"

For a second there, I lost concentration and slipped beneath the surface. I swallowed a mouthful of water in my panic, but then Matt was there, lifting me up, helping me to stand in the knee-high water.

"You did it!"

I felt like I'd conquered Everest. My panic fled, and in its place was pride in my achievement. Matt's arm was around my shoulder as he led me toward the shore, where my parents were standing, both of them applauding. Matt's parents were smiling and clapping too.

It was an amazing feeling, one that I've never forgotten.

K.C. WELLS started writing in 2012, although the idea of writing a novel had been in her head since she was a child. But after reading that first gay romance in 2009, she was hooked.

She now writes full-time, and the line of men in her head clamoring to tell their story is getting longer and longer. If the frequent visits by plot bunnies are anything to go by, that's not about to change anytime soon.

K.C. loves to hear from readers.
Email: k.c.wells@btinternet.com
Facebook: www.facebook.com/KCWellsWorld
Blog: kcwellsworld.blogspot.co.uk
Twitter: @K_C_Wells
Website: www.kcwellsworld.com
Instagram: www.instagram.com/k.c.wells

A friends-to-lovers novella that came from *Out of the Shadows*, because Nate and Dylan needed a story....

Nate and Dylan have been pals for a long time. So what if their friends think they've got a little bromance going? Doesn't mean there's anything more to it than that, right? And even if there is, Nate and Dylan are totally oblivious....

Until the night they share a drunken kiss—and everything changes.

# www. dreamspinnerpress.com

DREAMSPUN
DESIRES

# OUT OF THE SHADOWS
## K.C. Wells

*Can he step out of the shadows and into love's light?*

Can he step out of the shadows and into love's light?

Eight years ago, Christian Hernandez moved to the Jamaica Plain area of Boston, took refuge in his apartment, and cut himself off from the outside world. And that's how he'd like it to stay.

Josh Wendell has heard his coworkers gossip about the occupant of apartment #1. No one sees the mystery man, and Josh loves a mystery. So when he is hired to refurbish the apartment's kitchen and bathrooms, Josh is eager to discover the truth behind the rumors.

When he comes face-to-face with Christian, Josh understands why Christian hides from prying eyes. As the two men bond, Josh sees past his exterior to the man within, and he likes what he sees. But can Christian find the courage to emerge from the darkness of his lonely existence for the man who has claimed his heart?

# www. dreamspinnerpress.com

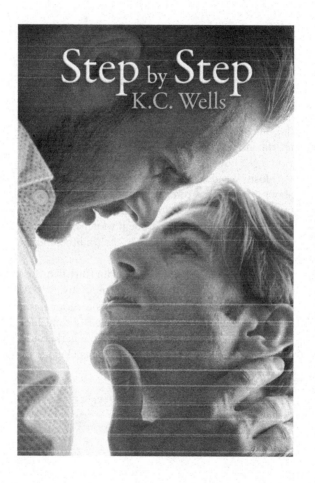

# Step by Step
## K.C. Wells

Jamie's life is one big financial mess, and it really isn't his fault. However, the last thing he expected to find in the library was a Good Samaritan. He might have been suspicious of Guy's motives at first, but it soon becomes apparent that his savior is a good man who has been lucky in life and is looking to pay it forward. Guy being gay is not a problem. Jamie's not interested… or so he thinks.

Guy is happy to help Jamie, and the two men get along fine. But when Jamie's curiosity leads him from one thing to another, Guy finds himself looking at the young man with new eyes. What started out as a hand up is now something completely different….

# www. dreamspinnerpress.com

DREAMSPUN DESIRES

THE
SENATOR'S SECRET
K.C. Wells

Politics, puppy dogs,
and passion, oh my!

Politics, puppy dogs, and passion, oh my!

When his Republican opponent outs him with a photo in a Facebook post, Senator Samuel Dalton doesn't have many options open to him. It doesn't matter that the photo is totally innocent. He has no choice but to come clean… until his staff suggest putting a spin on it that leaves Sam reeling.

Sure, he'll end up with a lot of sympathy, not to mention the possibility of more voters from the LGBT community, but it still seems a pretty drastic solution.

Now all they have to do is persuade Gary, the other man in the photo, to play along. It sounds so easy: convince the constituents of North Carolina that he and Sam are engaged.

No big deal, except for the fact that they've only just met….

# www. dreamspinnerpress.com

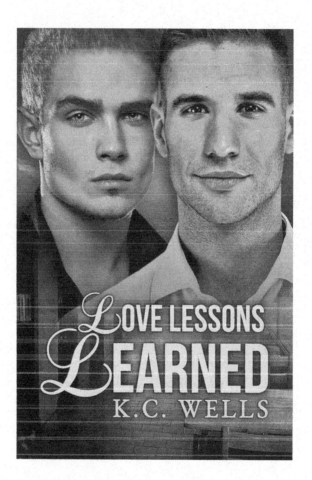

LOVE LESSONS
LEARNED
K.C. WELLS

John Wainwright is having a momentous day. To start off, he lands his first teaching job. Then his brother, Evan, and Evan's husband, Daniel, take him out to celebrate in Manchester's gay village. An encounter with a sexy man forces John to admit what he's been denying for too long—he's gay. His coming out proves he's supported and loved by his family and roommates. What more could a man want? There's just one small problem: John's dishy Head Teacher, Brett Sanderson, and John's gigantic crush on him. Too bad Brett is straight.

Brett Sanderson leads a double life. At thirty-three, he is the Head Teacher of a primary school. But for seven years now, during every school holiday, Brett has fled to Brighton, where he becomes 'Rob,' a man who has a different guy in his bed every night but has never had a relationship.

Once he's back in school, Brett is firmly back in that closet, until his newest staff member starts prying open the door. When John pulls out all the stops to get Brett's attention, neither man is prepared for the consequences.

# www. dreamspinnerpress.com

FOR **MORE** OF THE **BEST GAY ROMANCE**

DREAMSPINNER
PRESS
dreamspinnerpress.com